Joyce Windsor was ~~~~~~~~~~~~~
leaving school, wen~~~~~~~~~~~~~
Revenue, subsequen~~~~~~~~~~~~~
ations necessary for promotion within the
service. Moving to Liverpool, she became part
of a fascinating circle, living next door to Fritz
Spiegl and just around the corner from Beryl
Bainbridge. A shortage of money in no way
impeded the determined party-givers of that
era and, as a devotee of the Liverpool
Philharmonic Orchestra, she was delighted to
meet people like Efrem Kurtz and François
Poulenc.

She then moved south, first to Putney, then
Dorset. In 1982 her husband died and she
retreated to the Isle of Wight 'to die', but by
chance hit upon a flourishing and companionable community of writers. Thus began one of
the happiest periods of her life, which culmi-
nated in the publication of her first novel, *A
Mislaid Magic,* which is also published by
Black Swan, as is the sequel, *After the Unicorn.
Arriving in Snowy Weather* is the third and
final book in the Savernake sequence.

Also by Joyce Windsor

A MISLAID MAGIC
AFTER THE UNICORN

and published by Black Swan

ARRIVING
IN SNOWY WEATHER

Joyce Windsor

BLACK SWAN

ARRIVING IN SNOWY WEATHER
A BLACK SWAN BOOK : 0 552 99797 8

First publication in Great Britain

PRINTING HISTORY
Black Swan edition published 1998

Set in 11/13pt Melior by
County Typesetters, Margate, Kent

Black Swan Books are published by Transworld Publishers Ltd,
61–63 Uxbridge Road, London W5 5SA,
in Australia by Transworld Publishers (Australia) Pty Ltd,
15–25 Helles Avenue, Moorebank, NSW 2170,
and in New Zealand by Transworld Publishers (NZ) Ltd,
3 William Pickering Drive, Albany, Auckland.

Reproduced, printed and bound in Great Britain by
Cox & Wyman Ltd, Reading, Berks.

For Susan Netton with love

Chapter One

The buses were on strike. A hooting, screeching mass of traffic crawled around Marble Arch and into Oxford Street; the pedestrians looked weary and depressed. I hadn't meant to be shopping in London at all. That morning I had come up from Sussex for the day to visit my grandfather, who was ill. I saw at once that he was drifting towards death. He was, of course, an old man. That made not a speck of difference to my grief. In my childhood I had experienced a scarcity of love. Without consciously thinking about it, I knew that Grandfather loved me. My feet hurt with trudging in and out of shops. Longing to sit down with a pot of tea in a pleasant café and grapple with the approach of sadness, I made for my usual haven. Since my last visit it had become transmuted into a coffee bar with Espresso machines, posters of Spain, compulsory music and boys and girls in jeans.

Hustled, bumped and disappointed, I turned into a side street and found myself alone, or almost. On the corner of Wigmore Street stood a tall woman wearing a white-spotted silky dress the colour of lightly pati-nated bronze. It had an expensively elegant air. Her hair was closely wrapped in a scarf and although the late May afternoon was cool and the sun sporadic, dark glasses with white frames hid her eyes. She glared wildly around her as though she were lost. After a moment's hesitation she bent her head and started walking towards me. The genteel placing of her feet put me in mind of someone. My eldest sister, Portia, walked in just such a manner, but she lived in Leicestershire, rarely came to London, and never wore enviable clothes. Yet on closer inspection, Portia it was. I doubt whether she would have noticed me, or a rogue elephant for that matter, if I hadn't stopped squarely in front of her. The purpose of the sun-glasses was immediately evident. She had been crying. This was as astonishing as the beautiful dress. Her nature was stoical. Public displays of emotion offended against her canon of good behaviour, as did practically everything. I assumed at first that, like my own, her grief was for our grandfather. Then I recalled that she had been unreachable by telephone since his illness began because, according to the exchange, her line had been disconnected. Struck by her extreme pallor, I said, 'What is it, Portia? What's happened? Are you ill?'

Never before in her life had she been pleased to see me, but she was then. She clutched at my arm. 'Amy, thank God.' A stray tear ran down her cheek and into a fold of her scarf. 'This awful strike, I should have ordered a taxi. I'll never get home. Perhaps the Tube, though the crowds are so confusing. Would you, could you come with me?'

'Of course.' She shocked the response out of me. Dignity, hauteur and rank carried Portia through all situations, however obnoxious to her refined sensibilities, and her opinion of my usefulness was low. 'You *are* ill, poor dear. You look awful. We'd better try to find somewhere for you to sit down. If there's nowhere else it'll have to be the coffee bar.'

She didn't argue. I took her hand and she ambled meekly along at my side. The place wasn't as crowded as I had anticipated. I sat her in a corner and obtained cups of froth masquerading as coffee, and a couple of rather nice, sticky, lemony buns. 'Try to eat one of these. I bet you didn't have lunch. How long have you been in London?'

'I came down this morning to see – oh no, never mind. It's so sickening, I can't possibly talk about it. I've been subjected to the most atrocious humiliation.'

Very calmly and gently I said, 'Whatever it is, Portia, you'd better tell me. At least I'm family and I might be able to help.'

Her tears had dried. She took off her sun-glasses, stowed them in her handbag and sat staring in silence at the chocolate grains on the top of her cup. After a moment she picked up a spoon and carefully removed them. 'I'm not ill,' she said in a dull voice. 'I rather wish I were. Disgusted beyond measure, but not ill. It's bound to get out, things always do, but I can't face it yet. I'd better go. Perhaps I can walk to St Pancras. There's a fast train in two hours.'

An unwelcome dilemma presented itself. I lived with my husband and two sons in Sussex, but we had another haven, selfishly guarded against all save invited guests, a flat above my husband's theatrical agency in Bloomsbury. It was scarcely Portia's kind of place. She, who had married a duke and lived in a castle, a fate far worse than death in my opinion, chose not to approve of my marriage to Rudi and snubbed him when chance threw them together. Yet I shrank from letting her go off alone and uncomforted and unaware of Grandfather's illness. 'Must you leave London today?' I asked. 'You could get a room at the Connaught, they know you there. Or is Botolph expecting you at Hindlecote?'

Forgetful of the mixed company around us, Portia sat upright and, enunciating with awful clarity above the thrum and shriek of the juke-box, said, 'Botolph is in a clinic in Austria: heart, lungs, other things. If

9

there's any justice in the world he'll stay there. Always.'

Heads turned. But Portia possessed a distinguished brand of beauty and for once she had managed to avoid dowdiness. She could have been an actress incognito. The glances wilted before the glacial blue directness of her stare. 'What about the boy? Is he at home?'

'Beau? In school, naturally. He'll have to be told, he might have to leave. Oh God, how can I tell him, but if I don't someone else will, won't they?' She began to cry again, silently. I couldn't begin to imagine what might be causing her so much anguish. No love remained in her marriage to Botolph, nor had done for years. Duke and Duchess co-existed under the accommodating roof of Hindlecote Castle for the sake of appearances (on which Portia was enormously keen), caring nothing for each other. How, I wondered, had he managed to reduce her to this state of nervous misery?

My other sister, Claudia, made of coarser clay, would undoubtedly have put down her condition to sex starvation and have asked what on earth Portia expected to happen if she kept a padlock on her knickers; but as a family we weren't given to nerves and complexes. Meanwhile the tears were enough to touch the hardest heart. 'You certainly oughtn't to be on your own,' I said. 'Stay with me, at least for the night. We can decide what to do next in the morning.'

'I haven't any night things and I'm not sure that I want to go down to Sussex. I'm so dreadfully tired.'

'Not Sussex, London, and we can buy whatever you need on the way; there's a Marks & Spencer in New Oxford Street. In any case, Grandmother's been trying to reach you. Grandpa's very ill, dying.'

'That's cruel,' she said quietly. 'He's the rock I hoped to lean on. Grandmother must be distraught. She'll be

10

alone after all these years. How on earth can we comfort her?'

I shook my head. That morning Grandmother had pulled in her several chins and said, 'It's best that Robert goes first. Men are sad creatures on their own and it won't be a long parting.' The insincere assurances that might have comforted a lesser woman would not do for her. The world offered her nothing that she wanted. Already she had begun to withdraw from us to follow Grandfather, the one love of her lifetime.

I said, 'It oughtn't to be a shock, but it is. I never remember about people's ages. They're both very old, almost ninety. If only we could make them immortal.'

'He's been so good to me. Before I married he talked to me for a long time. Not that I listened. I'd convinced myself that I was in love. Botolph could charm when he wanted to and I quite thought that I could change what I didn't like. Ridiculous, women never can.' The juke-box played 'Magic Moments'. Portia, closer to confiding in me than she had ever come, stopped abruptly and looked down, stroking her fine kid gloves into shape. She still hadn't told me what was wrong. 'I shall have to see Grandmother before I go back.'

'It's better if you stay with us. Come along. You need to rest and you need company. If I can't help, you might try talking to Rudi. He's wonderfully comforting.'

'Really, Amy,' she said, quite in her old manner, 'I can scarcely discuss my affairs with a man and a stranger. What a suggestion!' But she unfolded her tall frame and allowed me to lead her away. I didn't point out that Rudi was her brother-in-law and that it was entirely her fault that he was still a stranger. Portia lacked defences against a world no longer ready to bow before duchesses. I couldn't hit her while she was down.

11

The last occasion on which she had been cosseted and spoiled a little must have been long ago, perhaps not since childhood. Rudi was still in his office, so we were alone. She sank gratefully into a hot bath. I was about to leave her when she said, 'Would you mind staying with me, Amy? To keep me awake.'

I had never seen her naked before. She was elegantly put together, with long legs and slight, childish breasts, though much too thin for her height. Her skin was so intensely white that it looked transparent over the prominent bones of her spine. 'Of course I'll stay. How slim you are. You can't have put on an ounce since you were twenty-one.'

Relaxed, she lay back, covering herself modestly with the sponge. 'Amy, do you think it possible that some people are born without souls? Who do evil and feel neither shame nor guilt? Who lie to themselves and even to God? I believe they exist. They can't be helped, they can't even be truly loved, though they expect to be.'

'I've noticed that one or two extremely callous murderers become quite indignant to be punished, as if they aren't like the rest of us and ought to be let off.'

'Yes, that's it, an enormous self-conceit that excuses its own vileness. Humiliating to others, because such natures can't be altered or concealed. Now that the doctors have finished with me I must try to feel properly clean again and I don't, not yet. They asked me about marital relations. No-one should have to talk about such things, not even to specialists.' She shuddered and sank deeper into the water, muttering so low that I scarcely heard her. 'You know how my marriage has been. I told them that for ten years it has been no marriage, except for one occasion two years ago. He forced himself on me. They insisted on an examination. I could have died of shame.'

I shrank from considering an event so horrifying, thinking that Hindlecote Castle, beautiful as it was, concealed for her only ugliness and torment. Her remarks, filtered through a concealing cloud of steam, were scarcely explicit. I made a broad guess. War and service with the Navy had been remarkably educational and I didn't doubt that Botty's life-style had been as promiscuous as that of any sailor. The clinic in Austria, rather than London, suggested that part at least of his suffering was of a kind to be backed away from rather than soothed with duty visits and grapes. 'Portia, am I making a mistake over this?' I asked. 'We're talking of Botolph's illness, aren't we? Is it what I think it is?'

'Down there,' she said. Stupidly I glanced at her feet, forgetting for a moment the squeamishness of her attitude towards sex and her inability to mention body parts by name. 'Now you know. Monstrous. I could have loved him, but a marriage needs its soul. Sometimes he came home with – well, he made me shudder when he touched me.'

Still uncertain (it might, after all, turn out to be nothing worse than athlete's foot), I said, 'It's over now. He'll be looked after, treated. For your sake the doctors had to be sure.'

Although it was barely five o'clock in the afternoon, I helped her into her new nightie and put her to bed in our spare room with a mug of Horlicks to which I added some brandy. 'The taste is odd,' she said, 'rather nice. Nothing seems quite the same since the War, but I may have forgotten what it used to be like. I feel so sad about Grandfather. Everything is very sad just now.'

'Yes, yes it is. These times come, I think, and have to be lived through somehow. Are you hungry? Would you like a Bath Oliver or some bread and butter?'

'No thank you, I don't want to make crumbs in the bed. I'll just rest for an hour.' Her poor, tired, haunted gaze slid past me as, miserably, she confirmed the correctness of my guess by adding, 'He left it too long and spread it around. Foul of him, but then he is, of course. One of the women named him.' She closed her eyes as I shut the door. I listened a while for sounds of weeping, but there was no murmur from her other than a single long sigh. She must have fallen asleep at once.

At six o'clock I heard Rudi say good night to his secretary and come upstairs. As I opened the door for him I rehearsed in my mind how I should explain the presence of Portia, considering rather late the awfulness of my involvement. He was pretty patient with my family and their vagaries. He had borne Portia's snubs and snobbery with amused fortitude, but I had never before allowed anyone to invade the rare occasions when we could be alone together. He kissed me as though we hadn't met for a hundred years, then looked at me closely. 'Hallo, something's up. Is it your grandfather?'

'No, nothing's changed. He's very weak and just about holding on. It can't be long.'

'Then you've brought home a swarthy Latin gigolo, or given all our worldly goods to a beggar.'

'How is it that you always know?' I asked crossly. 'It isn't fair.'

'Aha, kisses are a perfect barometer. I trust I shan't have to throw a rival down the stairs, it's been a tiring day.'

'Of course not, idiot. Rather worse in a way and not nearly as much fun. And do keep your voice down. Portia's here, asleep in the spare room.'

His look of woe reproached me. 'Not the Duchess? She's the Savernake I considered us entirely safe from until the day that I become ennobled and buy you a castle. Please, please say you're joking.'

14

'I'm not and I don't want a castle. It's just for a night. I expect she'll go home tomorrow, or perhaps she could stay with Grandmother. Truly I'm sorry. I only meant to get Piers a dressing-gown; he's growing out of everything so fast and it doesn't seem fair to make him wear Roland's hand-me-downs. The bus strike held me up.'

'I shall have to forbid you to shop,' Rudi said. 'There's something irrational about setting out to buy a dressing-gown and coming home with a duchess. And why, oh why, is she asleep at six in the evening? It's not at all sociable.'

'She was wandering near Wigmore Street, in tears and dreadfully upset. Portia never manages to call a spade a spade, but I believe that a revolting thing has happened. If I've got it right, the Duke has caught a disease not discussed in polite circles, and passed it on. Not to her. But I expect she'll be a pariah as well as him if it gets known, and Little Botty may have to leave his school. He's in a clinic in Austria – Old Botty, that is, not the boy – and she calls him Beau – the boy, not Old Botty, I mean. Why will people pass on these awful family names?'

'Take a breath, my darling,' Rudi said.

'Almost finished. Then I had to tell her about Grandfather as she hadn't heard. Oh dear, and I've just remembered, I suggested that she might like to confide in you since you're always such a help.'

We brooded silently a while. My maternal instinct had exhausted itself, likewise sisterly concern. I considered all the occasions when Portia had squashed me and preached the sanctity of blue blood and been generally hateful. Did I really want to help her? No, I didn't, not one bit. There was no reason in the world why she shouldn't long ago have divorced Botolph and been rid of a connection that had brought her little save misery. Except, of course, that to yield her status

15

and the right to live at Hindlecote Castle would have been her utter defeat. 'What a fool I am,' I said. 'May I have a very large gin and tonic, please? Not too strong.'

'You're possessed of a kind nature which, in your family, is a handicap,' Rudi said. 'Portia's problems are usually so unimportant, the impertinent behaviour of servants and the impossibility of accepting unmarried mothers in the Hindlecote Mothers' Union. What can I do? I might manage to get her a walk-on part in *Pygmalion*, but I'm far too common to advise her on serious matters.'

Ice clinked comfortingly in the glass. 'She doesn't cry over servants, she sacks them, and you're much cleverer than you know.'

'I adore your simple faith in me,' Rudi said. 'I doubt whether the Duchess shares it. If she's awake we'd better feed her.'

Before I served our evening meal I put my head around the spare room door. Portia was curled on her side. She clutched a fold of blanket against her flat bosom and breathed quietly. I retreated. After ten o'clock I heard her stir and went in. 'Amy?' she said, half dazed. 'How long have I been here?'

'A few hours. Are you hungry? Or thirsty?'

'I must go home; there'll be taxis now,' she said. 'I can't impose on you like this.' My heart began to rejoice and then I knew that I couldn't bear to think of her solitary and desolate, rattling through the night with a near-empty castle as her destination. Also I was deeply curious.

'Tomorrow's soon enough. You can telephone Grandmother. Put on your dressing-gown for now and come and talk to us. We forgot slippers. D'you mind wearing a pair of Rudi's? Mine are too small. And I'll make you an omelette, I'm rather good at those.'

Modest as ever, she buttoned herself to the chin.

Rudi looked once and saw why I was concerned. Without comment he stowed her in the most comfortable chair and put a glass of wine beside her. 'Fortunate that Amy ran into you, Portia. We don't see you in Town often enough.'

Our lovely studio room has a seductive atmosphere of peace. Portia essayed a smile and when her omelette was ready she attacked it with genteel enthusiasm and followed on with French bread and cheese. On my rare visits to Hindlecote Castle I had found the food pretty dismal. Knowing myself to be only a moderate cook, I wondered when she had last eaten a remotely enjoyable meal. A faint sparkle came to her eyes. The wine – Rudi kept it topped up – mingling with the brandy in her Horlicks, was having a decided effect. The Duchess hovered on the edge of mellowness, combined with mild belligerence.

'If Claudia laughs over this I'll hit her,' she declared with such suddenness that I jumped. 'We're sisters, yet she hates me. You and she are as thick as thieves. There's no way in the world of keeping it from her.'

The antagonism between the two had begun early and arose from opposing temperaments. It was unsafe to make promises for the erratic Claudia. 'You've always disapproved of us so much,' I said, smiling, 'and we have our pride. If you can bring yourself to trust us a little we might turn out to be not quite as bad as you think.'

'I've never thought you bad precisely.' Portia sounded surprised for a second, then driven as she was by wine and rage and misery, she talked unchecked. 'She'll hear it anyway. Heaven knows how many women that wretch has infected; he simply didn't care. They asked *me*. As if I could tell them, though I know that for years he's been sleeping with that foul Smythe-Fennel woman who hasn't an ounce of discretion.

She's too shameless to keep quiet.' Portia slapped butter on a piece of bread, topped it with a wedge of cheese and sank her teeth into it as though it were Botty's neck. 'Is there some wine left, Rudi?'

'About half a glass. Shall I open another bottle?'

'Not at all,' she said graciously. 'If Botolph had gone without treatment longer he would certainly have died. It's begun to affect his brain. He may die anyway, since he's developed severe heart trouble.'

'There are effective drugs nowadays, I believe, if it's not too far advanced. A quick death might, of course, be kinder.'

'Oh dear.' An expression of dismay crossed Portia's face and she lapsed into thoughtful silence. The notion of Botolph's early demise plainly did not absolutely please her. What on earth *did* she want? Her situation as it stood was precarious and unpleasant to a degree. She had clear and ample grounds for divorcing Botolph should he survive, yet she never would. Her only hope of release was his death. She explained. 'It's money, you see. Botolph would never listen to his lawyers and he borrowed without telling them. Keeping him in the clinic is ruinous, yet the minute he dies all the loans will be called in and then we'll be faced with death duties so enormous I can never hope to pay them. There'll be nothing left for poor Beau to inherit.'

'Beau? Oh, your son, yes. That's awkward, extremely so. Apart from the debts, does the land pay?'

'Less and less. Some of the farms have been sold to the tenants. Extras crop up from time to time. Botolph accepted an offer from a film company to use the castle in one of their productions. They paid a prodigious amount. I managed to see that the money went into the trust towards Beau's school fees and wasn't squandered. And an international team of archaeologists wants to dig up the Wodsbridge field.'

'Anything that could be sold? A trifle by Vandyke or Rembrandt, perhaps, a rare something or other up in the attics? It's a common solution.'

Acid entered Portia's voice. 'I'm quite sure that Botolph will have sold off any portable treasure. Since he didn't confide in me I have no idea of what forms part of the entail and what can be disposed of.'

Rudi lapsed into thought. Portia returned to munching and finished off the loaf and the last of the Stilton. My attention wandered. No solution of any kind occurred to me. I remembered that I hadn't managed to get a dressing-gown for Piers and that tomorrow I would have to shop again.

'There's no help for it,' Rudi said. 'The castle must be made to pay, not occasionally, but over and over again. Think of Woburn Abbey and the rest, tourist attractions nowadays and quite the thing.'

'It's the absolute limit,' my sister said. Hers was a token protest. She and Rudi exchanged speculative looks. 'Would it work? Would people come, and actually pay? We don't have a rare animal park or anything of that nature.'

'But a great deal of history. You underestimate the public thirst for blue blood. A bedroom slept in by Queen Elizabeth, a walled-up nun who walks by night, deaths by boiling oil; the castle must be renowned for something.'

'Roses, that's all I can think of. And Vikings. We're not too far from Bosworth Field where the last battle of the Wars of the Roses was fought. The first Hindlecote roses were planted then, after the death of Richard the Third. They and the glasshouses are famous in gardening circles. We're constantly troubled by writers and organizations wanting to take photographs or films. The head gardener gets furious.'

'He'll have to be spoken to,' Rudi said. 'Plants must

be potted and brought on, if that's the correct expression. Anybody will pay twice the price for a rose-bush born in a castle. Well, that's certainly a start. More will be needed.'

'The idea is repugnant to me.' (Where on earth did Portia pick up such Victorian expressions?) 'Becoming a peep-show; and how do I know it will be worth while?'

Rudi said, with a smoothness that I didn't quite trust, 'If you can extend your tolerance a little further and give whole-hearted co-operation, the situation and Beau's inheritance might be saved. Always providing the Duke has the tact to stay alive a little longer. You'll need professional help. If you wish I can recommend a team and, who knows, you may find the exercise interesting. The castle must be lonely without your son.'

'Yes.' Portia stood up. 'Will he approve, I wonder? It may interest him. He finds the holidays dull enough and me rather stick-in-the-mud.'

'We're fated to bore our children,' Rudi said. 'Why not sleep on it? Things may look less dark in the morning. They often do.' He rose to open the door for her, bowing very slightly from the waist as he did for Dame Edith Evans, whom he adored. Surprised, my sister glanced back at us and smiled.

Chapter Two

Early the next morning we were drinking tea in bed, or I was; Rudi had finished his and lay back looking at the ceiling. A question hovered at the back of my mind. 'Who will you suggest to Portia for developing Hindlecote? It's a nice old place if you like that kind of thing, which I don't much, and it oughtn't to be spoiled.' He closed his eyes and gave a theatrical snore. I dug him in the ribs. 'Don't pretend to be asleep, you're an abysmal actor.' His silence was eloquent. 'Oh, Rudi, not Merve Promotions surely?'

'Why ever not, my dearest? Rescuing castles from the taxman isn't in my line, as you know, and it's absolutely in theirs. They're the best and they're available. Think of the wonders they worked for that undistinguished and gloomy manor in Kent. Coining money, I believe. Half London flocks to the Elizabethan banquets, convinced that it's gnawing its way through the local swan population. Never has one cottonwool neck and head done such sterling service. The greedy are, I'm afraid, endlessly gullible.'

'Serves them right. I'm not crazy about swans, they're rather fierce birds, though too beautiful to be eaten by ugly people. But Merve and friends, aren't they rather *extreme*? Won't Portia misunderstand them and take fright?'

'Apart from the fact that all decisions rest with the lawyers, I think we should give the Duchess a chance. Merve will make money for her in one way or another, and arrange it so that Botolph's creditors won't be able to touch it.'

Small doubt of that, I thought. He was good, extremely so, and his partner, Reggie Bowmaker, controlled his wilder flights. But Merve in middle age had elected for the trendy and Portia, as far out of the swim as it was possible to get, might easily take fright at his Edwardian suit and gorgeous pink-tinted blond quiff. Presently I stopped fretting. For Beau, Portia would walk barefoot over red-hot coals. At his insistence she had, she confided, bought the dress I admired, and others too, so that she would look suitable for his school's Parents' Day. Whatever his motive, pride or snobbery, I warmed to him. Selflessness is all very well, but in my opinion Portia overdid it, concealing her beauty as though it were a shameful thing.

I said, 'Then I'm going to leave it to you, Rudi. Portia intimidates me and so does Hindlecote Castle. I absolutely *know* that I shall hear myself inviting her to stay with us in Sussex or share our holidays, though I don't one bit want to. Then Claudia will be furious, and the children will squabble with Little Botty.'

'Beau, please,' Rudi said. 'Try to remember. What a blessing that I have exquisite tact and no family. Perhaps I'd better pick up a scold's branks and ensure your silence.'

'You'll find one in the castle dungeons, together with assorted instruments of torture. The dukes used to be prosecution, jury, judge and executioner all rolled into one, *and* they got first go at the virgins.'

'Really? How splendid. I mustn't forget to tell Merve. He'll be thrilled. The Hell Fire caves at Medmenham Abbey have been made as spooky as you please – terror without tears. Is there a ducking stool and a moat? Are there peacocks?'

'The little river's rather pretty – it has widgeon and

moorhens and punts – and so are the woods. The moat's dry. There are bits of Roman wall all over the place and a lake and fountains that don't fount. I don't think I ever saw the Wodsbridge field.'

Rudi grasped my head and pulled it down onto his chest. 'Fields look much alike,' he said, 'grass mainly. You offer me a wealth of treasure. The moat can be filled and fish and exotic water-fowl procured. The splash of fountains, eerie lighting and disembodied voices in the dungeons, oh yes, I see it now: Hindlecote, the crown of middle England, and Portia its jewel. Kiss me.'

'The jewel of middle England has just gone into the bathroom. You'll have to shave in the kitchen.' Rudi shot out of bed with a groan. He liked to shave slowly, regaling me at the same time with his version of 'Where is the life that late I led?' from *Kiss Me, Kate*, or other favourites. While Portia was still at breakfast I telephoned my grandmother. She had sat all night beside Grandfather's bed and the confident boom of her voice was muted and infinitely sad. I had suggested nervously that Portia should not mention the reason for her presence in London. 'As if I would at a time like this,' she said, with an unfriendly stare.

'Sorry. Of course you wouldn't. Can you make up a small lie, d'you think?'

'There's no need for that at all. Naturally we shall be thinking of her, of them both. My problems can wait.'

She now put down her coffee cup. 'Before you hang up, let me speak please.' I allowed her to take the phone and listened admiringly as she dispensed comfort in a calm, low voice. I had forgotten how splendid she could be, instinctively saying and doing the Right Thing. Although slightly shaken in her faith, Portia believed in correct behaviour, the Royal Family, the innate virtue of noble blood, and the organization of God's humbler creation into unions, institutes and guilds under her presidency, yet she deferred to our grandmother as we all did. They spoke only briefly. 'Shall I come and sit with you, dear?' Portia asked.

The reply was resonant and clearly audible to me. 'Thank you, but no. Time is very short now and I wish this to be a private parting. Naturally you will be advised of the funeral arrangements. They will be kept quite simple.'

Portia put down the telephone. 'How dismal it is. What about the funeral, Amy? Should I take Beau out of school or not?'

'Not, I think, unless you're particularly keen – rather much strain for a tired old lady. Claudia certainly won't bring her children. Vaisey's too young. The twins are delightful girls, but quite irrepressible, and Alexander breaks his heart over the death of any living thing, including mice and beetles. I shall set our two to choosing some flowers and a suitable card.'

'In my opinion Claudia's twins have inherited their mother's character,' declared Portia. (This was not a compliment.) 'I thought perhaps Grandmother might find the young a consolation. She's particularly fond of Beau, the eldest great-grandson, you know.' I nodded. Some years had passed since I last set eyes on her boy. He had been a page at my wedding and Portia a matron of honour. Each year on the anniversary we invited the principals to a celebratory dinner. Portia and Beau came to the first. Thereafter she turned us down without troubling to find an excuse. I dare say the boy had improved with growth. I still did not envisage him as a comforter. 'Well, I can't hang around here doing nothing,' she went on, just as though we were detaining her against her will. 'I shall need to look out suitable mourning and see what the gardeners can do in the way of flowers. I dare say they can manage a creditable wreath between them.'

The hothouses and gardens of Hindlecote were indecently fecund. I nodded, uneasily imagining something in the nature of an outsized horse collar. It's entirely my fault, of course, that huge arrangements of flowers seem to me expressive of nothing at all. Portia meant well. 'You'll come back?' I asked.

'For the funeral, naturally. I shan't stay. Grandmother won't be up to guests. Hotels are expensive and since Botolph never paid a bill I imagine we owe most of them money already. It will be quicker and cheaper to use the car.' Before I could offer our spare room again, she added, 'Kind of you to put me up, Amy, but you're very cramped here and you have no servants. I prefer to go home.'

Sometimes it's painfully easy to dislike Portia. I wished she would hurry up and leave so that I could continue my search for a dressing-gown that would pass muster with a seven-year-old and get down to Sussex again. Snappish replies came to mind, but before I could utter them Rudi intervened. 'Speaking of money, Portia, I should like to see the castle before I suggest any kind of development. I'll just arrange the day with my secretary then I'll drive you home.'

'All the way? That won't be necessary, the train serves perfectly well. But surely you've visited Hindlecote?'

'You have never done me the honour of inviting me there,' he said, smooth as silk and laughing to himself. 'Of course, if you do open to the public I shall certainly buy a ticket.'

Portia gave me a look of faint pleading. She felt reproached and so she jolly well should, I thought. Then, with an about-face that made me sorry for her all over again, she said, 'It's a long time since I felt able to entertain. You know, Amy, when I married it seemed as though I had everything: love, position, a castle, acres and acres of land, yet none of it's in any sense mine. I have no rights, only duties. I own nothing, nothing at all, and it's a cold, unpleasant feeling.'

'You have Beau, Portia, and by salvaging his heritage surely you've earned a place at Hindlecote.'

'He can never get the castle back as it was. Perhaps it's as well there's little money. You can't know the agony of watching him and wondering what kind of a man he'll be. Like his father? God forbid that.'

It was not in her character to abandon herself to despair. No castle was worth it, and no husband. I didn't say so. The moment for rallying cries hadn't yet come. 'Beau has your blood too and the Mottesfonts'. The times are against the idle and dissolute. He'll come through,' I said. 'Let Rudi drive you home. He knows a great many people with a variety of talents and he won't let anyone upset or cheat you, I promise.' While Rudi brought the car round from the mews I fussed about, kissing her goodbye, packing her few things back into the Marks & Spencer bag and putting in some bars of chocolate in case she got peckish, though I guessed that they would stop somewhere for lunch. It was blissful when she had gone.

Grandfather died that morning, before Portia reached home. A week later the families, Mottesfonts and Savernakes, gathered for the funeral, half-filling the sooty Victorian church across the square from the house where Grandmother would now be living alone. Beatrice, an ageing Mottesfont cousin, waved to me rather more vigorously than the occasion warranted and wept copious tears. Ferdy, her second husband and a source of scandal, gave a furtive nod. 'That man, how dare he come?' muttered a voice behind me. Yet

Grandfather, who had looked after Beatrice and her money, had not gone to extreme lengths to prevent the marriage. His understanding was deeper and more compassionate than my grandmother's, who had said emphatically, 'You're a fool, Bea. The man's a common little gigolo and marrying you for your money.'

'Of course he is,' she agreed amicably. 'Why else would he bother with an old muddler like me? But he's kind. He'll never do anything to hurt me or make me look ridiculous. We're fond of each other.'

Ferdy, so hopeless at being a confidence trickster, pretended to be foreign but hailed from Ilford. As he aged, the insecurity of living on waning charm and such small wits as he possessed frightened him badly. Beatrice gave him respectability and a place. Scandal rather dogged her. Her first husband, a judge, had died suddenly in a Liverpool brothel. Under cover of darkness his corpse had been discreetly conveyed back to the Judges' Lodging on a handcart and, had he not seriously upset the coroner on more than one occasion, the truth might have been hidden. Instead, to poor Bea's chagrin, the full story came out at the inquest and had to be lived down. I suspected that, in spite of an unprepossessing exterior, Ferdy cherished a stronger sense of honour and decency than the judge and, in his way, loved her.

Since the miseries of the War our occasions had been happy ones, weddings or christenings or anniversaries. Once again we faced painful loss. There were a great many flowers. Portia became mildly put out when she saw that the only wreath on the coffin was a simple affair of yellow roses from Grandmother. 'I should have thought the Hindlecote lilies,' she murmured, looking proudly at an immense construction, bearing on a broad black ribbon across its lush bosom the instruction, 'Rest In Peace'.

27

Claudia surveyed it with a baleful expression. 'Leicestershire deforested again,' she muttered. I gave her a nudge in the ribs to shut her up. She and Portia wore deepest mourning and looked entirely beautiful, though Claudia's dress was of a fine silky chiffon and Portia's appeared to have been run up out of an old black-out curtain. Since I look hideous in black, mine had a broad white fichu collar that drew disapproving glances.

The long drive to the cemetery through clogged streets and drizzling rain frayed tempers. The air felt cold and melancholy. As if snow at Easter wasn't enough, 1958 seemed determined that we should be neither warm nor dry. At the gates, a Mottesfont female made the mistake of complaining to my Uncle Henry because Grandfather's medals and orders were not displayed on the coffin. He was already sad and in a huff. 'Don't know what you're moaning about,' he said. 'Robert was a modest chap, unlike his abominable relations; one of the few remaining men who understood port. I ought to be up there with the pall-bearers, carrying my old friend to his rest. The young ones pushed me out, damn them.'

His wife leaned across him and apologized. 'Now please stop being absurd, Henry. Of course they turned you down. It's bad form to drop a coffin and you have your work cut out picking up *The Times* nowadays.'

Henry fixed her with a faltering eye. 'You're right, Phylly, I'm not a fit man, but you don't hear me complaining, even though that woman's wearing the most God-awful hat I've ever encountered. Can't think why they must go into black – makes them look like crows, even your brother's girls.'

'Do get on, Henry, dithering all the time. You're not obliged to pass comment on everyone.'

'They're getting a bit long in the tooth now, of

course. Portia must be fifty if she's a day. Is that blasted penguin with the hideous wimple Amy, may I ask?'

'You may not, and Portia is forty-five,' Aunt Phyllida said as we moved towards the graveside. 'Another word and I shall be sorely tempted to push you into the hole first.'

'That's a fine thing to say to a sick man. You won't have me for long now. I'll get pneumonia hanging around here in the rain, bound to. As soon as I'm gone you'll prance off like Beatrice and marry some rotter who'll give you a dog's life, I shouldn't wonder.'

'An interesting prospect,' she said, removing his hat and thrusting it into his hand as the committal began.

Portia, Claudia and I, the recipients of so much quiet kindness and love, shed tears. Cristabel, my brother's wife, stayed close to me and held my hand. Grandmother didn't weep. Refusing Rudi's arm, she stood like a monolith, showing signs of irritation with our muffled whimpers, only unbending to ask Cristabel, who was several months pregnant with her third child, whether the standing tired her. Later, when we were back at the house and most of the guests had gone, she said, 'The world is becoming uncommonly frightened of death. Too much to lose these days. Heaven offers nothing to compare with frozen peas and television sets.'

'The immortal soul's out of fashion,' Aunt Phyllida said. 'There can be few as great as Robert's.'

Grandmother nodded. 'Rest is a great blessing. That occasionally wearisome fellow Spenser asked quite sensibly, "Is not short pain well borne, that brings long ease?" So much better to accept the bargain of death after life than to live all one's days in terror. Robert was very tired and so am I.' A chill came over me then. The generation that had cemented the family together and been our shield against danger and rough weather was

29

falling away, leaving us naked. I started doing miserable sums in my head. Rudi was already fifty-six, seventeen years my senior. How much more time did we have together? Twenty years, or thirty? Perhaps a kind fate would see that I died relatively young, before he did, and so be spared a loss I could scarcely bear to contemplate.

My brother, Valentine, said, 'There's no hope of persuading you to come back with us to Gunville Place I suppose, Grandmother?'

'None, thank you, my dear. Get Cristabel home before she becomes exhausted. Robert and I have lived in this house for more than sixty years. If we have spirits, this is where his will be. A visit, perhaps, later in the summer when the baby arrives.'

Black clouds filled my sky. This is awful, I thought; she doesn't mean to be here then, she's letting us down gently, saving our consciences. Rudi noticed the watery look in my eyes. 'No more tears,' he whispered, 'they're a burden to her. Shall we go? I'm longing to be home.'

The company of mourners was becoming animated, as always happens at funerals, and exchanging news of little interest. Portia looked wraithlike. Claudia, who grows savage in times of grief, watched and ground her teeth with irritation. We said goodbye to Grandmother, who gave a grateful nod, then we slipped away before our intention was noticed.

Chapter Three

My thoughts, which had been morbid and chaotic, calmed as the car turned out of the narrow lane and skirted Underhallow green. Hallow Hill sulked under cloud. Pewter threads of water ran down the lower slopes in channels dug by the incessant spring rains, the trees and grass stood out violently green against the grey. Hattie Doolittle came out of the door of Parsley Cottage, trundling a handcart. She had not lived there for long. In a shed behind the house she made pots and tried to sell them door to door without a great deal of success. They were fairly hideous. Her long hair was coming unpinned, her green cloak flapped around her feet, picking up a rim of mud from her wellingtons. I wished she would wear stockings under the boots. Her legs turned purple in cold weather and there was a sore patch at the back of each knee where the tops rubbed. Claudia and I had almost known Hattie once. That was when we were small and not yet disgraced and still sometimes invited to children's parties. Our mother was alive then. After Mother's death Claudia learned to swear fluently and lapsed into unsociability. I didn't mind being ostracized. I was shy, and sudden jollity frightened me into fits. The Doolittles enjoyed a wealthy life-style and Hattie was welcomed everywhere until her father suffered reverses in the City and they moved away from Dorset. By the time that scandal struck them after the War I had virtually forgotten the Doolittles.

Hattie, who now lived alone, had developed a tenderness for Reggie Bowmaker of Merve Promotions, who disliked her intensely. Always neat himself, he resented untidiness in women. His affections had, in any case, lately become fixed upon Dora Slade, who kept the village shop. The headquarters of his firm was in a house in London, owned by Merve. When in the country, the partners shared a Victorian mansion set on a bank at the corner of our lane and belonging to Reggie. He was a strand in a cobwebby relationship that extended throughout the whole of show business. Filaments connected him distantly to American politicians, minor and defunct European royalty, a family of Romanies and the owner of a chain of seaside cockle and winkle stalls. As far as I could judge, the partners' relationship consisted of friendship and common interests. Some witless village youths said they were homosexuals, though in less polished terms. I'm not sure how they explained Reggie's obvious partiality for Dora. Aside from their main business, the partners were well known to researchers, writers and devotees of the theatre. Divided between the two houses, they kept an extensive library and a bizarre collection of costumes, prints, playbills, drawings and assorted knick-knacks. They supplied information to anyone who asked. They were unique. I wanted Portia to like them.

The three villages of Hallow had grown rapidly in the past ten years. Grouped on the outskirts of Underhallow, where once had been pasture, now stood a dozen exclusive 'executive' homes of varied architecture, the Manor Court Estate. They sported double garages and Spanish-style wrought-iron work. Their names were determinedly rural, in the vein of Meadowsweet, The Cotte or Badgers' Den. The houses were frequently burgled, for which the tenants of a large new council estate at Hallow Wickens were blamed. I wasn't so sure. The newcomers were not exactly popular. They joined the Residents' Association with the aim of turning us into a kind of running production of *Merrie England*, and brought in friends who snapped up cottages as weekend retreats and proceeded to ruin them with hardboard, ornamental shutters and painted wagon wheels.

The lady at The Paddocks tried to lure away Kettle, my part-time gardener, with the promise of hourly wages at almost twice the going rate. She envisaged, she told him, a symphony of colour against a background of divinely noble trees. 'Every darned old tree for a mile got cut down to put them houses up,' he muttered. 'They takes their time agrowing, do trees. Try to get 'er to see it, silly cow. Paddocks is it? Bollocks more like.'

I never quite knew whether I was supposed to hear and take notice of remarks of this nature, delivered semi-audibly, so I had cultivated a series of non-committal noises that could have meant anything or nothing. He was an uncouth old devil, but good at his job. I didn't want to lose him. In all ways I found the Kettles an uncomfortable family. Mrs Kettle, a Londoner, was as determinedly jolly as her husband was miserable. Her conversation was larded with wartime catch-phrases from the wireless, and occasionally, when she could be persuaded to move her considerable bulk, she 'obliged' me and the vicar's wife. Greeted with the cry of 'Can I do you now, sir?', the vicar, a serious man, winced and fled into the safety of his church.

The Kettles had seven children. From the time that Horace, the eldest, could walk with reasonable steadiness, he had been burdened with the care of one or more of his six sisters while Mrs Kettle toured the cinemas, jumble sales and newly arrived bingo halls. His opportunities for play were nil. Except when he was in school, a filthy and gradually disintegrating perambulator had gone before him, attached to his skinny arms like a growth. Poor Horace was, I think, a natural martyr. No sooner was he free of sisters than he found an exacting religion, the Brethren of Micah. They met in a tiny brick chapel in Uphallow. After morning service each Sunday Horace set up a rickety kind of pulpit beside the pond on the green and preached in a demented fashion, usually to no audience other than the ducks. I quite enjoyed the threatening messages on his posters. My favourites were, 'They Shall Lick The Dust Like A Serpent', and 'I Will Cut Off Witchcrafts Out Of Thine Hand'.

Then, one night, crossing Hallow Hill after evening service, Horace saw a heavenly vision in the form, he said, of a spaceship. It hovered, shining, above him, emitting beams of light. To him had fallen the honour of receiving the new annunciation, a warning of the second coming of Christ. He prepared another poster: 'Though He Tarry, Wait For It'. Poor Horace, nobody believed in his experience, with the possible exception of Hattie Doolittle, who sometimes saw dryads and hamadryads in the woods and whose hold on reality was already tenuous. An improbable friendship developed between them. While Horace shot pigeons for the pot, went ferreting for rabbits and sought to convert her to Christ, Hattie preached astrology and vegetarianism and persuaded him to look after her ancient and unreliable boiler. 'Brethren, chapel, bleeding spaceships,' Kettle grumbled. 'I need a word with Mrs Kettle. He's no flesh of mine.'

I went into the house by way of the side gate. Piers knelt on the damp ground, inspecting a rose-bush that he had bought out of his pocket money and planted himself. He liked gardening. So far the bush had produced only a single red rose. 'Are you all right, darling?' I asked.

He frowned slightly at the endearment. 'We're going to give it a good old load of pig-shit,' he said. 'That'll perk it up no end.'

'Yes, I expect it will,' I said, wondering whether there was any point in trying to ban the use of such technical terms to my seven-year-old. 'Have you looked after Aunt Dora and made sure that she's comfortable?'

'Course I have. She's having five minutes with the newspaper in the drawing room. She let me weigh the sweets for a lady in the shop and take the money and have one for myself. It was a maple brazil. I didn't like it much. Then I kicked a ball around for a bit, not in the shop, in the yard, and Mr Slade banged on the floor with his stick and told her to stop that little sod from thumping about 'cos it was giving him a headache. Aunt Dora says he's a rude old devil and if he weren't her father-in-law she'd put him in a home. Where's Dad?'

'Putting the car away. I found you a smart dressing-gown, dark blue towelling. You can try it on later. And sod isn't a very polite word, so please don't use it.' He looked so grubby and sweet that I longed to pick him up and hug him, but I didn't dare. With Piers, unlike Roly, who at the same age clung affectionately, it was necessary to wait until he came to me.

'I won't then. Aunt Claudia wants to talk to you.'

'Already, are you sure? We left her only a couple of hours ago.'

'I'm sure. She spoke to Aunt Dora on the telephone, then I talked for a little while – not too long mind – and I asked did she enjoy the funeral, like you said I'd got to ask people, and told her some things I'd done. Then she asked why wasn't I at school and she was having a rest from brats. Do you know some someones called Bee and Porsheler?'

'It's Portia, darling, she's your aunt too, though you haven't seen her since you were tiny; and I suppose she meant Cousin Beatrice. Did she sound cross at all?'

'Just funny, like always. She wants to talk to you about those ones and find out what the hell is goin' on. Can I sit up while you talk to her?'

'I don't think so, Piers. I shan't ring her just yet. Come in now, bath, then supper. What would you like to eat?'

At Grandmother's there had been no chance to talk over the state of affairs at Hindlecote, even had I wanted to. I wondered what Claudia had heard. Also I wished that she wouldn't talk quite so forcibly to my children. Roly, a nervous baby, used to scream if she so much as looked at him, though school had toughened him satisfactorily. He infuriated her now by scoring little points off her with logic. Apparently they had begun to teach one-upmanship to boys at an early age. By the time that Piers arrived, I no longer fretted about dropping him or making mistakes in his feeding. Consequently he displayed a blissful calm. My chief dread was of them growing up and not needing us any more. I imagined and yearned for a daughter. At thirty-nine my time for child-bearing was beginning to run out. Had I tried again and produced more sons I might not have been able to conceal a sense of disappointment, so I had learned to do without her.

Piers gave a last fond look at his rose. 'Grow, grow, grow, dear old darling,' he said softly. Balanced on one foot, he hopped into the house, shedding his shoes in the kitchen. 'Aunt Dora gave me my supper, didn't you, Aunt Dora? Fish fingers and tomato sauce and cake.'

Dora was dozing lightly, looking like a resting empress. She woke with a slight start and said, 'Your sister rang, did Piers tell you? He's been as good as gold. I'll get back now. Hattie Doolittle's trying to interest me in a new range of art pottery. If she wakes Slade he'll screech again.' She lowered her voice to a whisper. 'When she brought me those *marmites* things, he yelled through the door that when he wanted a new pisspot he'd tell her so. Most of the village heard him.'

'Pisspot,' said Piers quietly, trying it out.

Dora quelled him with a severe look. 'That's enough of that, Piers. Don't be a parrot. You're old enough to know what not to repeat. Funeral went off all right, I hope?'

'Sad. I do hate them growing old and leaving us.'

'Eighty-eight's a good age. That generation grew up in comfortless times, yet once they got safely past four-teen it took a lot to kill them. Slade's well over ninety. If I'm not careful he'll outlive me from sheer spite. Goodnight, Piers.'

'G'night. It was lovely. Thank you very much. I'll kiss you if you like.'

Dora contained her enthusiasm behind an enigmatic smile and presented a smooth, pale cheek. 'A kind offer, Piers. You smell rather earthy, but it doesn't matter. See you both tomorrow.'

When Piers had fallen asleep on Rudi's lap and we had dined, I telephoned Claudia. She seemed irritable. Her way of wrestling with sorrow was to pretend that nothing had happened until she was sure that all her softer emotions were under control. 'Where have you been? I've been sitting here on my own waiting.'

'Isn't Bill with you?'

'He stayed in Town. He's getting so damned import-ant it isn't true, what with the panic over the Common Market and where we're to sell and buy cereals.

37

Forever at meetings with ministers. They want him to stand for Parliament next time, God forbid.'

'Wouldn't you like it? Lots of parties and pictures in the papers, you know the kind of thing, William Deering, MP and Lady Claudia Deering, caught in an informal moment at their gracious old manor house.'

'Where have you been living, idiot?' she enquired fractiously. 'Our titles cut no ice nowadays. It's far more likely to be farm labourers flinging dung at our windows because they want more money, or Bill in trouble because the price of wheat has risen a groat.'

'Well at least we could all wear posh frocks and have tea on the Commons' terrace and stun them with our witty conversation.'

'Politicians depress me. They make such fools of themselves. I like Bill the way he is, thanks. The urchins are in bed, I hope?'

'Kindly don't refer to them as urchins. Piers is asleep and you know that Roly boards. Is education strange these days, d'you think, or am I simply behind the times? So much space travel and loud music and sport. Roly's crazy about cricket and rugby, and when the Manchester footballers died in that air-crash he insisted on a black armband. Yet he scarcely turned a hair over poor Grandfather.'

'Schools have a lot to answer for,' Claudia said. 'Sometimes I feel that everything from cruelty to animals to the atom bomb is entirely my fault. They encourage the little brutes to read newspapers and be public-spirited and to despise their parents.'

'Weren't we forbidden newspapers? I can't recall ever seeing one, not until the Great Stepmother Scandal and of course the divorce.'

Claudia made a loud snorting noise. In spite of the passage of the years she had never become reconciled to our father's second wife, Sonia, a disaster if ever there was one, and now history. She said, 'Sometimes I sneaked a look at the cook's *News of the World* and tried to fathom out what the accused scoutmasters and vicars on serious charges had been up to. I didn't properly discover until the War.'

There came a pause while she marshalled her forces and I indulged in a wistful dream wherein Claudia grieved over our sister's plight, thought of schemes to give comfort and pleasure, warmly invited Portia and Beau to share our holidays, and generally behaved beautifully. I said nothing of this. My occasional fits of sentimentality usually make everyone, particularly Claudia, hate me. 'Well,' she said, 'that's enough chat. Now you can tell me what's going on.'

'How d'you mean?' I asked in what I hoped was a casual tone. 'Piers said you mentioned Bea and Portia.'

'Come off it, rat, I'm not totally dim. You usually manage to nose out everything. Don't you know that Beatrice has been taken up by the ducal set since she married Ferdy?' I said that nothing so unlikely had crossed my mind. 'Well, they think him quaint. It's so hard for them nowadays to find someone to patronize that they grab at any chance. Not that Bea gives a damn. She's using up the old judge's moneybags as hard as she can go, but she could buy and sell the lot of them if she felt like doing so idiotic a thing.'

Mercenary ideas came into my head. Perhaps Cousin Bea could be induced to divert some of her money towards the rescue of Hindlecote. I could almost see Ferdy in smart Coritanum livery, showing visitors around the castle and boasting like mad of his aristocratic friends. He had tried to talk to Portia at the funeral. Regrettably, after a decent interval for courtesy's sake, she had moved away from him, nipping in the bud his efforts to be chummy. Yet the marriage of Bea and Ferdy certainly possessed a soul. It was present in the kindness of the looks they exchanged, and in Bea's generosity, and in Ferdy's eagerness to perform small services for her. I said as much to Claudia, adding, 'And Bea suffered such indignities in the past that one can only be happy for her. I shan't say a word against Ferdy as long as he behaves.'

'Why on earth are you drivelling about souls? You're getting touchy these days. Please shut up. Ferdy's entirely by the way. The thing is, I was standing beside Portia and wondering how she could possibly become more boring each time we meet, when Bea accosted her. I distinctly heard her say she was sorry to hear that Botty's dying, and was it really leprosy, as she understood it had died out in England in the Middle Ages: more likely it was constitutional, though if it was catching she perfectly understood why Portia had sent him abroad alone.' Claudia paused for breath. 'Are you listening there, or have you gone to sleep? You're not saying anything.'

'I'm not getting much chance. Have you finished?'

'No. My first thought, naturally, was that Beatrice had gone batty again. She's supposed to be on the wagon since Grandfather got her dried out, but I'm damned if she is.'

'Are you sure? She rambles a bit but she never seems at all tipsy.'

'Of course she doesn't. Bea resides on a kind of alcoholic plateau, neither entirely drunk, nor entirely sober. Anyway, Portia burst into tears and jabbered away and I distinctly heard her mention you and Rudi.' Claudia paused dramatically, then barked at me, 'So what have you to say to that?'

'I suppose you'll have to know sooner or later. Portia said you were bound to find out,' I said. 'The full truth is a secret and I warn you, it isn't nice. If I tell, you're neither to laugh nor mock nor say I told you so, because I more or less promised you wouldn't. And you're to help, not turn your back and say it's nothing to do with you. Agreed?'

She badly wanted to know. 'How do you mean, help?' she asked cagily.

'Visit her, invite her to share our holidays, write now and again, telephone regularly, that kind of thing. This is a shockingly lonely time for her and the boy.' I could almost hear her rummaging around in her head for a foolproof way of escape and not finding one. Portia's tears had bothered her even while they irritated. I thought, If there comes a question of involvement she'll want to be as far from it as possible. But this time I was wrong.

'Holidays, good God, you're crazy if you mean the sea. There isn't room in the Studland house. And you realize, I suppose, that the twins would make Little Botty's life an absolute misery, and Portia would hate the way Alex always fills the place with rescued slugs and dying seagulls.'

'Stop hedging. And do try to call Little Botty Beau now he's growing up. We could take a year off from renting by the sea and try Leicestershire instead, or you and I could go to Hindlecote on our own. There are endless possibilities.'

'Endless,' she repeated glumly. 'What a lively summer it's going to be one way or another. You won't believe it, but the government's sending Bill to Canada for three months and me with him, unless I can get out of it pretty smartly. Canada, I ask you! What am I supposed to do in Toronto while Bill's at those interminable meetings? I'm not in the least bit good with wives. They go in for baby showers and sewing-bees, whatever they may be, and I must say they sound the utter end in boredom. They're bound to take an instant dislike to me. What a grisly prospect!'

41

I didn't want her to go to Canada. It seemed only fair to suggest that perhaps she shouldn't miss such an opportunity and that she might enjoy the spectacular scenery. 'I loathe and abominate scenery, *and* abroad. Listen, Amy, I'll do my best, but I don't think it's fair to change the children's holiday. They love the sea.' She had a point. For two or three weeks in summer our families rented a large, decrepit old house on the Dorset coast, near Kimmeridge. There were no sophisticated touches like mains electricity and water, and we got it cheaply. The children had empty beaches, cliffs, heathland and total freedom.

'If Bill's not going to be there we could invite Beau.'

'I don't think so, not with the twins. Those wretched girls can argue over anything, and they compete. The fuss they made when I refused to let them march to Aldermaston with Michael Foot and other assorted crackpots! And all because Little Botty boasted to Grandmother that he was going. They hate to be outdone.'

'Good Lord, Little Botty – I mean Beau – banning the bomb? How surprising. Better not mention it to Portia; I don't think she knows.'

'Stop waffling and tell me what's really up with her. Not that I want to go to bloody Hindlecote, don't think it.'

'Well,' I said, 'if you really prefer Canada, I won't try to dissuade you.'

So that was it, the boredom of Portia versus the boredom of Canada. She swore a bit, but Portia won. I rejoiced. Carefully I related the story as it had been told to me, adding nothing of my surmises and allowing Claudia to reach her own conclusions. It all seemed far worse with the retelling. If Portia had a true friend among Botty's set (which I doubted), she could scarcely correct the rumours without broadcasting her plight to the world. Let her at least be able to rely on her sisters.

After a brief consideration Claudia said, 'Why did you think I might laugh? It's tragic, isn't it?'

'We have rather made fun of Portia in the past, you know, and not been sympathetic.'

'She's so irritatingly passive. Putting up with the worm-eaten Botolph, and trying to please, was wrong. I can't imagine why she's so miserable now. If he dies, she's free.'

'And the estate will be bankrupt. Botty has to stay alive a little longer, not for his sake but for Beau's. Hindlecote Castle can become what I believe is now called a tourist attraction, cream teas, tasteful souvenirs, punting on the river, a glimpse of the young heir playing croquet on the lawn. Rudi thinks the possibilities are endless with the right organizers. The government gives grants as long as the public is allowed in.'

Claudia livened considerably. 'I really don't see why not. It's a marvellous idea. Look how Val's managed to turn our hideous old home into an hotel and make it pay. If Portia's got an atom of go in her she'll stop grizzling and enjoy herself.'

We talked on for a while, discussing the funeral, and Grandmother, and Uncle Henry's decline into old age, then she hung up abruptly. The rain stopped and the moon came out. In the distance, on Hallow Hill, a nightingale sang. Nice bird, I thought, knowing that for once in our lives I had argued with Claudia and won.

Chapter Four

Over the period of change at Hindlecote, Portia confounded my gloomy prophecies. Mothers can be savage in defence of their young. Having made up her mind to salvage Beau's inheritance, her character, admirable though never congenial, hardened, and she pursued her goal without repining. She wasted no energy on hating the Duke. Her struggle for Coritanum's reputation and the stability of his house was lost. Once she mentioned the bad faith of his mother, who presented her son in a much whitened image. 'I never heard of brainwashing until after the War, but that was mother-in-law's technique. I can't blame her. She feared for Botolph as I fear for Beau and believed that marriage would redeem him.' She shook her head as though she were shaking off those distant influences. 'Happiness lies in duty well done,' she said drily, 'and what arrant nonsense that is!'

Ever the eldest sister and the duchess, her attitude to me remained commanding. Occasionally I was summoned, but my contacts with her were necessarily intermittent. In consequence my view became keener. Rudi asked me to be on hand for her first meeting with Merve Promotions. 'You can stand by with the smelling salts, or whatever ladies use nowadays for crises,' he said. 'If not for your sister, then for Merve. He's a jangle of nerves.'

Neither needed me. The partners fell in love with Portia at first sight, and she, in her cold detached way, with them. 'But it's wondrous,' Merve trilled, 'you, this gorgeous castle, so grand, so noble! Utter, utter perfection. Duchess darling, you shall be rich, shan't she, Reggie, shan't she, Rudi? A huge government grant wisely invested, the public happy, and Hindlecote firmly on the coach tour itinerary.' Reggie smiled. Merve executed a few dance steps. 'And now to explain us. *Not* queers, in spite of appearances. Reggie as straight as you please, and the poor self a nothing, a dire case of mumps in adolescence. I wish it were other, hearth and home and little ones at the knee, but it's too late for repining. The balls are shrivelled irrevocably, dear Duchess.'

I quailed at his awful frankness. Why ever hadn't I warned him to be discreet? Why hadn't Rudi? Portia, with rescue within her grasp, examined Merve's radiant hair and suede boots without flinching and positively soared. If only Claudia had been there to see her! 'Indeed? Scarcely my affair, I think. I'm assured you are the best, and my sole concern is that the enterprise should pay. Do you wish me to conduct you around the estate?'

'So gracious, but may we be bold and ask to wander at will?'

'Certainly. Please avoid the Wodsbridge field beside the stream. Archaeologists are at work there. It's important that the site isn't disturbed. You will see their tents and huts and a notice on the gate. When do you expect your preparations to be completed?'

'That depends to some extent on the amount of construction and the contractors. Not before next spring. We shall agree a date with the trustees as soon as we can.'

'Good. The digging will be over by then.'

Half absent, I stood by the window, looking out over the castle acres to the low and distant hills. It was an exhilarating day. A strong wind blew. Vast clouds boiled and broke, racing across the sky like mad things. The children will love it, I thought, and was brought up abruptly against reality. So beautiful had seemed my idea of a grand reunion of sisters and their families that I had nurtured it despite the gallons of cold water poured on it by Claudia. Now, listening to Portia's precise businesslike tones, I knew the folly of dreaming.

With a nervous tremor in my voice, I said, 'I did wonder whether this year Claudia and I might arrange a visit with the children. We rarely see you and Beau. Of course, we wouldn't expect to stay here. I imagine Leicester has a pleasant hotel.' Any hope that she might fall on the idea with enthusiasm vanished when she looked at me as though I were a raving idiot and didn't answer. 'Claudia asked me to say how sorry she is that Botolph has the – that Botolph's illness is causing so much upset. She sends her love.'

'Yes,' Portia said. The word emerged with a dry scepticism that caused me to set aside my idyll with haste. Rudi grinned at me. Somehow I never learn.

'It's two o'clock,' he said. 'Will you all be ready to dine at seven? I've reserved a table at the Red Cow and I hope that you'll do us the honour of joining us, Portia.'

'Thank you, I will. I prefer not to put an extra burden on Cook. The archaeologists brought their own most ingenious field kitchen, but she has a partiality for one or two of the young men; they give her ingredients and she bakes for them. Showing off, but out here in the wilds one dare not forbid it in case she gives notice.'

The presence of a group of assorted Europeans on the sacred English soil of the Coritanums surprised me. It was the first of many astonishments. The old Portia would not have considered it. Her attitude to foreigners, especially those with whom we had quarrelled in the past, had always been snobbish and

46

suspicious to a degree. They may have paid her well. Money not only talked now at Hindlecote, it blew trumpets and brought down the walls of Jericho.

The leader, Gerhardt Nordmann, a quiet scholarly man from Heidelberg in Germany, arrived first and spent hours in the castle muniments room examining the archives. The Wodsbridge field, he thought, might once have been a burial ground. A rumour, recurring from one century to another, of hidden treasure did not much interest him. His main search was for a tablet recording a ninth-century revival of an ancient Danish custom, the building of a bridge to eternity by a mother for her dead son.

I'm not sure which came first, Portia's interest in the excavations or her comfortable friendship with Herr Nordmann. 'I have allowed my mind to rust,' she declared. 'Shared interests are so satisfying. We read the English poets together and Gerhardt promises that in time he will teach me enough German to understand Goethe and Heine.' Her friends had always been few. The great companion of her youth had been Botolph's sister. On the occasion of her wedding to a garden designer, the son of a bishop, Portia had been chief bridesmaid. The union proved to be temporary. A lady with royal connections and catholic tastes trapped the designer in an arbour and quite took his mind off horticulture. After a second marriage and a second divorce, Portia froze out her sister-in-law. It seemed a pity, since she now lived an idyllic life in Beverly Hills with her third husband, an American film producer, and filled her house with the great, the funny and the clever of two continents. But Herr Nordmann was a likeable man, spare, almost monkish, in appearance, and possessed of a quiet, self-effacing charm that awakened no alarms. Certainly Portia achieved an ease with him that she had never managed with Claudia or me, or even with Botolph. It was pleasant to see.

Before the castle became the unquiet preserve of Merve Promotions, Portia removed to the Dower House. Although quite large, it contained a warren of uncomfortable rooms, most of them small and inadequately lit by leaded panes within deep stone mullions. In the garden stood an old round brick kiln. At some time it had been converted into a pleasure pavilion and fancifully extended by the addition of a second circular room behind the first. At head height the stone facing blocks were decorated, mysteriously, with incised animals, flowers and symbols. On the lintel a phoenix flew to the sun. There were no windows. The unknown builder had added fireplaces, plastered the walls and painted them with a frieze of dancing figures, fauns and maenads lightly clad in vine leaves and bearing grapes and wine. A lantern, constructed above the roof, threw brilliant light on to floors of polished, honey-coloured wood. Portia sat there in preference to her drawing-room. As I first stepped over the threshold of that curious and beautiful building, a creep of sheer pleasure touched me, a sense of happy anticipation, as though I were revisiting a place once known well. A memory returned of night and voices. 'Gifted with the second sight perhaps,' said Gwennie, then my nurse and now my present stepmother, and my father asking if she was angry. But I had never been the slightest bit psychic. I shivered violently and grinned. 'What is it, Amy, are you cold?' asked Portia.

Noticeable was a gentle warmth, as though the old fires that baked the bricks had left an imprint. The temperature, I discovered, scarcely varied in rain or frost or snow. I shook my head. 'A goose walked over my grave.'

Each day Portia visited the excavations. Every

evening Gerhardt Nordmann and some of his colleagues came to the pavilion for drinks and a discussion of the day's finds. 'It's quite fascinating,' she told me, 'the various layers of civilization, Anglo-Saxon, Viking, Roman, lying under the grass where we grazed cattle. What a pity you never went to school, you could appreciate more the importance of knowing the past.' Undoubtedly she was right. Ignorance sent my brain off on tangents. To dig up the dead, even after twelve hundred years, seemed faintly sacrilegious. How long would we lie undisturbed? I didn't voice the thought. I've noticed that Christian burial is the only one deemed to count and those buried with other rites have to expect to finish up, a neatly labelled selection of bones, in a museum.

Rudi and I returned to Underhallow and Portia got busy. She became almost as fervid a telephoner as Claudia, the world's worst troubler of the wires. We were weighed down with every detail. In the interests of research, she travelled to those great houses close at hand, disguised in headscarf and dark glasses, to sample their delights and pick up ideas, entering in a notebook the prices charged in the tea-rooms and the quality of the provender. She sent pictures and large ornamental objects to auction rooms for sale, realizing astonishing sums. 'I've kept the Coritanum family portraits,' she said. 'They'll belong to Beau when Botolph dies, and no-one would want to buy them anyway. Such an ugly lot!' When she ran out of information I asked after Botolph's health. 'Much the same, I believe – still alive. How strange of you to ask.'

'You don't intend to visit him then?'

A silence ensued. Portia was good at telephone silences, allowing the foolish time to consider their folly. I gathered that Botty need not look forward to her early arrival and that those of her acquaintance who felt compassionate enough to visit would incur her displeasure. Eventually she said stonily, 'He took my fortune and my jewels to buy other women. Let them visit him if they choose.' She gave Merve *carte blanche* to keep or discard the castle's mountain of furniture. Scenting scandal, the neighing, braying ladies of the ducal set called at Hindlecote and were repulsed with the intelligence that her Grace was not receiving at present. A few hardy spirits succeeded in tracking her down. She excused herself coldly by pointing out that she couldn't possibly entertain them in view of the pokiness of the Dower House. The drab Duchess had somehow become formidable and they didn't persist.

Claudia loathed the idea of spending time at Hindlecote, but she deeply resented not being wanted. '*She* doesn't want *us*? My entire life was blighted for weeks with dread. What absolute cheek.'

'Well, you didn't want to go,' I pointed out. 'She's reluctant to invite anybody until she's thought of a way to tell Beau about his father and why she's opening Hindlecote to the public. You know how she chokes and strangulates over mentioning sex, particularly to the boy. I gather she's confided in Herr Nordmann, the archaeologist I told you about, and expects that he'll do the telling for her.'

'That's the oddest thing I've heard in years,' Claudia said. 'The woman's a plague sore. Why not the vicar or the school head? Why not Val or Bill or Rudi or even Father, though he's remote these days? Does she want all Europe to know? Mark you, if we can never make head or tail of what she's driving at, I give small hope for a foreigner.'

'It's his lovely calm manner, I think. He gives confidence. And I have a feeling that he finds Portia *gemütlich*. Scholars do have a way of overlooking externals. But you're right, I'm an ass.'

Claudia huffed noisily down the line. 'It's lucky that one of us has common sense. The twins positively refuse to go anywhere near Portia. They say she hates them. Of course they did take Little Botty on their mud-slide when he was staying with Val and made a bit of a mess of him.'

A plaintive girl's voice broke in. 'He liked it, Aunt Amy, truly he did. It was fun. We were only small and he was quite a big boy. He could have said no, couldn't he? Aunt Portia said that we're grubby little hooligans and trust our mother to give us outlandish names. And her with a Botolph! Unreal!'

The names were not Claudia's fault. She had considered christening her daughters Laura and Dora, then Pansy and Primrose. Bill opposed her. 'I refuse to be coy and amusing at their expense simply because they're twins,' he said. 'My mother's family names have died out, we can use those. Lindsay and Grainger – distinctive, don't you think?' By then Claudia was bored with looking through the births columns of *The Times* for ideas and agreed.

'Get off the line, whichever miserable eavesdropper that is,' she called.

'It's Lindsay, dearest aunt, your favourite. Lots of kisses.'

Another voice said, 'Give me that. She's not your favourite, Aunt Amy, is she? I am, me, the sweet-natured Grainger.'

Claudia's patience gave out. 'Stop being so damned winsome, you fiends, and go to bed. It isn't too late to send you to your Aunt Portia, whether she wants you or not. Little Botty can show you his train set and stamp collection.'

'*Seriously* ratty! Good night one and all.' A click and silence.

'You're so lucky to have two daughters, Claudia. I

adore the boys, but I'd dearly love a girl as well.'

'If only you'd said at their birth; you could have had one before I got used to them.'

I stifled a sigh. She doted on the twins, on all her children in fact, though she would have had her finger-nails pulled out with red-hot pincers before she admitted it to me. The girls could be torments and they were dreadful liars, but I loved them. 'I'm glad we're to have our holiday. I'll get some new jigsaws, huge ones, and bring books in case it rains. You can spell out the long words for me. Goodbye, Claudia.'

Studland Bay was a child's paradise in fine weather, which it failed to be in that abysmal summer of 1958. Cold winds and storms far out in the Channel drove the sea against the shore in curling, foamy breakers. The sky loured dismally over us. I hadn't noticed in other years how heavily we relied on Bill and Rudi to carry coal and wood, build fires, pump water, and even to cook the huge, simple meals required to satisfy the appetites of six finicky children. But Bill was in Canada. The prospect of three weeks without elec-tricity or mains water began to seem endless. The gas stove was ancient and either roared at us or burned with flabby yellow flames, and the gas lighting didn't extend to the bedrooms. Rudi came down with us, though he intended not to stay beyond the first week, and chopped up driftwood, filled an old copper in the kitchen for emergencies and lit the fire underneath.

When Claudia suggested to the twins that they might help with washing-up and peeling potatoes, two ident-ical faces took on a look of deep pain. 'It's our holiday; we're doing tasks already.'

'Such as?'

'I'm writing a perfectly lovely essay on What I Did In My Holidays, and I certainly don't want to say "washed up". Lots of girls go to Spain and places and fall in love with waiters. Then Grainger and I have to look for interesting and instructive objects to take to school for a college about the beach. You stick things on paper. I've got a crab claw already; it's empty.'

'And I found a piece of gold tobacco paper and a red strap from a bathing suit; oh and some seaweed. It smells a bit, but I expect it'll look nice. There's a prize for the best. I don't know why we can't go to Spain.'

'If I thought I could foist you off on some unsuspecting waiter, I'd take you like a shot, though knowing my luck he'd be bound to return you after two days. And it's *collage*, not college. Now wash up.'

'We promised to make a sandcastle for darling little Vaisey and darling little Piers and take Alex up on the heath to look for sand-lizards and snakes.'

'Then why is Alex crying? Have you been tormenting him?'

'He's too young to tease, quite a baby really,' Lindsay said from the lofty eminence of her eleven years.

'I'm not, I'm seven and a half,' Alexander wailed. 'She saw a poor hoppity frog in the road, all run over, and she's going to bring it back and put it in my bed. I don't want a dead frog in my bed, Mummy, I don't, I don't.'

'Stop howling, Alex. That frog, damn it, had to die to make room for all its baby frogs or they wouldn't have enough to eat. If every frog lived for ever there'd be no room for you. Bring it home, Lindsay you ghoul, and I swear I'll make you eat it!'

'What an unnatural mother we have, to be sure,' she said to her twin. 'If we grow up to be totally ignorant and die young without ever winning a prize, she'll be desperately sorry for her cruelty and wish she'd encouraged us.'

'Please don't raise your hopes,' Claudia said,

throwing a tea-towel in their general direction. 'Your Aunt Portia was a great prize-winner and it did very little for her, other than turn her into the dullest woman in the world.'

After three days of rain and cold the sun shone. I sat on the rickety verandah, sewing buttons on shirts. From behind the house came the rhythmical clack clack of an axe splitting wood and Rudi singing, 'Farewell and adieu to you fine Spanish la-ha-dies,' in time to his chopping. Claudia was upstairs, slopping iodine into a graze on Vaisey's knee. Poised on the ridge of heath above the shore, Grainger shouted, 'We've got the stumps in. Come and play cricket.'

I looked up at her. Roly, forbidden swimming which he loved, paddled in the shallows, his back turned to the sea. His eyes creased and he smiled. On his knees as usual, Piers inspected with absolute concentration something held in the flat of his hand. From fifty feet away, I saw the slow wave form, climb and crash down, racing in to land and knocking my two sons flat on their faces, dragging them back into the glassy depths.

I don't think I made a sound. I was up and running, to hurl myself at that monstrous green enemy. I swim, but not strongly. The heavy draw of the waves pulled me outwards. Roly's head came up and he floundered, trying to strike for the beach. Clutching his arm I put it around my shoulders. At first I couldn't see Piers at all. Then I felt a soft bump bump against my side and glimpsed the red of his trunks. Thin arms and legs spread, he drifted like a turtle just below the surface. A wild despair tore through me like a physical pain. I grabbed at him and missed, and then the twins were with me, diving and surfacing like dolphins, their fair hair slicked to their heads, bringing up after an interminable age a small, limp bundle that was Piers.

'Hang on, hang on,' I muttered to Roly, 'hang on,' as I thrashed and paddled my way back towards Lindsay's outstretched hand and safety.

Grainger knelt astride Piers, rhythmically pressing his back. Dead, I thought, he's dead. Agonizing centuries passed. Then he choked, dribbling sea-water with a moaning cry. She turned him gently onto his side. 'Breathe softly, darling, breathe. That's good. Alex, run and get a rug.' I sat down on the wet sand with Roly's head on my knees, thinking, This dress will shrink, wool always does. I reached out and touched Piers's small cold hand. His fingers curled around mine. A tiny pink shell dropped into my palm. 'Hospital,' Grainger said. 'Mother's coming. She's the fastest driver, she'd better take them. We've got our robes, we'll go as we are. Sorry, Aunt Amy, we can't wait while you change. You can follow.'

'It's going to be all right,' Claudia said, bending over me, 'they'll be fine. Just not to take any more chances.' She kissed me and then I was alone, sitting on the wet sand with little curls of foam washing my feet, salt water dribbling from my hair and face, mixing with the bitter salt of tears. Rudi picked me up and carried me into the house. He was white and shivering as he stripped off my clothes and rubbed me with a towel, wrapping a blanket around me, murmuring all the time as though I, also, was a child. My fist was clenched tightly over the pink shell. He eased my stiff fingers apart. 'He'll want it when he comes home,' he said, and laid it carefully on the table.

Chapter Five

That was the end of the holiday. My sons were unharmed. Tragedy had not happened, though I was infected with a hovering sense of panic and impending loss that made me miserably afraid. Once recovered, the boys were proud of their adventure. Roland, quick-witted and selfish in defence of his own interests, recognized the danger that lay in anxious mother-love and took immediate steps. 'I'm going over to Miss Doolittle's this morning to help with the potting,' he said, two days after our return from Dorset. 'Lighting the kiln makes her nervous. I bet that's why her pots are so awful. Shan't be in to lunch. Some of us are cycling to Chichester. There's an Elvis on.'

'A what, darling? Oh, I see, Elvis Presley, that's nice. It looks as though it might rain again; wouldn't the bus be better? Or if there aren't more than four I can run you over and pick you up afterwards.'

'Cool it, Mum, we're all right now, Piers and me.'

With some effort I avoided begging him to eat and drink nothing offered to him by Hattie. She was the product of an expensive girls' school, then a casualty of her father's scandalous amatory and financial mis-dealings. She might, I feel, have survived his imprisonment for fraud. His bigamous marriage and the discovery that a clutch of half-brothers and half-sisters had, for much of her life, been living within five miles of her home, somewhat damaged her perception of the world. Both Mrs Doolittles were piqued to learn of the existence of the other. The true Mrs Doolittle in particular regarded the arrangement as unfair, since she had only one child and the usurper had four. She withdrew into the security of nervous illness. Hattie elected to be alone. Untrained for any vocation, she tried to live off the land. Elementary food hygiene was unknown to her and she went in constant danger of poisoning herself. Herbal messes boiled to extinction on the gas stove. Welded to the draining board and kitchen table, ancient fragments of left-over experiments lay quietly mouldering to compost. Aside from her potting, Hattie was engaged in writing a life of Kemal Atatürk. Frequent visits to reference libraries left her little time for homemaking.

Roland's attachment to her had a freakish inconsequence that I made no effort to fathom. She was his favourite person. I suspected that part of the attraction was that she let him filch small lumps of damp clay to be thumped into models of rockets and space satellites and mannikins holding guitars. He waited on her in his holidays with dogged devotion. I wondered aloud about the craze for rock and roll. 'You're a mum, you don't dig,' Roly said. 'Stay square. See you later, alligator.' Thousands invested in teaching our children the beauties of the English language and they preferred gibberish from nowhere, leaving my generation to ferret out their meaning.

I mentioned this to Claudia who had taken to telephoning daily, expressly, it seemed, to be rude. ('How are we this morning, fish-face?') She confessed herself baffled. 'Centuries of noble blood and we spawn slaves to bawling American truck-drivers with dislocated hips and overtight trousers. Wretched degenerates! We were interested in improving subjects.'

'Like jazz and sixpenny novelettes?'

'What else? They improved me enormously. Better

by far than the *Girls' Own Paper* and those tiresome heroines full of derring-do. Saving the Empire with prayer and hockey-sticks? Extremely plausible, I must say.' She gave an indignant snort. 'The boys are fine then?'

'How can they actually boast about almost drowning and treat me as an enemy to freedom? It was terrifying.'

'Plenty more terrors to come,' Claudia said, 'so you might as well stop behaving like a wet week and accept that parents are helpless, not to say redundant. We're going away for a few days.'

'Why not? The twins had their holiday thoroughly spoilt.'

'Not that us – you and me, fathead. It almost choked me to ask favours of the damned Duchess, but as you're so keen on sisterly love I forced myself. Talk about haughty! It's like trying to sell her a dud vacuum cleaner or a pair of brown bootlaces. I'm to convey her sympathy for your distress, blah, blah.'

The point of Claudia's phone calls and inconsequential chat now became clear. 'Oh lord, you're taking me out of myself, is that it? Of course I can't go away. Piers is still a little boy and he doesn't understand caution. He needs me. Losing a child is the worst of all losses.'

She gave a patient sigh, of the please-God-spare-me variety. 'But you haven't lost a child, have you? You've had a shock, probably the first of hundreds. We'll stay in Leicester. Bring Rudi if you want to, as long as I can do the driving. It's ages since I drove any distance. What's all that whispering going on?'

'It's at your end, not mine. I thought there must be someone with you.'

'There is,' she said, 'those pestilential girls are listening in again. I'm going to have the extension cut off. Wait a moment while I knock their heads together.'

'Don't punish them, please. I haven't properly thanked them for saving Roly and Piers.'

Lindsay said, 'Yes you have, darling, four times already. Had you forgotten? And Uncle Rudi thanked us, and Roland. It's going to Grainger's head. She's taken to bothering old ladies with kind acts and they don't like it much, so can we please not be thanked any more? What we want to know quite desperately is whether we're to have our cousin carnival.'

'Cousin car— whatever can you mean? Claudia, do explain.' I was beginning to fall into the confusion of childhood, when people had conversations around and across me and I struggled to guess what they were talking about.

'It's perfectly simple,' she said. 'Your boys, together with my tiresome rabble, are joining forces with Val's two, just for a week.'

'Eight of us,' Lindsay put in, 'isn't that an idea of heavenly brilliance? Annie Bowells is coming with us and Aunt Cristabel's going to slot us in. I don't think I've ever been slotted before. Oh, and Uncle Val says not to worry, their nurse would have made a good prison guard for the Nazis. She'll take care that we behave. And the swimming-pools are for the guests. If he catches one of us within fifty yards of either he'll tan our bottoms.'

'But Aunt Cristabel is – er – busy.'

'No, she isn't, not at all. She's only pregnant and bored because nobody lets her do anything much. She's looking forward to us. Please, please, don't say no.'

In the background Grainger said, 'Dearie me, there's no time to lose, Aunt Amy, not a single second. We're all living under the shadow of the bomb, d'you dig me?'

'Grainger,' I said, smiling at her lugubrious tone, 'I'm a mum, I don't dig.'

'Poor, poor you. What hell to be old persons. Jive to stay alive, twist until you bust, we say. Ow, Ma!'

'Speak politely to your aunt, you festering brat, and do it in English,' Claudia said, 'or I'll box the other ear and pack you off to boarding school.'

There were distant noises of the twins clattering downstairs, grousing vigorously. Old persons indeed! And how pityingly my sons looked at me, as though I should be bent and grey and wearing a knitted shawl. Challenged, I determined that thirty-nine was not at all old and that I could reasonably regard my sparring sisters as counterpoise to the weight of years. I made conditions to which Claudia answered, Yes, yes, before blithely forgetting and arranging things in her own way. Rudi was more enthusiastic than I expected. 'Claudia's ideas usually fill me with alarm,' he said, 'but this one contains an element of sense. Unless it's ladies only I shall come with you. I've been so abominably scared, Amy. At one moment it looked very much as though I was going to lose you all, and that's an unbearable prospect.'

He had dealt so considerately with me that only now, to my shame, did I notice how strained he looked. 'Why, when I know that I'm tiresome, do I always expect you to forgive my follies?' I asked. 'I thank fate that nothing worse happened, I really do. The boys think we're dreary old dodos of course.'

'Of all dodos alive, though I believe mostly dead, I'm probably the happiest,' Rudi said, touching my hand. A small ache in the region of the heart nagged at me. The ghost daughter I would never have moved behind me with a swish of imaginary skirts. Damn! Two children were quite enough to worry about.

We found Hindlecote Castle aglow like a painting by Constable. Across a sky of watery blue, blowsy pillows of cloud moved like sleep-walking sheep. Clotted shadows lay under the trees. On the pale stone of the walls the famous roses spread a shawl of colour and light. The first impression was of tranquillity. We then became conscious of a concert of noise and movement. The repair of moats is destined to remain a mystery to me for ever, but men, ladders and machines worked far down with loads of clay and gravel and heaven knows what. On an undistinguished piece of grassland now stood a medieval pavilion, tasselled and broadly striped in red and yellow. There seemed to be the beginnings of a small railway track. Over the considerable confusion rose the springing tower of Merve's bright quiff, as he squatted crosslegged on a pile of trestles, screeching and gesticulating. Rudi defected at once without excuse. 'Shall we see you later?' I asked.

'Of course, darling. Enjoy your talk. Make my devotions to Portia; she'll prefer to have you to herself.'

Claudia gloomed at his departing back. 'Men always manage to weasel out of things and make it seem a virtue.'

For all the colour and animation of the scene it was a wake, the death of a way of life for which Portia had sacrificed her youth and happiness. With what regrets did she see the splendour die? As we passed through the Dower House gate into the unkempt garden, I prayed silently for no unfortunate remarks from Claudia and assumed an expression of determined cheerfulness. Our reception was cordial, if not warm. While it would be untrue to say that Portia burned with an inner fire (she would have regarded that as very bad form), some alchemy warmed her pallid skin and gave animation to her manner. Her clothes played a part. Gone were the dull tweeds of yesteryear. Over straight black velvet trousers she wore a shirt by Chanel, cut like a man's, with topaz links at the cuffs.

The effect was odd, passionless and at the same time devastatingly feminine. Her hair had been shorn. Pale as a new sovereign, it curled neatly and naturally about her ears.

Claudia was put out by the unexpected competition. 'What's happened to the fawn cardigan then? I thought it was good for another ten years. And who cut your hair?'

'Merve. He asked if he might. Did you know, Amy, that he used to be a hairdresser in Mayfair? He's full of gossip about Botolph's friends and their wives; you wouldn't believe the things they told him, intimate things.' Portia wore a faintly guilty expression. 'Wrong of me to be consoled by the sins of others, I suppose, but I am.'

We sat in the outer room of the brick-kiln pavilion, looking over a tussocky lawn and low wrought-iron railings towards the river. Portia made us coffee in a streamlined glass pot and served with it heart-shaped honey cakes. Delicacies formed little part of Hindlecote baking, which tended towards the wholesome and filling. 'Lovely, Portia,' I said. 'Did your cook make these?'

'Gerhardt, Herr Nordmann you know, very kindly brought them for me from Germany, and the pot and the appropriate coffee. He went home to visit his wife. She's rather a lonely person, unable to have children, and unhappy when Gerhardt is away from home.'

'Who's Gerhardt Nordmann?' asked Claudia.

'Amy's met him. He leads the archaeological team. If the dig is successful it will be an extra attraction for Hindlecote.'

'I suppose you don't keep a butler now?' Claudia said, her eyes roving in a quest for sherry. 'Or a cook?'

'Cook's still at the castle, but when the buttery and snack-bar are opened, she'll be one of several under the supervision of a chef. I shan't trouble her to give us lunch. The promoters provide a buffet meal for the construction workers and I usually share that. Will you take a turn up to the castle first, to see what's planned? I expect we'll find Beau there.'

'Certainly,' Claudia said, nudging me in the ribs to draw attention to the Jane Austen phraseology, 'as long as there's some food left when we get to it. And something fermented, in a bottle.'

A small bubble of anger formed in my mild bosom. I nudged her back. 'How greedy you are. You can't be hungry already.'

Portia stood up. I saw the shadow of lost defencelessness return for a moment. She had the nervous, offended air of a borzoi hound. 'Damn,' Claudia said. 'Sorry, Portia, you look so heavenly I think I may be the tiniest bit jealous. Don't mind telling me that I'm dreadfully common, I *do* know.'

The hard frost of Portia's utterances had melted, though an odd icicle clung to the fringes. 'I trust you're not common, Claudia. If you are, so am I, having been "nursed upon the self-same hill", to quote Milton.' (The poetry readings were doing good service.) Out of her blue eyes an eager light shone. 'Do I truly look well? I have a little money now, but with Beau's future to consider I don't feel comfortable spending it on myself.'

Claudia turned her around to face a long glass on the wall opposite the fireplace. I got a very queer feeling indeed. The glass was old and uneven and the downward light cast unexpected shadows. Cloudy shapes moved to and fro. My sisters' reflections wavered, were lost and found again. A crown of stars gleamed around Portia's head. I pulled myself together sharply. They were simply the raised pattern of the fireplace moulding, appearing and vanishing with the intermittent

63

sunlight. A gentle sighing in the room gave way to Claudia's brisk tones. 'To quote somebody else – I don't know who: "Mirror, mirror on the wall, who is the fairest of us all?" All right? Good, then do please show us what's going on.'

Merve had ransacked the castle, finding treasures that Portia herself had forgotten. 'What a place,' he said, 'cupboard upon cupboard stuffed with Sèvres and Limoges and Derby and Worcester. I grew up in a terraced house in Hoxton with souvenirs of Southend on the mantelpiece. Now I have the run of a silver closet as big as our ground floor. Heaven of heavens!'

In the vast dining-room, a boy in jeans and sweater bearing the message 'CRAZY FOR ROCK', was distributing along the table a gorgeous Crown Derby dessert service. He looked up as we wandered in, walked to Portia and gave her a casual hug. 'Hallo, Mother. Aunt Amy, Aunt Claudia, how nice. Isn't this the most?'

'Beau? You've almost grown up when I wasn't looking,' I said, studying him with interest. As a child on the podgy side, he now had the starved appearance of difficult adolescence and a prominent Adam's apple. He regarded us warily, as strangers.

'Completely,' he said with some diffidence. 'I should like to leave school and look after things here, but I know I must finish and try for Oxford.'

'You don't mind all this, giving up the ducal life-style before it's begun and having your estates taken over?'

Portia and Claudia had wandered past. Beau lowered his voice. 'That stuff's uncool, misery-making; it doesn't take much brain to see it. I play piano, oboe and guitar – at least, I'm learning, and Merve's arranging rock concerts once a month in the season. And when the locomotive for the little train's delivered I get

64

to drive it. The chaps are sick with envy. I think Merve's great, the absolute greatest.'

'Doesn't your mother want a career for you? The diplomatic service, I thought. What does she say to the guitar?'

An air of sullenness clung to him. 'It makes a bit of a fool of one to be worried over so much and the last thing I want is to be a diplomat.' He put an arm through mine. 'She's going to be all right, do you think, Aunt Amy? I feel responsible, you see. Everything for me, sacrifices I never asked for. I haven't the nerve yet to tell her that what I'd like is to bum around the world, play music, earn my living somehow and mix with all sorts.'

'You care what happens to Hindlecote though? It's been in the family for so long, hundreds of years, and once this enterprise gets going there'll be plenty of money to run it.'

Beau's shrewd dismissal was an engaging mixture of extreme youth and worldly wisdom. 'While curiosity lasts, Aunt Amy. How long do you suppose? Twenty years? Fifty? We're bound to lose in the end, when people are tired of us and stay away. Then it's caretaking for the State.' He grinned. 'You *do* look surprised.'

'I am, Beau, tremendously. Your mother frets so, and I quite expected the traditional attitudes. You must have thought about it a lot.'

'The one really useful thing they teach us at ghoulish school is to think – that and how to take a beating. Swing, swing together stuff is the oldest of old hat. If Mother has lots of money and spends it, that's fine with me.'

'She looks quite different already, stunning in fact.'

We stopped in the shadow of a lifesize marble of Atalanta stooping to pick up a golden apple, watched

65

by Milanion and Aphrodite. Beau patted the goddess's draped bottom abstractedly. 'It's an awful thing, but when this place starts to pay I hope that my father dies quickly so that we're both free of him. I hate him. He's never given a damn for us, yet I don't want anything that Mother wants for me. How do I tell her so?'

At present he fought a losing battle. Maternal devotion, as I had cause to know, is more passionate than tender, an agonizing, obsessive anxiety that must be a mild form of torture to the subject. 'Too much love's a burden, I expect.'

'And being young and trapped and ignorant of life can be hell, don't you think?'

'Yes, it can,' I said, remembering the fears and torments, and remembering too that in the blood of this gangling child lay as much of me, as much of all of us siblings, as either Portia or Coritanum. He could turn out to be any kind of man, good or bad. 'It passes of course, Beau. Come and see us if you feel like it, or telephone, or write.'

'Thanks, Aunt Amy, thanks awfully. I might.'

I discovered Claudia alone, surveying with acute distaste a hand-sewn tapestry carpet, three hundred years old. It had been lifted from the floor, and cleaned and now hung on the wall within a frame of thick, tasselled cord, looking venerable and rich. 'Doesn't heritage make you sick?' she said, glancing around the great hall. 'I quite thought that damned carpet would have been thrown out by now. And who do you suppose took the trouble to cart all those great white lumps of marble across the continent? The place looks like a cemetery.'

She hadn't behaved too badly, all in all, but sociability was beginning to tell on her. 'They're great art and worth thousands,' I said. 'Definitely allegorical.'

'They lurk about like ushers at a public meeting. Can

Hercules really have had such a tiny winkle, d'you suppose, Amy? All those labours and feats of strength seem to have drained him.'

'The idea is to admire the skill of the artist and the beauty of the stone. You're not intended to carry out a detailed examination of the private parts.'

'Then they shouldn't stick the damned things at eye-level,' said Claudia, being fractious and lubricious at the same time.

'You *are* missing Bill, poor thing, and I expect you're hungry too. Come and eat.'

There was quite a crush around the long table. The crowd parted deferentially for my two fair, aristocratic sisters and closed again before I could get through. One could easily starve for being small and unimpressive. All of a sudden I felt a grasp on my waist and I was lifted off the ground by a young man in overalls. His face was angelically handsome. 'Here, darling,' he said, pushing a pie into my hand, 'you can sit on my lap and eat that.'

Behind us Rudi's voice, even and calm, spoke. 'I think that Lady Amity would prefer to choose her own food.'

'Blimey,' croaked the angel, 'sorry, lady, I didn't know you was one of them. Sorry again, mate, is she yours?'

It isn't often that I get propositioned. I smiled at him, faintly regretful. 'It was a kind thought, just the same. Thanks very much. You'd better have the pie.'

Rudi got me a plate of food and a glass of homemade lemonade. 'Now you flighty wench, sit down and try to behave. I ought to get Merve to sack that youth.'

'Don't you dare,' I said, 'he was only being sociable.'

After that he stuck like a burr for the rest of the day. We were taken by Portia down to the Wodsbridge field to examine the dig and meet the diggers. Gerhardt

Nordmann showed us what was happening. His English was amazingly good, with only the occasional stumble. 'The finds so far are much of Saxon and Roman,' he said. 'I suspect that we are excavating in the wrong area. There may have been a bridge only in the imagination. The custom is out of the ancient times when the dead must cross from earth to their soul's destination. It is said that Odin created the rainbow, Bifrost, as the passage to Asgard. But we have no rainbow, Portia, only rain! We may not end at the day set.'

'That's no problem to me, Gerhardt. It may be to you, of course, but you know best how much time you can spare.'

'You are kind,' he said. 'Two of our good helpers are at work on the labelling and the bringing together of fragments in the muniments room, but if you wish I will come and explain the finds most gladly.'

Portia shook her head, acknowledging his offer with a light touch on his arm. Claudia and Beau were arguing the respective merits of jazz and rock with more intensity than I thought either subject deserved. Presently Claudia began to yawn. She stumbled through the tour of the various trenches with growing restlessness and inattention. Rudi said, 'Will you spend the day with us tomorrow, Portia? Beau wants to buy an engine driver's hat before the locomotive arrives and when he's finished his shopping we might lunch at the hotel.'

So that was arranged and I managed to get Claudia away before her patience fractured. 'I notice definite signs of money,' she said in the car. 'The government must have stumped up handsomely.' Then she nodded off and snored a little. Rudi, who was driving, watched the road but managed to squeeze my knee in a loverly fashion. The attentions of the angel in overalls had done me some good. But my attention kept wandering back to the brick-kiln and the Wodsbridge field and the mysteries of human feelings. Was there a magic abroad? Something extraordinary, the unlikeliest event, had happened, of that I was certain. Gerhardt Nordmann, the dry-as-dust archaeologist, had fallen deeply in love with Portia. Emotion lurked in the tired, faded grey of his eyes and echoed beneath every unexceptional word he spoke to her. Claudia, unobservant yet given to flashes of insight, had noticed nothing. And Portia? In her nature lay an untouched innocence and integrity unscathed by the corruption she had witnessed. The very mention of sex (and her experience with Botolph must have been shaming and unlovely) made her flinch and freeze. Throughout the wasteland of her marriage she had kept her vows. I doubt whether her canon of good behaviour encompassed romantic dalliance or the conventions of flirtation. The time was late for learning. There was no way of guessing what might happen should she awaken from her long anaesthesia and find herself desired by a man she truly liked. It was an interesting area for speculation.

Chapter Six

Portia arrived in Leicester with Beau and a long shopping list of her own. Her style was an object lesson to weaker women. Where I might have slunk away with profuse apologies from a shop where I had examined most of the stock and bought nothing, she merely surveyed the offerings laid before her and said, 'Quite unsuitable, thank you.' The shop assistants, I suppose, knew her ways. Claudia muttered under her breath, tried on sensible hats and bought a strange handbag in some hairy substance that she returned the next day. Beau and I blushed together in a corner. We were relieved after two hours to return to the hotel, where he tried on his peaked cap for our benefit. After lunch, Rudi drove him and Portia back to Hindlecote. We saw her only twice more, and briefly. With her archaeologists and the castle swarming with people, she had no great need of our company. It was almost as though Botolph were already dead or had never been, and my unhappy loathing of vast, lonely aristocratic houses caused me to regard Portia as fortunate in her misfortune. She was less haughty, yet remoter than ever. I don't believe in hauntings and influences from the past, but around that beckoning place, the brick-kiln pavilion, weird thoughts and ideas flourished. Try as I might, I could not rid myself of them. Overlying the ordinariness of the days was an impression that, as Portia crossed the threshold, something happened to her, some subtle yet significant change. These thoughts

I kept to myself. I'm never all that keen to be laughed at and Claudia could be scathing about my supposed fancies and fictions.

As an oblique revenge, I dragged her off to view the antiquities of Leicester. She expressed annoyance. 'Not more walls? Didn't I spend hours in a muddy field listening to assorted foreigners going on about walls? And churches don't do much for me either.'

'This is where King Lear was supposed to have lived. It's our history. Do try to take an interest.'

She scowled. 'History stinks. And Portia's having a lovely time, everyone bowing and scraping and dropping in. Why did you make me come all this way for nothing?'

'I didn't make you, you made me,' I protested, wondering whether she wasn't the slightest touch disappointed by Portia's new style, and jealous of the devotion of Merve and his men.

'It was your idea in the first place. Let's go back tomorrow. We can call on Grandmother and I'll stay a night or two with you.' We were emerging from the cathedral and her expression was thunderous. Happily at that point a young clergyman accosted us with an offer of information and Claudia plunged into a mild flirtation that restored her temper. 'The useful thing about the clergy is that they're safe for us married ladies,' she said. 'Committing adultery with them is as unthinkable as shooting a sitting bird.'

In my experience, if not in hers, they weren't always so much different from other men. 'You're not thinking of adultery at all, I hope.'

She smiled a wide and wicked smile. 'One always thinks about it, given the right circumstances. I bet Bill's thinking about it like mad in Canada. Doing it is another matter entirely.'

The idea of acting as chaperone to Claudia on the

71

rampage filled me with alarm. We went back to London the next day. She drove brilliantly at what seemed to me a manic speed, bursting into snatches of tuneless song, her mood improving the further south we went.

Grandmother was in far better spirits than I expected. 'My wish is to die peacefully as soon as possible,' she said, 'but I'm not to be permitted. There's work to do. Beatrice would marry Ferdinand against my advice. Now that graceless Smythe-Fennel trollop declares that he has stolen her diamond bracelet and she threatens him with prosecution.'

'But Cousin Bea has diamonds to spare and pots of money. Why did he steal it?'

'He didn't. It's spite and bluff. The creature has established herself as a ready assistant to tired wives, including Portia, if I'm not mistaken. It piques her that Ferdy declines to be seduced. No doubt she regarded him as what I believe is referred to as a push-over.'

'You and Cousin Bea aren't thinking of buying her off, surely?'

'Not at all, just a few modest arrangements. I don't care for extortion. Mrs Smythe-Fennel has tried that trick before on a larger scale and on someone we know.' Claudia and I sat up. Rudi showed mild interest, but thankfully no guilt. Grandmother regarded us with cynicism. 'You need not be anxious, I don't refer to your husbands. The lady made a very determined bid for your half-brother, David, an exceptionally wealthy and attractive young man of course, and engaged in the kind of business that could easily be ruined by any hint of dishonesty. Metkin Fine Arts has an international reputation to uphold.'

If it had been her intention to amaze me she succeeded abundantly, and I'm sure enjoyed doing so. Her dislike of Sonia, mother to David and, for a while, stepmother to the rest of us, had remained steadfast throughout the years, surviving the later divorce and a world war. I said, 'But you don't know Davy. After Sonia married Father you refused to go anywhere near Gunville Place.'

'There was small reason to visit, given his mother's insufferable patronage and the fact that he isn't my flesh and blood.' Grandmother accomplished the impossible and leered with refinement. 'I met and spoke to him for the first time at your wedding, Claudia, together with Mr Pandel Metkin, the principal of his business. David is not, I think, your flesh and blood either.'

We had no protest to make, no denial. It justified her steady rejection of Sonia that my father had raised a cuckoo in the nest, Pandel Metkin's son. Not that it mattered. To us it was ancient history. David was ours and we loved him. I asked, 'And after that, how did you meet again?'

'Who else should I trust to dispose of my great-grandmother's jewels? The collection was famous, of no use to me and a temptation to others. A few years ago I came upon a burglar in my bedroom. I decided the time had come to sell.'

'A burglar!' Claudia said. 'You might have been murdered in your bed. Why didn't we hear of it? The police were called, of course.'

'There was no need; you really must curb your ghoulish imagination, Claudia. Of the two of us, he was the more frightened.' Grandmother wore a faintly guilty air. 'I knew him and his father, you see, during the War. The mother was killed in the Blitz and he was such a dear little boy. A most inept burglar. Robert and I gave him a strong talking-to. He works in Marshall and Snelgrove now, and what he does on dull evenings is no concern of mine.'

'Don't tell me,' Claudia said, 'you gave him a reference. But you'll have to involve the police to frighten off Mrs Smythe-Fennel.'

Grandmother surveyed her with the ironclad stare that invariably reduced me to jelly. 'You've developed an uncommon faith in authority, I notice. Haven't I mentioned a burglar who is in my debt? The Smythe-Fennel bracelet is by Cartier and quite well known, what's more I'm convinced that it reposes safely in her jewel case.' Claudia and I babbled out questions and exclamations. Rudi, who was a great friend of our grandmother, simply listened, wearing an extremely amused and thoughtful air.

She had hatched a plot. It wasn't a bad one either, though tremendously risky and decidedly criminal. Her burglar, armed with a copy of the day's newspaper to establish the date, was to break in, not to steal, but to photograph the wretched bracelet *in situ* in the Smythe-Fennel boudoir. Blackmail against blackmail; I could see the point. 'But if he's not an awfully good burglar he might be caught again. What then?'

'Should he be discovered and manage to escape with his virtue intact, he is to blame me. I have never seen the inside of a prison; it will be quite a new experience before I die.' I became aware that secretly she was laughing; at us and our gaping faces; at herself; at the thought of one last exercise of power. Affection swamped my worry. Claudia protested vehemently. At that point the elderly maid rattled in with a tea-trolley and abruptly cut short the conversation.

The tea cooled in my cup. I brooded, wishing miserably that David would confide his problems to me. He and I were particularly close. My abiding love for him carried with it always a certain difficult, protective jealousy. Grandmother watched my betraying face. 'David is sensitive to your opinion, Amy,' she said. 'No young man cares to look foolish to those who are dearest, and you are the world's champion worrier. Console yourself with the thought that he snubbed Mrs Smythe-Fennel with commendable thoroughness.'

I nodded. 'He's thirty now. I wish he would marry. Pandel had little joy of his son. A grandchild would please him. You'll tell us about the rescue of Ferdy, won't you please?'

'Certainly, unless I'm apprehended. Then you can read about it in the newspapers.'

'"Hie you to the cell,"' Rudi said, kissing her hand. 'Please take no undue risks.'

'"Hie to high fortune!"' she replied, which I took to be another of those sadly unfunny Shakespearian puns. 'Our man-eater lives in a glass house and would be advised not to throw stones.'

When we arrived in Underhallow it was early evening. David was on my mind, but I knew him to be in America and temporarily out of reach. I had not, however, heard the last of him for that day. A pair of long legs in violet-coloured tights stretched across our threshold. 'It can't be a bailiff,' Rudi said. 'A present d'you think, or a waif and stray?' Claudia, chafing with eagerness for sherry or gin, shuffled her feet and huffed impatiently.

Attached to the legs was a stranger, a small, fair, disconsolate girl, slumped on a carpet-bag that had seen better days. She seemed to be dozing. 'Hallo, are you looking for us?' I said.

A pair of large blue eyes opened and filled with tears. 'Thank God you've come,' she said. 'I spent last night on a bench by the pond and hardly slept a wink. A dog put its nose into – well, it woke me up – and there was an odd kind of man staring at me. He had sandals on and two corn-plasters.'

Horace Kettle, I presumed, who had trouble with his feet, due to tramping back and forth over Hallow Hill in the service of the Lord and the pursuit of miracles. 'The pub would have found you a room. Who on earth are you anyway?' I was too travel-weary to be polite.

'Oh dear, sorry, I should have said at once. David sent me. I'm Meggie Openshaw. I didn't like to risk the pub as I've run away and this time I won't let them find me. I seem to have lost my purse too.'

'Openshaw? Openshaw?' I repeated. The name had a familiar political ring to it, of demands and protests and threats and meetings. Cotton suggested itself, thread-workers and a union. And I had seen posters on the London news-stands, caught with half an eye in passing, that nudged my brain. 'Oh dear, now I know; you must be "Socialist Agitator's Daughter Again Missing From Home".'

'That's me, or if you subscribe to the left wing press, "Respected T.W.O.T.S. Leader In New Domestic Puzzle". What an embarrassment that union is!' The girl grinned and shivered. 'I say, would it be all right to go indoors for a moment. It's a bit chilly for August, don't you think?'

'Freezing,' Claudia said. 'I met old Openshaw once at Tolpuddle, drivelling on about the martyrs, so I imagine you're not here to steal the spoons. Rudi, take the bag and let's move at all speed towards the hot and rebellious liquors.'

I added my voice. 'Come in, Miss Openshaw, and explain to me about David. Wasn't he off to America in a great hurry?'

'He was supposed to be posting a letter to you on the way to the airport. I expect you haven't got it yet if you've been away.' There it lay on the hall table, over-taken by events. Not a great deal of point in reading it now. My brow furrowed, brooding over the tiresome business of making up beds when what I wanted was a pot of tea and a long sit down. In a small voice my uninvited guest said, 'Could you call me Meggie, d'you think? I get this awful sinking feeling over the name Openshaw, especially now I see that I'm being a nuisance. I'll explain how David comes into this if I can just wash a bit first. I tried the pond this morning and got more mud than water.' She apologized for the carpet-bag. 'Father locked up my luggage. This was my grandmother's. She was in domestic service, but I'm not supposed to tell anyone now that Father's always in the newspapers. He's a dreadful old snob. At least Gran was a real person and lovely and not something made up.'

Meggie, washed and brushed and gleaming, emerged as an original kind of girl, viewing the world from under the edge of a fringe of straight, fair hair that conformed to no known fashion. (In the village, Gloria Hopkins's salon preferred to deal in profuse curls or, for the elderly, regimented waves that would last. Charlie, her husband, barbered in the basement where she could keep an eye on him.) She had changed her violet tights for scarlet ones. Running away seemed to be something of a hobby with Meggie. Although her mother, a doctor presently in Africa promoting birth control among a baffled population, took pride in espousing the cause of women, she effectively abandoned her daughter to the Socialist Agitator and the union of Thread-Winding Operatives and Twist-Spinners, or T.W.O.T.S. ('To the pure, all things are pure, I dare say,' sighed Meggie. 'Why ever can't they change their name?') Mr Openshaw did not desire freedom for his daughter. He preferred her to be biddable, pliant and marriageable, having had, one supposes, his fill of assertive career women. His spies were everywhere. No sooner did Meggie secure herself a bed-sitting-room and a modest job than her father descended, paid any sum required in lieu of notice, and hauled her home to sit in their modern mansion on the fringe of Bolton and receive such suitors as he chose for her.

'If you've ever been truly close to a foreman twist-spinner,' she said, 'you'll know how comforting the grave. Getting a clerk's job with Metkin's was the rarest luck and only happened because David fell for a girl I knew at school. She didn't last. I rather think she betrayed me to Father out of pique. Being somewhat desperate, I threw myself on David's mercy and I wasn't one bit disappointed.'

And I wasn't one bit easier in my mind. Harbouring a runaway, even if of age, for an indefinite period had its worrying side. For the moment I was securely bolstered by my troops, in the persons of Rudi and Claudia, but I had small confidence in my ability to repel singlehanded a militant Mr Openshaw. 'How long is this to go on, Meggie?' I asked. 'As you seem to be front page news, I rather think that freedom is likely to be shortlived, unless David has a more permanent solution.'

'In two days, three at most, he'll be back in England. I trust to his cleverness, Amy. May I call you Amy? Oh good. It's going to be absolutely all right.' Her round blue eyes looked into heavenly distances. 'I hope you won't mind; I'm going to marry David.'

'Oh!' I struggled to find something to say in the way of congratulation and pleasure. Nothing came. For all her charm, Meggie conformed not at all to the leggy sophisticates of David's harem and I wondered why his sudden urge towards matrimony. Surreptitiously I studied her middle.

She twisted a hand through her fringe and smiled.

'It's all right, he doesn't know yet, and I'm not pregnant; pure and unsullied, more or less. It's going to be
hard work to get him. On top of being so devastatingly
attractive, he can't see a beautiful woman without
immediately wanting to go to bed with her, which
makes me cross and miserable. And, naturally, they all
want to go to bed with him too. The Chelsea set is
queueing up to the last woman. Love's a great nuisance, or do I mean sex? Luckily I've inherited some of
Father's pigheadedness and I've made up my mind.
You don't utterly hate the idea, do you, Amy?'

'Not utterly,' I said, considering the ill-spent life and
approaching death at fifty-three of Botolph. 'I want
David to settle down and be happy and not just turn
into a sad old philanderer. Oughtn't he to choose,
though?'

'He will,' Meggie said with high confidence, 'when
he can see me properly. You can't know how abjectly I
adore him. His life will be happy and fun and I'll look
after him all my days, I swear.' So that was that, and
nothing I could do about it, either to help or to hinder.
One advantage occurred to me, Meggie didn't intimi-
date me in the slightest. The Chelsea set in full pursuit
of pleasure most certainly did.

Claudia awoke from a light slumber and muttered,
'Only mistresses have fun, not wives, and girls can't
keep their hands off married men. If he's unfaithful
you'll suffer.'

'I become so clumsy when I'm upset,' Meggie said.
'Beautiful objects just slip through my fingers and
sometimes hit people, such as girls, on the head
and smash to fragments.' She nodded at Claudia, who
seemed impressed with an oddity that came close to
matching her own. 'Not that I expect to run down the
stock of Metkin Fine Arts. David's no cheap old forni-
cator, crawling out as the sun sets. He keeps his word.'

When Rudi and I at last got to bed, I lay awake going over the day in my head. As my eyes began to close, I spotted the fatal flaw in Grandmother's criminal plans. I shot upright. 'Are you awake, Rudi?'

'Now I am. You're not hearing suspicious noises, are you? I don't want to get up again.'

'Grandmother's burglar, it isn't going to work, is it?'

'Of course not. If she doesn't notice herself, one of us will have to tell her, but which?'

'Too late to telephone now. In the morning – I'll ring her in the morning.' I humped up close to him and rehearsed my speech, all about exchanging innocence for guilt and playing into the hands of Mrs – who? I forgot and drifted into a peaceful land where there were neither grandmothers nor sisters.

Chapter Seven

During our short absence life in the village had heated up. 'Merriment tonight,' said Dora Slade, presiding over the bacon machine with a sheet of greaseproof paper balanced delicately on her left palm. From a wireless set in the private sitting-room behind the shop came the voice of Frank Sinatra. He was singing 'Love and Marriage', accompanied by irritated thumps from old Mr Slade's walking-stick. He always listened to *Housewives' Choice* and, in general, loathed most popular songs and American singers. Dora wore her regal air. I felt subtly flattered, as though I were receiving groceries at the hands of Queen Victoria. 'Twelve slices, there we are. You'll be coming to the social?'

'Oh dear, I'd forgotten. I'll have to consult. Claudia's here, and a friend of David's turned up unexpectedly.'

'Do try. Gloria Hopkins is on her way round with tickets. She asks for trouble, but I can't help feeling a bit sorry for her. She's up against it this time.'

'Charlie again, I suppose?'

'Edie Farnsworth's got her claws into him and she means business. Marriage no less. After all, she's an outsider. Gloria's one of us and badly upset.'

In my early days in Underhallow I sometimes wondered why Gloria and Charlie Hopkins didn't divorce and be done with each other. Neither had the temperament for open rows. The simplest conclusion was that the periods of sulks and silence they enjoyed were in some way health-giving to their emotions. Certainly Charlie's infidelities paid generous tribute to his constitution. Topsitogs (everything for the kiddies: your knitting-wools ordered), Mrs Farnsworth's new establishment, was next door but one to the Hopkinses' hairdressing salon, and handy for nocturnal prowlings. As for the bold Edie, a greedy, come-hither gleam lurked in her eyes. The non-existence of a Mr Farnsworth caused some interesting and wildly slanderous speculation, particularly from Gloria.

Not that her own record was entirely unsmirched. Mr Slade had switched off the wireless and pushed his wheelchair into the doorway where he could overhear in comfort. 'You don't want to feel sorry for that one,' he said. 'She had her turn in the War, playing pass the parcel with the Yanks. Her bedroom curtains never got opened. Anything they fancied for a pair of nylons and a packet of Camels.'

'That's quite enough of that kind of talk, Father. Just because you don't like her it doesn't mean those tales are true.' Dora gave the wheelchair a firm push with her foot.

Mr Slade moved it back again. 'Who says I don't like her? I can't bloody stand her, that's what, and I never went much on Camels either. Giving fags a name like that makes you wonder what's in 'em. Where's my elevenses?'

'It's only half past nine. You've just had breakfast.' Dora once more pushed him back into the room and this time closed the door on him. 'Now, it was eggs, wasn't it?'

'A dozen, please. Perhaps I'd better say no to the social, Dora. I do rather hate recriminations and rows.'

'They'll not come to blows with the vicar there. Reggie's bringing me and he'll like having Rudi to talk to. Anything from the freezer?' I shook my head. Dora wrapped my purchases and told me that the social club committee (Gloria dissenting) had voted to ask Mrs Farnsworth, the possessor of a maturely impressive bust and a piercing, though true, soprano voice, to sing and do her impressions. Pleased to be chosen, she donated a furry rabbit and eight ounces of knitting-wool as raffle prizes. Before her arrival in Underhallow it was Gloria, also a soprano, who was accustomed to favour us with songs. The slight gnawed at her soul. In a cold fury she took the Farnsworth rabbit and threw it into the village pond, followed, ounce upon ounce, by the wool. No wonder then that blood was up and tempers running high. 'We won't clap Edie more than a little,' Dora said. 'No point in making bad worse and I can't endure her voice anyway. It goes through my head like a pneumatic drill.'

Before I mentioned the social to the others, I telephoned my grandmother, enquired for her health and then, with extreme diffidence, said, 'About Mrs Smythe-Fennel, darling, your plan's very clever and exciting.'

'Do you think so? How nice.'

'I do feel though that it's unnecessarily complicated and rather playing into her hands to give her irrefutable evidence of breaking and entering. If you simply approached her directly, well, you have an intimidating, no, I mean commanding, presence. I'm sure you could threaten legal action for slander and frighten her away.'

Somehow between sleeping and waking, the gentle arguments and well-turned phrases had deserted me. The words sounded bald and blunt in my ears. And, alas, in Grandmother's too. 'How kind of you, Amy. I had no idea of my own strengths. A dragon am I, a Gorgon able to terrify with a look? And I imagined I was all heart.'

I gathered my courage. 'You know I didn't mean that, and you *are* all heart, but not with the Smythe-Fennels of the world. Oh dear me, we love you lots and we don't want you to be rash. Please, please, behave.'

A silence ensued into which I read (wrongly) high dudgeon and hurt feelings. After a suitably chastening interval she exacted revenge by saying, 'You're a good sort of girl, Amy, though deficient in tact. I mustn't tease you. Plotting was agreeable enough. Second thoughts are sounder, if a little dull, and your grandfather would certainly have disapproved. Pray don't worry. I shall be circumspection itself.'

We could breathe again. I gave the news to Claudia and Rudi. I think that Claudia had rather looked forward to the drama of getting our grandmother out of jail and was the slightest bit disappointed. I offered the social as recompense. 'Boring,' she said. Had I not then gone on to mention the tense situation between the Hopkins and Farnsworth camps, I could have got out of it nicely. Scenting blood she changed her mind at once.

Later Gloria Hopkins knocked at the door with tickets. She was in the worst of tempers and gunning for Edie Farnsworth. 'Four?' she said. 'You've got company then?'

'My sister and a friend.' The name of Openshaw would have to be concealed. Gloria read the newspapers and, being quite as suspicious of nature as Mr Slade, couldn't be trusted with secrets. I decided to put Meggie into the care of our young scoutmaster, Humphrey, a nice reliable boy and a budding chartered accountant. He would tell her about scouting and his recent visit to America. It would make a change for her from thread-winding.

'I'll put you down for four meat suppers then. Hattie Doolittle only wanted us to get nut cutlets in special.

The meat's there, I told her, and if it's not good enough for you, you'll have to make do with salad.' Hurriedly I pressed money into her hand, not anxious to prolong the conversation. 'Ta muchly. On the quiet, you'll not be missing a thing if you leave before the entertainment. *Some* persons are forever pushing themselves forward in the belief that they have talents.'

The evening, a teetotal affair, began pleasantly. Humphrey carried Meggie off to meet his fiancée and to join a group of young people. There she attracted no curiosity, becoming simply another tree in the wood. Claudia, fortified in advance by old sherry, showed evidence of enjoying herself. I have never entirely managed to follow the process of her relationships and the sudden camaraderie that sprang up between her and Hattie Doolittle was pleasant yet baffling. Hattie had exchanged her wellingtons and cloak for a satin cocktail dress with sequins, rather too small for her, and a pair of exceptionally dirty white satin shoes. Her legs remained bare. She said to Claudia, 'I remember hearing about you in nursery days. You were a byword among the nannies. It was too bad, by the time I was old enough to go to those foul parties, you'd been put on the blacklist.'

'So I had,' said Claudia. 'When my mother died, I decided not to bother with best behaviour. Are you a true Doolittle or a dud Doolittle?'

'True. You wouldn't like the others at all. The mother's very pushy and seems to imagine that being bigamous and having four illegitimate children gives her some kind of distinction.' Hattie went on to describe the philosophy behind her potting, her artistic aims and the progress of her life of Atatürk. Claudia's eyes glazed, but she bore up manfully. 'It sounds a lot of rot to me, Hattie. Who's going to read a book about a Turk written by an Englishwoman? If you must write, why not a novel with loads of sex and excitement? Everyone likes those.'

'I don't know anything about sex,' said Hattie, sadly drooping.

'Then it's high time you found out. If that's beyond you, make it up. There's been plenty in your family to go on with – and in mine, come to think of it.' They were talking still as we took our seats for supper. In a spirit of benevolent interest, Claudia watched as Hattie produced a stained package of greaseproof paper from her velvet Dorothy bag and shot the contents on to her plate. 'Dear God, what is it?' she asked.

'A lentil patty. I'm a vegetarian. Eating the dead flesh of our fellow creatures is utterly gross. We were meant to eat natural things, herbs and berries, as early man did.'

An expression of pity, coupled with faint unholy glee, appeared on Claudia's face. 'Halcyon days, Hattie. I see it all. Drog the Hideous and his band of brothers toil home after the hunt, proudly dragging a mammoth carcass back to the cave. But Mrs Drog tells him to take the nasty thing out of her kitchen this minute as she's spent hours boiling him up a delicious root and a few leaves for his dinner and she's not about to cook dead flesh for him or anyone else.'

A certain heat entered the conversation. 'I didn't say that at all. What I said was that my way of life, the healthy way, excludes meat, and there's nothing funny about that. This is natural food, seasoned with herbs from the wild.'

'That explains why it looks like a cow-pat, but not why you're prepared to eat it. Highly poisonous, I should think. Try the duck pâté, it's very good.'

Claudia enjoyed probing at weakness. I tried to catch her eye before she went too far. Then in one of those sudden mood changes that take one by surprise, the pair of them exchanged amicable looks. 'Drog the Hideous, where did he come from?' Hattie said, and laughed. 'My patties never seem to stick together. It's quite fit to eat, but I must have gone wrong in the mixing, a constant hazard with me.'

Reggie Bowmaker held Dora's hand underneath the tablecloth. Hattie didn't even notice. I concluded that her mild pursuit of him arose from loneliness and that she wasn't much interested in men at all, only in some fanciful, cherished view of the simple life. When we took our places for the entertainment, she stayed with Claudia, dismissing an attempt by Horace Kettle to interest us once again in his theory of the Second Coming. I couldn't see Meggie anywhere. Rudi went to investigate and found her with Humphrey and the rest, playing Monopoly in the committee room. 'She's happily abandoned and buying hotels as hard as she can go,' he said. 'The Agitator despises capitalist games. He thinks it's enough for a girl to sit on a cushion and sew a fine seam.'

The programme followed an accustomed pattern. A confident child with plaits launched the proceedings, reciting 'The Little Doll' by Charles Kingsley, with actions and expression. In a strained bass, the verger sang 'Asleep In The Deep' and 'Excelsior'. Yet more recitations followed and a lady, hampered by a tendency to giggle, gave us her bird songs, all of which sounded remarkably alike. Monica Berry's Dainty Blossoms, the local dancing class, followed, thudding dutifully to and fro, being butterflies, fairies, toy soldiers and assorted woodland animals. The Blossoms looked endearingly sweet and drew a chorus of oohs and ahs. I found myself thinking, heaven help me, that my daughter would have made the daintiest blossom of them all, had she ever managed to be born.

Then Mrs Farnsworth was announced. She simpered

at Charlie Hopkins, who fidgeted and clapped, relapsing into bashful inactivity when no-one followed his lead. Gloria, wearing a pale green dress spikily patterned in white and red and suggestive of a cactus, stood up. Her pale contemptuous eyes looked us over. Ostentatiously she stumped out of the hall and could be heard in the kitchen, clattering dishes with unnecessary violence. Someone got up and shut the door. Gloria opened it again. The pianist hurriedly played an introduction. Aboundingly confident, Edie inflated her bosom and launched a violent attack on 'One Night Of Love', leaving it for dead. Sparse applause. 'If I Can Help Somebody' followed, a smug kind of song in my opinion. I was indifferent to its fate. Whatever Mrs Farnsworth chose to do to it was perfectly all right with me.

Before her impressions there was a short hiatus, filled by the pianist with his interpretation of a storm at sea. Claudia began to get restive. 'Not the bloody storm at sea again,' she complained. 'Why can't they learn another piece for a change?'

'Shut up, it's almost over. Mrs Farnsworth, then the Queen, then cocoa at Dora's, a navy brew, with rum.'

The impressions were predictable, but not bad at all. We had Jeanne de Casalis, Elsie and Doris Waters, Suzette Tarry, and, raising a few knowing titters, Gracie Fields singing 'Walter'. That was not quite the conclusion. For her finale, Edie, a brunette, donned a blonde wig, deeply waved, and said in a nasal voice, 'Would you like lacquer, dear? How about a hairnet for nights, to keep it in?' Unmistakably Gloria in her salon. 'Yes, dear, I did hear about her and that boy from Hallow Wickens. The way those two are going on they'll have to get married. I ought to have a word with her mother. Not that she'll thank me. There's no gratitude for trying to help people these days.' Gusts of laughter exploded in the hall. Charlie Hopkins, an expression of horrified alarm on his face, stared straight ahead as Edie got fully into her stride. It was a cruel caricature. 'For heaven's sake, shut the door,' somebody said, but it was too late. Gloria, with a tea-towel in her hand, was there, listening with a face like stone to the mockery and contempt of her enemy. Then she was gone. Charlie left soon afterwards, but not for home. He got exceedingly drunk in the Castleton's Oak and towards closing time was collected by Mrs Farnsworth and taken to her rooms above Topsitogs.

On the following morning I woke early. Rudi groaned, turned over and went back to sleep. No sound of movement came from Claudia's room or Meggie's, but the sun shone, our resident blackbird was yelling a cat alarm at the top of its voice and, for a Sunday, the village sounded full of noise and movement. I made tea and took it onto the terrace. Before I managed to drink it, Dora came quietly through the side gate. 'I wondered if you were stirring. You won't guess what Gloria's been up to in the night. Come and see before the police get there.'

A crowd was gathering, swelled by churchgoers diverted on their way to matins. Latecomers perched on the churchyard wall. While Charlie slept in the Farnsworth bosom, Gloria had certainly been busy. Flattened tubes of shaving-cream littered the pavement. Thickly white on the plate-glass window of the salon was the message: 'OWING TO A CHANGE IN MANAGEMENT FREE GIFTS FOR ONE DAY ONLY. UNWANTED STOCK.' The corners around this announcement carried some brief comments of a personal nature. 'C.H. IS A DIRTY BARSTAD' (either Gloria's spelling or the awkwardness of writing back to front had let her down on that one); 'C.H. CAN ROT IN HELL'; 'E.F. HAS GOT NITS'; followed by 'E.F. IS AN UGLY FAT COW'. Above, nailed firmly to the shop sign, hung bunches of pale beige balloon-like objects, lightly inflated, linked by a festoon of small square envelopes. On the door of Topsitogs, obscuring an advertisement for Chilprufe liberty bodices, drooped a generous monochrome nosegay. 'Come on, Gloria, where's the free gifts then?' called a voice from the crowd.

An upstairs window opened. We glimpsed her head, still neat in spite of the night's labours, and her furious, abandoned grimace. 'Coming down. This offer cannot be repeated.' I noticed that the disparaging whine had gone from her voice. 'Here we go.' A rain of small hard articles showered down on us: shaving sticks, packets of razor-blades, tubes of cream, tins of violet-scented brilliantine, brushes, combs and the remainder of Charlie's stock of never-spoken-about-except-in-a-whisper contraceptives.

Overnight Gloria, the cactus, had arrived at her full flowering. She watched with benevolent interest the scramble that followed, laughing aloud when Mr Kettle's fingers were stamped on by his eldest daughter and a minor fight broke out. Two pairs of trousers then fluttered down into the lane, followed by a storm of shirts, jackets, ties and handkerchiefs. 'One thing you can't fault Gloria on,' remarked a woman's voice, 'is her laundry. Just look at those whites. She certainly keeps his clothes nice.'

We moved back to a safe distance as shoes began to clatter about our heads. The door of Topsitogs creaked open and the shop bell tinkled. Charlie emerged, clutching his brow and held fast by Mrs Farnsworth's arm. 'She can't do this to me,' he wailed. 'Look at it, all my stock; two gross gone to waste, and the sundries, every damned thing. I'm ruined.'

'Never mind two gross,' Edie said indignantly, 'what about my door, I'd like to know? A kiddies' shop, too. Disgusting I call it. Come back inside, Charlie, don't give her the satisfaction.' But he shook off her detaining hand and sadly walked the few paces home, picking up garments as he went. The crowd gave a collective sigh as the door closed behind him. No shouts or screams were heard, no sound at all. After an interval the upstairs window closed and the curtains were drawn. Charlie knew when he was beaten. All eyes turned to Mrs Farnsworth and a low hissing began, gaining in volume as she elevated her bust with proud contempt. It was the end for her. She tore down the unwanted decoration, leaving a few shreds of rubber still firmly stuck in place, retreated into Topsitogs and slammed the door. A few days later a removal firm from Chichester collected her furniture and she departed in a taxi, leaving behind only a sign announcing that the business was for sale.

Chapter Eight

Dora decided that the reconciliation between Gloria and Charlie had been thoroughly satisfactory. By mid-day, when Claudia became conscious, all trace of Gloria's handiwork had been removed and she was seen on Charlie's arm, taking a decorous stroll to Hags' Gibbet and back. 'Let's hope it lasts for a while,' Dora said. 'At least I shan't have to listen to Edie Farnsworth shrieking her head off any more. That's something to be thankful for.' Claudia complained bitterly because I had let her sleep and miss the drama. I bore her reproaches with fortitude. Had I wakened her she would have been savage all day.

Meggie, in green tights and a wide hat, went to the eleven o'clock service, as it was church parade and she wanted to see Humphrey in his scoutmaster's uniform. While she was out David telephoned. 'I'm sorry about Meggie,' he said. 'My letter arrived, I hope?'

'You should have rung me. It's too bad of you to play a trick like that. We were away and got Meggie first.'

'There simply wasn't time. If I hadn't made a last check as I was on the point of leaving for the airport she would have been locked in the stockroom for the whole weekend. I had no idea who she was, except that we employed her. She told me the story in the car. I suppose I ought to have dumped her at the nearest hotel, but I simply didn't think of it.'

'Clearly you didn't think much at all. I should rather

like to hear what you mean to do with her now, having committed yourself.'

'Have I? Damn! I can see that she's going to be a wretched little nuisance. Is there any way of persuading her to go home, Amy? I half promised to speak to her father, but I represent the capitalist enemy. He'll have evil suspicions. Meggie's a child, and innocent as a kitten. She needs a proper mother, not that prosing absentee medic.'

The gods had smiled on Davy at his birth. He is one of the joys of my life and inexpressibly dear to me. He is also a man, with a masculine selfishness, obtuseness and blithe self-satisfaction that irritate me to bits. Poor Meggie, deeply in love, faced a problem with her image in his eyes. 'Innocent, I don't doubt,' I said. 'She may lack the worldly wisdom of those hungry predators you favour and she's too fastidious to leap into bed with every attractive man that comes her way. But she isn't a child, nor a stray kitten, nor a piece of property to be shunted to and fro. Think of her in those terms and you insult and wrong her.'

'I hate it when you scold,' he said in an injured tone. 'What have I done except try to help?'

'Taking people up and then dropping them isn't helping and solves nothing. I expect Mr Openshaw's a lonely man. He must be persuaded to give Meggie a reasonable degree of freedom or he'll lose her completely in the end. Tell me, do you have any plan at all, or is she on her own?'

His silence was almost as long as one of Portia's. 'Dearest, she can't possibly live here with me. It would be misunderstood. I rather hoped that you might think of something.'

I had thought of course. Somebody, and I knew very clearly that it wasn't going to be Rudi or me, must speak to Mr Openshaw. David's looks and wealth would put him under suspicion. Not that I meant to weep over him. Let him be chastened, except that it would be of no benefit to Meggie. 'Who do we all turn to for help in our direst emergencies?' I asked. 'You had better get in touch with Pan right away and ask if he feels up to tackling the situation.'

'My father?' Although Davy was a partner in Pandel Metkin's firm, the matter of his illegitimacy still rankled and it touched his pride to ask for favours. 'What can he do?'

'I've no idea, except that technically he's Meggie's employer and his beginnings were even humbler than the Agitator's. They'll understand one another. Meggie says her father's a snob as well, which is useful. Unless Val objects, a meeting with Pan can be arranged at Gunville Place. Emphasize that he's being entertained by a viscount, hire the lords' suite and ply him with luxury.'

'And in the meantime?'

'Give Meggie leave of absence on full pay and ask her whether she would like to keep Cristabel company for a while, until the baby's born. Unless, of course, you can think of something better.'

He said, 'Always my good angel. Thank you, Amy. I believe I may not deserve you.'

It was fortunate that he couldn't see me and the pleased smile on my face. 'Never mind buttering me up,' I said. 'And David, until this is resolved, please get rid of whichever female stick-insect is occupying your bed. Try celibacy until Mr Openshaw is appeased.'

There was no harm, I thought, in clearing the field for Meggie. He grumbled a little. 'Stunners don't grow on every bush, Amy, and this one is definitely stunning. By the way, I suppose you know that Portia's selling some nice pieces from Hindlecote. We've bought some of them through the trustees. What's up?'

'Not now – when we meet,' I said. 'Meggie's out. I'll ask her to ring you and you can tell her about Gunville. The boys are staying there. If she likes the idea we can take her down tomorrow when we go to collect them.'

And that was what happened. Meggie was ecstatic. I felt entitled then to retire and leave her to pursue love.

'Confess,' Claudia said as we started out for Dorset, 'you haven't worried about Roland and Piers once.' I didn't mention that in Leicester I had telephoned the Gunville Place Hotel each evening to make sure that they were safe. She would have been disgusted.

No ripple disturbed the surface calm of Underhallow as the summer gloomed towards its end, yet an atmosphere of restlessness still hung over us. Horace Kettle had become an object of ridicule to his family. A local newspaper reporter had got hold of the story of the spaceship and discovered from the Air Ministry that they had been testing by night a large new helicopter over the downs. The brilliant lights were designed to illuminate locations on the ground. Christ would not be coming after all. Horace lost his faith, gave up preaching and sulked. He sought comfort from Hattie Doolittle, who was deep in her life of Kemal Atatürk and designing a new range of pots in spare moments. She was kind, but absent, and growing stranger by the day. 'I'll do your horoscope when I get a moment. Your system's thoroughly poisoned with meat, I expect. Nature's the best doctor. Try drinking camomile with fennel seed.' This advice was of no use whatever to Horace. When Hattie's boiler next broke down, he simply disconnected the water supply, leaving only a trickle in her cold taps. The stars failed to help her. 'I'm a Gemini, I should never put my faith in another water sign,' she told me. 'And of course he's Pisces, a difficult sign for a man, cold, you know, and not energetic. That's why he gets so many corns.'

'I thought that was because of wearing sandals and no socks. Do you want me to talk to him? He won't listen, I'm afraid. He thinks I'm a spy for his father.'

'Such a nuisance. I shall have to do something, I'm beginning to get dirty.' Setting aside the criticism that she usually seemed quite grubby, neighbourliness suggested that I should offer her a bath. I bit my tongue. What with football on the green and fishing for minnows, my sons created mud enough. The prospect of removing quantities of Hattie's clay from the plug hole lacked appeal. For this meanness I got my reproof. Early the next morning a scandalized and blushing police constable forcibly removed Hattie, naked and not much cleaner, from the pond. Though arguing the natural life, she had to submit to superior force. The constable wrapped her, dripping, into her green cloak, since she had brought no other clothes. Having propelled her without ceremony back to her cottage, he dismissed her with the warning, 'Don't you do that no more, miss, or you'll find yourself in court.'

I was startled in the night by Piers, shouting out in his sleep. I went to him and he woke. Unusually, he clung to me, burying his hot face in my neck. I waited. In a tiny whisper he said, 'I saw Miss Doolittle's top bits. Will I go to hell?'

Damn Hattie and her fads! 'No, Piers, definitely not, it wouldn't be fair, not for an accident. Whatever made you think that?'

'Horace Kettle. He was shouting a bit on Sunday about discovering nakedness and sinners who did it going to hell. I didn't mean to, but she was right in front of me and I couldn't help seeing. Then the policeman came, so I hid.'

Damn Horace too! 'I do wish people wouldn't make up sins,' I said. 'You've done nothing wrong at all.

Horace Kettle is a bit of a crank. And the policeman was cross with Miss Doolittle, not you. It was her fault, you see. She should have put her bathers on, shouldn't she?' Piers nodded and relaxed against me. I laid him down and pulled the covers over him. 'Will you sleep now? No more nightmares?'

'No more.' I was at the door when he said, bubbling with laughter, 'They were like two big puddings, all wobbly.'

'I don't need to know that, Piers, thank you. Forget about it. Good night.' He seemed so small and vulnerable, and in two days he would be going to school as a boarder. I wouldn't be there to calm his fears in the night. Thank heavens I had resisted Eton, where Val had been beaten by older boys, and the school where poor Beau was being beaten in his turn. I thought I might kill anyone who hit Piers. I began to snivel quietly.

Rudi woke. 'What is it? He isn't ill or upset about school?'

'No,' I said, 'I am – upset, I mean. He saw Hattie's top bits and had a nightmare. They were like puddings, wobbly.'

'And I missed them,' Rudi said. 'Some fellows have all the luck. We always get the truth from Piers, you know. He'll tell us if he's unhappy.'

The first day of term arrived. 'You're not coming with us, are you?' Roland asked for the tenth time. 'You promise? Some of the mums cry and carry on. Grim!'

'I've seen quite enough of you over the last weeks. We've already arranged that Dad will take you. He's waiting in the car.'

'Old Piers will be OK, I'll keep an eye on him. You did pack our tuck, I hope? Aunt Dora gave us each a huge bar of nut chocolate.'

Roland kissed me on the cheek. He had already said

97

farewell to Hattie Doolittle and been given a small blue pot that wouldn't stand up properly. Piers thundered down the stairs and through the door without stopping. He looked a little tough, with a short haircut and football boots slung round his neck. Rudi started the car. Suddenly Piers ran back and leapt at me, muttering, 'I'll send you some postcards if you like.'

'Lovely. Is it all right if I kiss you goodbye?'

'Yes.' He kissed me rather damply. 'Mum, can you look after my rose for me? Mr Kettle forgets about it.' I walked down to the car with him and waved to them as they moved off. They didn't wave back. Bereft, I went inside and cried and carried on quietly in the bedroom. Grim!

It would have saved the village a ridiculous amount of fuss if Hattie had taken the time to console Horace. Goaded beyond endurance by his father's jeers, he loosed off both barrels of his shotgun at the door of Kettle's shed, accidentally killing his dog. He did the dog a kindness. The poor creature was seventeen years old, blind, sick and in pain, and already under sentence of death. Kettle begrudged the money for having it put down. He was none the less outraged, as he was in the shed at the time and felt, quite rightly, that the shots had been aimed at him. He grabbed as a defensive measure a Mauser pistol brought back as a souvenir of the War. The thing hadn't been fired for years and wasn't loaded. Horace knew that perfectly well, but appalled by his slaughter of the dog he made off at a run for the police house to confess his crime, with his father close behind. The first intimation we had of this incident was an eruption of Kettles on the green, Mrs Kettle and the Miss Kettles far in the rear.

Horace burst in to the police house. 'Lock the door,' he said to the astonished constable, with a jerk of his empty shotgun. 'Come on, be quick. They're after me. I've got to tell you what happened before they get here.' At the desk the verger was reporting the theft of his bicycle. He backed against the wall and raised his hands. Slowly the constable did the same. 'Now then, Horace lad, no need to be upset. Just you sit down there while I get the sergeant.'

'What are you messing about for?' asked Horace, rather puzzled by his reception. 'Lock the door first.' The gun was aimed at a spot above the constable's navel. He obeyed. Across the green, old Kettle, surrounded by his womenfolk, hid the Mauser inside his coat, content to wait. 'I didn't mean to do it,' Horace said. 'I only meant to frighten the old devil. Get back over, will you, so's I can talk.'

'Sergeant,' yelled the constable, 'out here, quick.' The sergeant emerged from the back room where he had been enjoying a cup of tea and a piece of crusty bread with farm butter, took in the scene at a glance, and put his hands above his head. 'There's been a crime, Sergeant. Better ring through to headquarters.' The siege of Underhallow had begun.

'There's no need for all that,' Horace said. 'Just shut up and listen to me.' He talked. Gradually hands were lowered and a purple flush of rage spread over the sergeant's face. 'You blithering idiot,' he said to the constable, 'worrying me like that. As for you, Horace Kettle, don't you know by now it's an offence to carry a dangerous weapon in a public place?'

'That's not dangerous. It's not loaded. Didn't I just say I loosed off both barrels? The old swine was right behind me so I forgot to break it, that's all. Are you going to arrest me or not?'

'For killing a dog? That's a summons, you great booby, not an arrest. Get out. Tell your father if he don't hand in that pistol I'll be round to collect it.'

'Booby yourself,' said Horace, spiritedly. 'If ever you meet a proper criminal you'll drop dead with fright. And what you've got to tell you can tell yourself. I'm not going near that lot again.' The verger and Horace left together, hurrying in different directions, the one to spread the news, the other to take refuge in Hattie's cottage. That was the end of the siege. The police, feeling that they didn't show up in a very good light, kept quiet about the incident. Underhallow settled down for harvest festival and the long winter's sleep. Horace stayed on at Hattie's. He slept in the shed with the kiln, and cooked contraband meat over a makeshift brazier at the bottom of the garden while Hattie made her witch brews in the kitchen. They lived their separate lives. The convenience of having a repairer of boilers on the premises appealed to Hattie. She didn't try to get rid of him.

With Beau's return to school, Portia's communications became more frequent and more animated. 'I do wish you could see the water gardens. They don't compare with Chatsworth, of course, but the fountains are playing for the first time since the War. I hadn't appreciated how lovely they are.'

'You sound relaxed. Are you happy about everything now? Not troubled by the workmen or the noise? No regrets?'

'I'm not imaginative at all, yet I feel odd, as though I were a step away from adventure. The excavations fascinate me. Did you read in *The Times* about our Saxon hoard? Otto — you remember him, the Swedish professor? — unearthed it. It's treasure trove, of course, though I believe we receive a recompense.'

'And the bridge? Has it been found?'

'The first traces. Gerhardt believes that the stone dedication is still there. He's tremendously excited.

Work is supposed to stop at the end of November. I hope he finds it by then.'

Gerhardt found his stone in October. Portia relayed the event, as excited as a child. Looking back, I thought that I had never known her to show open enthusiasm, not even on her wedding day. 'It won't be raised until all the earth is cleared away and photographs taken. There's to be a party for the team. Merve's helping me to organize it. Why don't you come, just for a night or two, if you won't mind sleeping in the Dower House on your own.'

Being startled by Portia was a novel experience. Dashing across country for a party had gone out with Oxford bags and cloche hats before I was of an age to be invited, and she had disapproved from the depths of her conventional soul. 'Not if you'll be there too, no.'

'Nowadays I prefer to sleep in the pavilion on a day bed.' Her voice became faint. 'It's always warm there and quiet. I rest better.'

A quiver touched the back of my neck, a reminder. What spells visited Portia in that place of insinuating enchantment? The strangeness of the pavilion, the symbols around the outer walls that we could not read, the dancing figures within, the rising phoenix, beckoned and smiled. The lamps were lit. '"True love's the gift which God has given to man alone beneath the heaven,"' read Gerhardt Nordmann, not daring to look at Portia, and meaning every word. Hypnotized by soft, remembered voices, I pinched myself and came out of my dream with a jolt, reminding myself how much I hated going anywhere alone, without Rudi. 'I shall be lost among professors, Portia, and it's a long way.'

'Nonsense, you're intelligent enough when you try,' she said, wiping out with condescension the last trace of mystery. 'It's arranged. Reggie will bring you the day after tomorrow and take you home again. You'll be in time for the raising of the stone.'

'Yes,' I said, mentally kicking myself and for a moment sounding like Claudia. 'I expect I shall, yes. Fascinating.'

Reggie, who drove majestically wearing a tweed hat jammed firmly on his head and a light flannel suit, spent the entire journey talking of his love for Dora and his despair that she refused to marry him while old Mr Slade was alive. 'I could just about bear to have him live with us, but the old devil hates me.'

'He can't stop you; I mean he can't actually *do* anything.'

'Don't you believe it,' Reggie moaned dismally; 'that old fiend would think of something, he'd have a fit, start a fire, tell those soft-brained idiots at the welfare office that he was being poisoned. Dora's a saint. Such a pity that euthanasia's illegal.'

'Reggie! You wouldn't?'

'No, but I like to think about it.' He heaved a sigh. Usually I'm in favour of love and I'm immensely fond of Dora, though after three hours I'd begun to weary of her a little. My responses were lukewarm. I tried for a change of subject without success. Everything and everyone reminded him of Dora. Journey's end came not a second too soon.

Hindlecote had exercised a powerful influence on Merve. His Edwardian suit abandoned, he now affected a version of early seventeenth-century costume, based on a portrait of a dead duke. He shone with silk and satin, breeches caught at the knee with ribbons, a frilled shirt, embroidered waistcoat and buckled shoes. ('Handmade, Amy my darling, and a bugger to clean.') All that he lacked was a powdered wig. He carried a long cane. 'You look like the fairy queen,' Reggie said unkindly, 'and your roots need doing.'

'God, do they show? London next week without fail. I daren't trust the poor self to the local hairdressers. They know pink, but not this shade of pink pearl. Leave your bags there, while the Duchess shows Amy the water gardens. You can tell me what you think of the champagne.'

In my opinion, Merve had over-thoroughly tasted the champagne already. His cane began to wander between our feet. Reggie took it from him and would have thrown it in the moat but for Merve's anguished cry of, 'It's borrowed! Amy, cherished girl, it's going to be a gorgeous party and not to be missed. Portia's waiting for you on the terrace.'

The water garden was lovely, a place of intricate patterns and changing music, too lovely, I suggested, for discarded cigarette packets and ice-cream wrappers. 'Not everyone is a vandal,' Portia said, clinging to the good thought. 'If the dry weather holds, tonight the fountains will be floodlit.'

'Has the stone been raised yet?'

'It's being cleaned now. Everyone from the dig is wild with excitement, but Merve won't let us see it, not even me. He says it's to be properly presented.'

As parties go, this was the strangest. To four women, including two young archaeological students, there were thirteen men, which precluded dancing. How Merve achieved harmony and excitement mystifies me still. Perhaps it sprang from ourselves, and the sense of an end achieved. Or had a ghostly benevolence been released with the unearthing of the ancient dead? 'Champagne,' Claudia said, when I afterwards mentioned my puzzlement. 'Provide enough and even a poxy old stone can seem exciting.'

It wasn't only the wine. The fuss seems a little silly now, but Merve had set his scene meticulously. Braziers burned in the Dower House garden, which was lit with Chinese lanterns and a dozen ancient torch sconces rooted out from the castle lumber rooms. Rose petals (the gardener must have raged to see his conservatories robbed of their late flowers) showered down on us, coloured smoke drifted far out and mingled with the spray from the fountains. The stone lay on a cushion, covered with a nice piece of embroidery. Gerhardt Nordmann, uncomfortable with an extravagance not usually expected of the English, unveiled it without flourishes. Merve had wanted a fanfare. Aside from hiring trumpeters at enormous expense, he found no convenient way of supplying one. He shrieked instead. 'The cry of "Io" is ancient Greek, not Norse,' Reggie objected, miserable with frustrated love. 'I wish Dora were here. She has Greek blood.' Merve poured a libation. The archaeologists crowded forward, free at last to examine their find.

'Latin!' said Otto. 'Are we wrong after all?'

Gerhardt, who knew, bent forward. 'The inscription says, "Hedreda, wife of Lucian, made this path for Baldr, her lost son." Her history lies in those few words. We can deduce that this was a woman of education, married to a man of Roman antecedents. She may even have been born in this country, yet she cherished the customs and the gods of her homeland.' He looked at Portia, his thin face alive with interest. Throughout the evening he had kept as close to her side as he could, saying little, drinking little. 'This mother named her boy for Balder, son of the magician-god Odin. His beauty outshone all others. All creatures loved him, but for the evil Loki only, who caused him to be killed by a mistletoe arrow. He was, we would say, the principle of light and goodness itself.'

The others of the team burst into a spate of discussion in several languages. Music played from the garden. The figures on the walls of the pavilion appeared to move in the lamplight and the building gave out its strange warmth. Soothed and sleepy, I watched Portia and Gerhardt move together. Outwardly she had changed so much, from a draggled crane to a sleek and lovely flamingo, yet the deep-rooted innocence and guilelessness of her nature remained. She had no tricks of seduction. 'I've learnt so much from you, Gerhardt, and reading poetry together has been so great a pleasure,' she said. 'I shall miss you when you leave us.'

'We are not quite done,' he said. 'Export licences must be obtained and the mapping and cataloguing is in delay. Will it be an inconvenience that I stay to complete the work myself?'

'Oh no, but your huts will scarcely be suitable for the winter. You must move into the castle.'

'How good you are,' he said, 'how very good.' And it was a declaration of love and longing. Portia gave him a bright, friendly smile that might have maddened a lesser man. Is she never going to notice, I wondered, urging her on with all the romance in my soul, not even on a night like this, in this magic place? She moved away then and talked to others. Our energies began to flag and there were yawns and little silences. I said good night to one or two people and went to bed.

I switched off my light and was instantly wide awake. The room seemed dank yet stuffy. I got out of bed and opened the window, leaning over the sill to breathe the rose-scented night air. A swimming feeling in my head induced a sense of unreality that was rather pleasant. The floodlights in the water garden went out and Hindlecote Castle disappeared as though it had been spirited away by some supernatural agency. Only the brick-kiln pavilion at the Dower House boundary was lit. The door stood wide open, spilling no light past its threshold. It was like looking into a lighted cave, swimming in brilliance and overhung by darkness. The arched stone doorway framed an opulence of colour. Portia sat upright in her chair, facing me. A blue velvet cushion framed her bright hair like a veil thrown back, the black and silver skirt of her dress spread in a fan almost to the floor. Gerhardt Nordmann sat at her feet. They were still, like figures in a painting. I was, I suppose, waiting for something dramatic to happen. Nothing much did, though I thought that I saw Portia's hand move and rest for a brief moment on Gerhardt's head. Wondering how often and for how long they sat like that in silence, I went back to bed. I must have slept soundly. I didn't see the lights in the pavilion go out or hear Gerhardt leave. Instead of talking over the party at breakfast, Portia was brisk and businesslike, making lists of details she proposed to discuss with Merve. The night might never have been. Before Reggie and I left for London, I walked down to the pavilion and tried in vain to decipher the meaning of the flowers and faces and signs that circled the wall. What are you? I asked it silently. Are you haunting us with mysteries or is it all my imagination? Naturally enough, I got no answer.

Chapter Nine

Hattie Doolittle took over Topsitogs. On the first floor, where Mrs Farnsworth had seduced Charlie Hopkins with her magnificent breasts, she established Topsiveg, a vegetarian café. Custom was slow. Hattie's practice of snatching up clumps of assorted herbage at random did not inspire confidence. As Claudia had remarked, most of the healthful dainties did indeed resemble cow-pats, and the *omelettes aux fines herbes* were a kind of culinary Russian roulette. The enterprise was doomed. That is, until the morning when a stranger rode into Underhallow. It was around noon. Behind closed doors the village ate the midday meal, keeping an eye on the street for any occurrence of interest. Mr Slade's snoring resounded over the green and then stopped. The deserted road, the silence, might almost have been the opening scene of a Wild West film. Underhallow could not, naturally, offer exotic tumble-weed rolling over desert sand, but bits of newspaper shed by the dustmen blew in the puddles. The stranger did not have a horse. He rode slowly on an extremely dignified bicycle. His pin-striped trousers and dark jacket were of a cut rarely seen since the War and a hard grey hat sat foursquare on his head. Lace curtains moved behind windows and noses pressed against the panes. At the gate of Parsley Cottage he dismounted, carefully leaned his bicycle against Hattie's fence and rapped loudly. A slight confusion occurred, a hiatus. The door swung to and fro, the stranger stood firm with a foot over the threshold and eventually pressed inside, closing the door finally behind him. Guesses at his identity proved wildly wrong. He was neither a bailiff, a man from the football pools, nor a Mormon missionary. His sentence served, Mr Doolittle, an exemplary prisoner, was free again, only to find that both Mrs Doolittles had learned to enjoy their freedom and declined to have him back. He thought of Hattie, his sole legitimate child. She had not meant much to him in his palmy days, but he relied on his authoritative manner, undiminished by years in prison, to provide him with a temporary refuge. Underhallow awaited his dismissal with interest. Mr Doolittle declined to be dislodged.

Hattie became quite desperate. With suicide in mind she once again walked into the village pond, this time fully clothed. The police sergeant fell into a dreadful rage. Mindful of his uniform, he ordered his constable to get the lumbering bitch out before she poisoned the water, and then lock her up. The constable frowned and shook his head. 'She's a stout one; I'll never get her out if she don't want to come, and who's to pay for the damage to my trousers?' A small audience gathered and looked on peaceably. 'Just you stop this mucking about, miss, before you catch your death. I've told you before.'

'Go away,' Hattie said. 'If I want to drown it's no business of yours.'

'Ho yes it is,' screamed the sergeant. 'Suicide's a crime. You can go to prison for suicide. I'm not having my patch messed up by corpses. You want to drown, get the bus down to Selsey and do it in the sea.'

'Shan't,' Hattie said.

The two sides stared at each other with dislike. She was not in imminent danger. The water was no more than thigh deep, though matted with weed that clung in green trails to her skirt. She began to hum quietly. There they might have remained, deadlocked, had not Mr Doolittle emerged from the cottage, noticed his enemies, the Police, and found their interest uncongenial. Carefully he removed his polished shoes and black socks and rolled up the ends of his out-of-date city trousers. He ventured into the margins. 'Harriet, come here at once,' he said. 'This obsession with nature will bring you no good.'

The confident authority of his tone, an echo no doubt of Hattie's childhood, succeeded where the sergeant had failed. Her shoulders drooped. With a sigh, she turned and waded towards him, reaching for his hand. 'Kindly don't splash my suit, you foolish girl. It's high time we had a long talk. Thank you, sergeant, that will be all.'

The sergeant addressed himself to Hattie. 'I hate you,' he said, 'I bloody hate you, and I hate him too and anyone responsible for bringing you into the world.'

Mr Doolittle tried to stare him down. 'I could report you for that.'

'Ho, could you indeed? I know who you are, I was warned you was making for my patch. Just you watch yourselves. I'd nick the pair of you as soon as look at you.' Mr Doolittle smoothed his large features and didn't answer. He led Hattie inside and firmly closed the door. I think that he must have brought all his considerable administrative abilities to bear upon his daughter for from that day he became prominent in the running of Hattie's business, particularly in Topsiveg, which he renamed Village Delights. In prison Mr Doolittle had served part of his time in the kitchens. He cooked rather well. Having found Horace Kettle lurking in the shed, he instructed him to conceal his corn plasters, smartened him up, and pressed him into service as a cross between kitchen maid and waiter.

Horace was also encouraged to kill such birds and small animals as he could find. An arrangement with the butcher produced a supply of bargain meats.

To Hattie's distress, her vegetarian dream was no more. She retaliated by seeing the Green Man lurking in a clump of elder bushes beside the churchyard wall. 'You look constipated to me,' her father told her. 'A thorough clear out will cure that overheated imagination.' He drew her into Dora's shop, bought a bottle of syrup of figs and, presumably, persuaded Hattie to take it. The potter's wheel and kiln he transported for sale to Chichester, pocketing the proceeds. The life of Atatürk filled him with contempt. According to Horace, he said, 'Heroes, particularly foreign ones, need no biography. Why not write about Horatio Bottomley? There's an interesting man.' Bottomley was also a notorious fraud. Hattie lost weight and looked older. Gloria Hopkins snipped off her confusion of hair and with one of her bubble-cuts turned her into a matronly Shirley Temple. The wellingtons and green cloak were consigned by her father to the dustbin. She wore stockings, sensible shoes, and blouses with lace inserts. She was deeply unhappy, but she began to make money.

Mr Doolittle had another and more mysterious business. Its nature was obscure. 'It involves sending out letters,' Hattie told me, nodding her curls. 'I don't think they're begging letters, yet people do send him money, pound notes mostly, but addressed to Mr Dee. I'm so worried. I wish he'd go away. He insists on looking after the books and my mother once told me that with a set of accounts to falsify he's a happy man. We'll all finish up in prison.' But nobody went to prison and Mr Doolittle didn't go away. He had discovered a perfect and legal fraud, good luck at the modest price of one pound a time, his own brand of chain letter.

Village Delights became a popular rendezvous. Most of us lunched there now and again, young lovers held hands and made two cups of coffee last a long time, the ladies from the Manor Park Estate drove down for afternoon tea. Dora Slade made and sold to Mr Doolittle the cakes and jams he served in the café. 'I'd help the devil himself, if he managed to persuade Hattie to give up potting,' she said, smiling from her Olympian heights, 'though it's wise to refuse cheques and insist on cash in hand.'

Roland's friendship with Hattie was effectively destroyed by the new regime. At first he visited her in Topsitogs during the vacations, sitting on the cane chair provided for expectant mothers, but genial Mr Doolittle often broke into their quiet conversations, making them both feel foolish. In the end Roland simply stayed away.

In Christmas week, Village Delights advertised a bargain turkey dinner. Hattie was distraught. The local newspaper had reported the theft of a van-load of turkeys, trussed and prepared for the oven. 'They're here, in my café,' she said, 'I'm certain of it.' Rudi, who privately shared her opinion, pointed out that one dead turkey looked remarkably like another and suggested that she should ask to see the receipts. 'I did,' she wailed. 'Father keeps putting me off and saying he's mislaid them.' That night in the dead hours she might have been seen, by anyone still awake, driving out of the village. An anonymous donor left two dozen fresh turkeys at the door of the local orphanage and sped away without thanks. Mr Doolittle took his loss in good part. A notice appeared, stuck across the advertisement for the dinner: 'Supplies Exhausted Due to Popularity. Offer Must End 21st December.'

*　　　*　　　*

Valentine closed the hotel for Christmas and invited us all to stay for a week. As a child, I regarded Gunville Place, my home and the seat of the Earls of Osmington, as the ugliest, coldest and most comfortless house in England. Now it had been transformed. Stripped of fretwork, assorted plaster garlands, scutcheons and inconsequential crenellations, the house emerged as a pleasant, if overlarge, stone and red-brick mansion. Inside was the ultimate in luxury. My father, the present earl, lived in seclusion at Lulworth with Gwennie, his third wife, battling against ill health. But in the second week of October a son had been born to Cristabel, an heir in the direct line, displacing Alexander, Claudia's elder boy. Nobody fussed about this except my father. Certainly not Val or Claudia, and least of all Alex, who was nervous of his grandfather, cared only for animals and wanted to be a vet. 'You won't be much use if you're howling all the time,' Claudia said to this ambition. He burst into tears. My father, unused to being regarded as an ogre, found him irritating and didn't like him much.

I quite thought that Portia would be happy to accept the invitation. She had always been fond of Valentine, and Christmas alone with Beau at Hindlecote seemed a dullish prospect. 'We shall be in Austria,' she said, and I thought I detected a joyous note in her voice. 'Beau's longing to learn to ski and Gerhardt's sister and her family have a lodge near Graz. Gerhardt has arranged it for us and he's going home to Heidelberg for the holiday, which means that we can travel part of the way together.'

'You'll be the only absentee from Gunville. Even Grandmother's joining us. We shall miss you.'

She laughed without resentment. 'You won't, of course. I know I'm regarded as dull company and that I perpetually irritate Claudia. Perhaps travel truly does broaden the mind. I've only been abroad once in my life, before the War, so I have no way of judging.'

'You don't sound at all dull just now,' I said, liking her for being able to laugh at us. 'Excited, I think.'

'I am. I love the prospect of leaving rain and murk behind and arriving in snowy weather. It's a kind of good luck charm, the clean cold and the snow. And I shall be glad to meet Gerhardt's sister and nieces and nephews.' She hesitated. 'He's such a good friend. It will be a loss to me when he finally leaves us.'

The clinic that contained the unfortunate ruin of Botolph was in the Austrian mountains. I speculated on the chance of either Portia or Beau visiting him. Both appeared to have dismissed him from their lives and in their emotional freedom they might well find it easier to be compassionate. The subject was a sensitive one. I didn't ask.

David usually spent Christmas either in America with his wartime foster family or entertaining the current untaxing lovely beside the Mediterranean, but when we arrived in Dorset he was there, playing chess in the library with Meggie Openshaw. 'You make an appropriate couple,' I said, helping matters on a little.

'It isn't at all appropriate that she should always beat me,' David said. 'I resent it. I shall have to go on playing the wretched girl until I win.' Meggie gave me a secret smile.

'You're very mean with news, both of you. I never was told what happened with the Agitator.'

'Oh, Amy, I'm sorry. It's been quite hectic with the new baby and Cristabel's girls and dodging the attentions of the old pomposities. Men are fiends when they're on holiday. Thank heavens for David, who's gone right off sex and doesn't fancy me in the slightest, do you, poor darling?'

'I don't propose to pursue you lustfully across the

113

golf course, if that's what you mean,' he said with hauteur. 'Or any other woman for that matter.'

'A pity.' Meggie's blue eyes looked into vast distances. 'I'd almost made up my mind to let you catch me, just to test the rumours.'

Davy looked so put out that I intervened quickly. 'What about your father, Meggie?'

'Charmed to the utmost by Valentine and Cristabel. And as for the divinely handsome Mr Metkin, I'd lay down my life for him. Where would one ever find another such entirely gorgeous and sweet-natured man?' She turned a look of innocent enquiry upon David, who, I noticed, glowered back with resentful fury. Clever Meggie! 'Such a pity he's spoken for in other directions. My poor old dad eats out of his hand, breathing in the scent of money. In fact, he's joining us tomorrow. I'm to have a flat in London and go back to work for Metkin Fine Arts in the New Year.'

'If I agree to take you on again,' David said. 'And that's by no means certain. Your taste is suspect and I don't have time to look after light-minded schoolgirls.'

'At times you sound more like my father than he does,' said Meggie. 'Perhaps I should ask Mr Metkin to let me go to the Paris showrooms. I speak a little French and I expect he would teach me more.' David shut up then. Over the holiday he watched Meggie with puzzlement, and paid a lot of attention to Mr Openshaw, listening to the woes and joys of the thread-winders and drinking in the glories of Bolton. I wondered how long it would take him to recognize the difference between an embryo love and his transient desires for beauty queens, models and other predators. Even intelligent men can be dense when they don't want their life-style to be disturbed.

After their cousin carnival the children knew each other fairly well and spent much of their time out of

114

doors, playing invented games with elaborate rituals. The only casualty was Alex's hamster, which unaccountably died, as they do. The funeral proved rather a nuisance since the spot chosen by Alex was in the middle of a large and soggy flower-bed, made soggier by his floods of tears. On Christmas Eve we had to drive into Dorchester and look for a replacement. Then Alex wept again because he saw a puppy that had a sad face and Claudia refused to buy it for him. 'Why can't I? It needs me!'

'No it doesn't. Just look at those feet; it's going to be enormous. Also it's alive with fleas and wants worming. And Alex, before you think of whining again, shut up or I'm taking the hamster back.' He inspected Claudia's expression, decided that she meant it and shut up. By tea-time he was relatively cheerful.

We walked down to Gunne Magna church for midnight mass. Overhead burned the frosty stars. On the hills the graves humped up where the long-dead lay, mouldering into Dorset earth. The enchantment never failed me. A barn owl floated ghostly white along the hedgerow and in the distance one fox barked and another and another answered. Intense wonder made me lightheaded and free. We were early. For this service the church, even in the private pews, was always crowded. The organ played softly. I relaxed against Rudi's side, watching the oval flames of the altar candles and breathing in the characteristic smell of incense and paraffin heaters.

For a moment or two I must have slept. I stood alone in the brick-kiln pavilion. The clouded looking-glass reflected me and I saw myself, tall and fair, in a madonna-blue dress. Something was to happen soon. I waited with calm anticipation, feeling no strangeness at having become Portia. Night gloomed outside the door. Within, candles burned, shedding a soft golden light. 'We are born in a dream, we live in a dream, and if death be a dream, we die,' said a voice in my head. 'Joy and woe are woven fine.' That's not it, I thought, suddenly afraid, that's wrong. From the organ emanated a single thunderous chord. I sat up with a jerk. The leading treble began to sing the processional hymn, 'Once in Royal David's City', and the choir moved off in a sudden flurry of surplices and the smoke of incense. Rudi groped for my hand and hauled me to my feet. 'Tomorrow, write out a hundred times, I must not fall asleep in church,' he said.

It was already tomorrow, Christmas Day. How would Portia celebrate the feast without the Established Church that she loved? In a Lutheran chapel or among baroque Catholic angels? I imagined her, thin and tall, crossing a snowy landscape, crunching back to the ski lodge for a breakfast of hot rolls or spiced sausages or whatever Austrians eat. The little pavilion held no ghost of her. And I was short, insignificant and Amy, and glad to be so. I hate dreaming. It makes me feel haunted.

It was a lovely Christmas. Lindsay was concerned at the number of books Val's elder girl received as presents and the time she spent in reading them or scribbling in notebooks. 'You're not turning into a dreaded swot, are you?' she asked.

'No I'm not. Swots do sums all the time and I can't. I'm writing down things about everybody, then when my spelling gets better I'm going to do a book and put you all in it.'

'Am I going to be the beautiful heroine?' asked Lindsay, simpering round at us in a sickening manner.

'Of course not, I am. You'll be a haggard old creature who tells lies and cheats people out of their money.'

'What a nerve,' Lindsay said. 'I don't want to be in a rotten old book.'

'All right then, I'll leave you out. Let's go and play some records.'

If I shut my eyes, I might have been back in the 1920s when Claudia's gramophone blared out jazz and I read anything that came to hand, and watched behaviour and recorded it in journals for when I was old and grown up, a habit that I have never entirely lost. A different music, different children, and the misery of loneliness had gone.

Claudia's William was home from Canada with a trunkful of strange presents, including maple syrup, sweets in miniature log cabins, toy tomahawks for the boys, and Indian dolls and fringed doe-skin tunics for the twins. 'Not particularly authentic,' he said. 'I doubt whether Canadian Indians went in for scalping.'

The twins, who had hinted elaborately for Levi jeans and were regarding their dolls with disgust, brightened. 'Lovely tops,' they said in unison. They listened expectantly while Bill explained to Alexander that his toy bear was made of real skin from an animal shot in the Rockies. During the inevitable misery, quelled by Claudia with a menacing glare, Grainger quietly relieved Alex of his tomahawk. 'We are eleven years old, Lindsay, I believe,' she murmured, 'and I, for one, have never cared greatly for dolls. Shall we go?' Lindsay nodded. With the stealth of imaginary braves, they made off and untidily scalped their Indian dolls behind the stables.

We were all relieved that Bill was home. Claudia's mood had become increasingly gloomy as her grass widowhood progressed. At some time in the process of acquiring an education she had heard that Canada contained a good many Celts who embraced Calvinism and were thoroughly moral and good. In such an atmosphere she felt that Bill could be trusted. When he flew south to the United States and then to Mexico and Brazil, she became slightly peevish. 'If I'd known that he was going to be exposed to black-eyed señoritas, dancing the fandango and throwing roses, I'd have gone with him. In all probability he's languishing on strange bosoms in strange boudoirs and having a riotous time while I have to remember to wind the clocks and get the hedges cut and check the bank statements and not have a drink until the sun's over the yard-arm.'

'Nonsense' I said. 'You're simply a bit lonely without him. Bill's not a languisher and he writes practically every day. He won't care a bit whether you do those things or not, except perhaps for the drinks. He won't want to come home to a dipsomaniac.'

'How you exaggerate. As far as one can make out from films, those fresh-faced American country wenches in gingham dresses drink corn-liquor, whatever that may be, out of the bottle. Or am I thinking of root-beer? Never mind.'

Christmas Day found her sleek with happiness. Around her neck Bill fastened a charming necklace of amethysts. 'Wear them always,' he said, pleased to be back in the scratchy, unsentimental relationship so satisfying to them both. 'They prevent drunkenness. And I don't know that this has any uses except to remind you of me occasionally. It's simply a love token.' The barb scarcely mattered. The token was a ring set with a large Colombian emerald.

'All those unworthy suspicions about señoritas,' I said in her ear. 'I hope you're suitably ashamed.'

'They can't be ruled out. He wouldn't tell me about them, would he, or put their photographs on the mantelpiece?'

'If they existed except in your imagination I bet they didn't get emeralds,' I said.

My grandmother had effectively routed Mrs Smythe-Fennel. She first made certain of her ground by offering a liberal bribe in money and the promise of a better job to the one overworked domestic. The girl happily confirmed that the wretched bracelet was still in the Smythe-Fennel jewel box. Then, with her solicitor, Grandmother confronted the lady at home. She gave me no details of what passed between them except to say grudgingly, 'You were quite right, Amy, to believe that so blatant a bully would crumble before righteous determination and the promise of a suit for defamation.' She looked wistful for a moment. 'I very much enjoyed it, though my solicitor shuffled about as though his boots were on fire. He's rather a timid man.'

He had my sympathy. Personally I would prefer to face the wheels of a juggernaut than my grandmother at her most warlike. She had shaken the dust of the household from her feet and rolled away, carrying both lawyer and domestic with her. Now she seemed content, lapsed into a tranquil, waiting state. She joined us for meals. Otherwise she kept to her own rooms where she received us singly.

Her awareness of our activities was as acute as ever, and she questioned me closely about Portia and Hindlecote. 'Life has treated her poorly,' she said. 'Once thwarted, Mrs Smythe-Fennel became spiteful and spoke rather openly of Coritanum. According to her he has the French pox.'

Grandmother, though a Victorian, inherited the frank speech of an earlier generation. Anything with a vague sexual connotation she attributed to the poor French, which seemed a little unfair. Well knowing her loathing of delicate evasions and the ladylike, her openness ought not to have discomforted me, but under her sardonic scrutiny I blushed and nodded. 'That may be so. Other things are killing him; his heart is very weak.'

'Ah well, I pointed out that such gossip might well recoil and ruin her love life.'

'I hate that crowd, Grandmother, I really do. Portia's good and patient and she's been cheated and robbed and wounded. It's so unjust.'

'It is, but the idea of justice for women is still regarded as an affront by stupider men. These changes at Hindlecote are the best thing in the world for her.'

'People admire her and make quite a fuss and she's relieved of the worst money worries. I feel that she's more alive now than at any time since she married.'

'I should have done more, guarded her better after your mother died instead of nursing my grief. Portia's always been deeply shy. She needed kindness. A man who pursued evil courses to the very point of death was never within the compass of her understanding, never could be. Loyalty and sacrifice become a pointless waste. Cold lechery will kill the strongest love.'

'Yes,' I said, 'yes,' thinking that I couldn't have borne to be in Portia's shoes. At my father's wedding to Sonia, she had told us all that she wanted to be a nun. Hurt and showing off, I thought. And yet how well the life would have suited her, an Anglican nunnery, the opportunity to study all her life long, the quietness of the spirit. 'Her worst anxiety now is that Beau might become like his father, but I don't think so. He's more Savernake than Coritanum.'

'A pity there were no other children. Look after her, Amy, as I know you will.' Grandmother's well-supported bosom rose in a sigh. 'Don't expect too much. Sadness is never far away from us.' Was that a prophetic thought, or was it a reflection of grief for her

only daughter, my mother, whose face I had almost forgotten? In an obscure way reproached and chilled, I
wished that Portia had not gone to Austria. I willed
nothing bad to happen to her, feeling inadequate to
watch over a sister I understood so little.

Chapter Ten

On New Year's Eve I tried to speak to Portia and was told by someone, describing herself as her Grace's secretary, that she was still abroad. By the end of the children's vacation her silence was beginning to cause me some concern. I telephoned again. There is something decidedly irritating in worrying about someone only to find them in roaring good spirits. Portia seemed impatient with my tender enquiries. 'Of course I'm well, simply too busy to think, and, yes, Christmas was an enormous success.' I thought I would get no more, but after a pause she went on, 'The mountains are spellbinding, Amy, they make me feel renewed and young. I love the remoteness and Beau loves the skiing. He skates well, too.' She chattered at length about Emmi, Gerhardt's sister, and her family, then checked herself. 'But you won't want to hear all that.'

She had not, I thought, told me everything. 'I'm glad you enjoyed it so much,' I said, and prepared to tell her about our Christmas.

She detected the question in my voice. 'You may as well know that I visited Botolph, not willingly. There was little to say.'

'No improvement, I suppose?'

'None. He's coherent, though heavily drugged, bloated to my surprise rather than wasted, the condition that Grandmother would call dropsical. And he's angry, angry with *me*. Why? I stuck it as long as I could. I did my best.'

'Death is a bitter punishment, Portia,' I said. 'Won't it be that and not you that makes him angry?'

'It's corrupting. Until I can forgive I'm cut off from the grace of God. But he doesn't ask to be forgiven. His only regret, I believe, is that he's now reaping what he so thoroughly sowed. He sees no need for repentance.'

It's easy to be wise for other people. A confused idea that the crisis in her marriage ought to have come earlier swam around in my head. To some men infinite patience might signify consent. I said, 'In that case, Portia, I truly don't see why your conscience should be burdened or why you should even think of forgiveness. Won't it be soon enough if Botolph asks?'

'I ought not to leave it too long.' Her voice had a distant, alarming note. 'Time has a habit of running out.' For a moment I thought that she was about to give voice to some wretched prophecy of imminent death, then, relieved, I concluded that she was referring to Botolph.

'Did Beau go with you?' I asked.

'As far as the front door. He refused to put a foot inside the clinic or to see his father. I'm glad. It's not a pleasant sight. I don't know whether I can bear to visit again. I'll think about it at Easter. We're spending another two weeks with Emmi then.' She went on to say that Gerhardt was installed in the castle for the remainder of the winter. He and Otto had helped to prepare an exhibition of the finds and they were writing jointly a paper that was expected to be ready for publication by the end of February. 'Then, sadly, they'll leave us,' Portia said in a far gentler tone, 'though they'll come over for the opening of the castle in May. It's difficult for Gerhardt. Emmi says that his wife is quite seriously ill with a nervous mental condition and spends many months in hospital.'

I wondered whether the evenings of poetry reading

continued and whether Portia had discovered that Gerhardt was in love with her. Women are supposed to know such things instinctively. I haven't noticed it myself, but that may be (sad thought) because no-one other than Rudi has ever wanted me. Even more I wondered about her feelings for him. Botolph had effectively and rapidly destroyed her romantic ideals and chilled all youthful warmth out of her. She was left with little but a high conception of duty. Yet I felt that if ever that correctness and cold propriety were broken down, Portia would be capable of intense emotion and intense suffering. And I very much wished her to be happy. 'Shall we see you in May then? I should love to be at the castle on opening day, if that's all right.'

'It won't be a party so I shan't send formal invitations, but if you like to come the day before I shall be giving a small dinner in the private apartments. Merve will arrange it with you. And Amy, thank you for telephoning, but there'll be no need for either you or Claudia to trouble me for a while. I'll ring you.' A definite dismissal!

I hung up, picked up the phone again and rang Claudia's number. Lindsay answered. 'She isn't in, dear Aunt. Her exact words were, "I've been dragooned into opening a bloody bazaar, and don't let me hear either of you girls using that word or I'll break you in two." I expect she meant bloody, don't you? Bazaar's harmless.'

'Darling, you know perfectly well what she meant, so don't be tiresome, please. I've been talking to your Aunt Portia and she's left me in a twitter. Can you tell your mother, very, very tactfully, that she needn't telephone Hindlecote just now, and that Hindlecote will ring her?'

'That's a bugger.' Lindsay sounded so exactly like

Claudia at the same age that I wanted to laugh, but knew I mustn't. 'She always grouses like mad, yet she'll hate being told.'

'You're not to use that word either, Lindsay, well not to me, please. It's rather offensive. And I'd prefer that you didn't ask which one and try to make me repeat it. Say that Aunt Portia's busy and often away. Will you do that for me?'

'I didn't mean to offend, darling Aunt Amy, so don't hate me. You won't tell, will you? The last time Father smacked me, my poor bottom was sore for days. I'll write down the message, is that all right?'

'Perfectly, and of course I won't tell. If you absolutely have to swear, do it privately or Grainger and the boys will start and you'll get found out.'

'Start?' Lindsay said. 'You wouldn't believe the words Grainger knows. She collects them at school.' Arguing with either of the twins was the fast route to exhaustion and their grasp of bad language was, in the main, Claudia's fault. I gave up.

Mr Doolittle was an industrious man. His bicycle became a familiar sight in towns as far apart as Portsmouth, Bognor and Arundel. He rarely drove. I suspected that he had no driving licence. In Underhallow he delivered leaflets advertising building firms, fire extinguishers, charity appeals and cut-price insurance. We had been back in Underhallow for less than a month when he accosted Rudi on the doorstep, thrust a selection of advertisements into his hand and by force of persuasion invited himself into the house. He saw us, perhaps, as a route to respectability. Having once been a gentleman, his behaviour, though shady, was always ceremonious, and it took him three glasses of Rudi's second-best sherry to make his point. 'Since we have met, may I ask a great favour of you concerning my daughter?' he said eventually. 'She has, I regret to say, an unstable personality, and I feel that she should marry.'

Rudi likes most people, but he excludes those who prey on the gullible and unprotected. He disliked Mr Doolittle more than most. 'Hattie's troubles are due to your behaviour, I suggest, as is her mother's nervous condition. She may not share your enthusiasm for marriage.'

There was no penetrating Mr Doolittle's hide. An amiable shark, his mouth stretched to show an abundance of gleaming white dentistry. 'That is possible, though naturally I would refute your argument. My misfortunes can scarcely have affected her so deeply. She was not a young child. But Harriet, at least, has faith in your opinions and with your encouragement will make a sensible decision. It would be useful to the business and, I believe, beneficial to both parties, were she to marry Horace Kettle.' He held up a large pale palm, though Rudi did not speak and I was hypnotized into silence. 'Before you point out the disparity in their backgrounds and social class, you must also agree that Harriet's attractions are few. She can expect nothing better. And on their wedding day I propose to take Horace into my businesses as a full partner.'

'Rogues exist in every level of society,' Rudi said, with shrivelling contempt. 'I shall make sure that both Hattie and Horace understand the laws of partnership before they commit themselves. Your hat, Mr Doolittle.' The dentistry retreated behind closed lips. He held out his hand, thought better of it, bowed, and walked majestically to the door. Rudi didn't slam it. He frowned. 'That was pretty transparent, yet I know nothing of any significance and it isn't our business.'

'What is there to know?' I asked, feeling decidedly

bewildered. 'Isn't he just trying to off-load Hattie onto any available man?'

'There's a swindle of some kind afoot,' Rudi said, 'a common one and not nice. Our resident crook is planning to slide off with the money and leave two innocents to pay the reckoning. We can't have that. Hattie needs friends. Without Atatürk and vegetables she's a lost soul.'

I made a half-hearted attempt to discover Hattie's feelings on the subject of marriage and Horace and unleashed a flood of misery. 'We were all right with the arrangement we had before he came along,' she said. 'I liked my life and I don't want to be married, to Horace or anyone else, ever. And he doesn't want to marry me either. I'm ten years older than he is. Father's always spoiled things, for my mother, for me, and now for Horace. God, I'm so miserable!'

'He can't make you get married, Hattie. Just be firm and say no.'

'You don't know him. He wears you down in the end. It's frightening. We're rich, and where's the money coming from? I've never heard of the charities he collects for and I don't see how you can make thousands by selling insurance.'

Well, you can if the company is your own and the policies are spurious, but there was no point in making her feel worse. 'What about the police? Can't you mention your worries to them?'

'They hate me because of the pond. It's me they'd lock up, not him. I expect they think I'm mad. Perhaps I am; I wonder sometimes.'

And there, for some months, the matter rested. Mr Doolittle pursued his activities outside the three Hallows until his contempt for the weak, the frightened and the old led him to turn his attention to business opportunities on his own doorstep. He fell into the error of supposing that Mr Slade, Dora's father-in-law, was feeble of mind as well as body. That assumption was the beginning of his downfall. Mr Slade enjoyed watching bowls and on a fine April morning he hobbled with other elders to the green, where Dora and I settled him on a seat below the open window of the pavilion. Dora lit the urn and we prepared to dispense tea, buns and soft drinks at need. Armed with a sheaf of proposal forms for his thousand-pound funeral policy, Mr Doolittle joined the spectators. Seating himself next to Mr Slade, he laid out his wares. 'For a modest hundred pounds in easy instalments the society recommends an undertaker who will provide silver fittings on the hearse and plumed horses,' he said. 'A tombstone of marble is not beyond reach. A truly dignified departure, you'll agree, plus a clear fifty pounds for the table.'

The interruption irritated Mr Slade. 'What are you yacking about bleeding horses and tables to me for?' he said. 'Taking me mind off the game. Shut up or piss off.'

'Oughtn't we to stop this?' I asked Dora.

She settled herself in a basket chair and folded her hands in her lap, her expression deeply tranquil. 'A clever man, no doubt,' she said, 'but he doesn't know Father. Wake me if the discussion gets violent.'

'Forgive the observation,' purred Mr Doolittle, waving a smooth, plump white hand, 'but you are a gentleman of advanced years. You have lived long and happily. The end is nigh. Are you not deserving of the best obsequies that money can purchase?'

References to Mr Slade's age were never well received and he had a retentive memory. He raised his stick like a club. 'You're deserving of a smack in the mouth, mate, and I'm not too old to fetch you one. I know what you get up to, rattling the till, doing time.

Don't you start eyeing my savings.' He glanced round uneasily. 'Not that I'm saying there are any.'

Mr Doolittle sneered. 'Safe in the Post Office, I suppose? I hope there's enough to bury you.'

'They won't leave me lying about, that's a cert, and you won't be touching my money, that's another. Thieving git!'

'There's a law of slander, you know,' murmured Doolittle, moving slowly backwards along the row of chairs, but leaving on the air like the Cheshire cat the faint memory of his smile. 'Can it be possible that I'm losing my touch, or am I simply out of practice?' he enquired softly to himself. 'How very tiresome.'

That wasn't quite the last of the encounter. On the afternoon of the same day Mr Slade undertook a brief errand for Dora to the daughter of a crony at a house two doors away from the shop. She put a carrier-bag in his hand, made sure it wasn't too heavy and left him to it. When he arrived he found Mr Doolittle trying to sell the funeral policy to his old friend. He took serious exception. 'At it again, are you?' he asked, unable to use his stick since he was leaning on it at the time. Frustrated, he swung the carrier-bag in a flying arc. The result was startling. Mr Doolittle made no sound. He collapsed gently sideways and lay, studying the sky and clasping his right ear, half stunned by a frozen chicken. The two old men stared down at him with interest. 'Hit him a bit hard there, didn't you, Sladey? He don't look well.' They cackled with glee.

'You may laugh,' whispered Mr Doolittle as his head cleared. 'The authorities shall hear of this. You shall be sued.' But he had lost his audience. The house door closed on him and then Mr Slade limped away homeward, evilly grinning.

'This place gets on my tits,' he told Dora, who was worried enough about the consequences of the assault to tell Rudi and me. 'No sense and no guts. You going to sit down and let that Doolittle rob you all blind? 'Cos I ain't.' He bypassed the Underhallow constabulary and made telephone calls to Chichester and to Scotland Yard, following up by post with a selection of the Doolittle advertising leaflets and insurance forms. Nothing happened immediately. A week or so later a black car approached the police house, paused there for half an hour and passed on to Dora's shop. Hattie said, when the fuss had died down, that her father kept a bag packed, ready for emergencies. Recognizing plain-clothes detectives at a glance, he emptied the safe and the tills of both Topsitogs and Village Delights, and bestowed his best and whitest smile upon his daughter. 'Goodbye, dear, I must run.'

'He shouldn't have bothered about the silver,' Hattie said, with the ghost of a satisfied smirk. 'It weighed him down and left us very short of change. The police caught up with him in half an hour. He fell off his bicycle, trying to ride the footpath above Hags' Gibbet, and broke an ankle.' Mr Doolittle's solicitor called on her, assuming that she would be eager to help the defence when her father came to trial. She chose to give evidence for the prosecution.

At the beginning of May Rudi and I received through Merve an invitation to spend a night at Hindlecote. Claudia and William had to refuse as, beginning with the twins, the children one by one caught German measles and, in Claudia's words, made sure that the house was plague-stricken for as long as possible. Valentine drove down, collecting Grandmother Mottesfont and her housekeeper on his way through London. 'I have never visited an *attraction*,' Grandmother said, giving the word a faintly scandalous sound, 'and shall probably never do so again. Should I be so inconsiderate as to die in the night, my old companion will see that I'm laid out properly and removed without delay.'

We all wished she would stop talking about death. Merve told me that one of the fears of old people is that they will die away from home, but it irritated my grandmother, I think, that she could not loose her hold on life at will. 'She's about a thousand years old and full of gall,' Claudia said crossly, burning up the wires with frustration. 'I think she enjoys a quiet laugh at the sound of tumbrils. What do you bet that she has a lovely time?'

'I hope she does. You've always been her favourite, but she cares about Portia's troubles too. The lifting of a few burdens will satisfy her no end. Is that a dog howling?'

'A child. German measles does nothing to diminish their lung-power. I'd better go. Give me all the gen when you get back.'

Hindlecote waited placidly for the beginning of its new life. The sun struck sparks from the moat, ducks dabbled and swans glided beautifully, as though they had been trained for nothing else. I had never seen such flowers or such green and manicured grass. The gardeners, coaxed, flattered and bullied by Merve, and no doubt better paid than at any time in their lives, stood ready with plants for sale and free advice. The little train rested in its station on the perimeter of the grounds, embowered in greenery. At a rustic kiosk tickets might be obtained for the nature trails, with prizes for observation. Even the swings and seesaws in the children's playground were painted with roses to match the signposts. While Merve pushed my reluctant grandmother in a wheelchair ('The ground is uneven, dear lady'), Portia took us to see the sandwich

131

and ice-cream bar (The Castle Snackery, ye gods!) and the self-service café in what was once the buttery. Within the walls and overlooking the enclosed inner garden, Merve's men had created a grander restaurant, all blue and gold. Here would be waiters and a wine list and souvenir books of matches. 'With an enterprise like this,' Merve said, 'one can only throw one's soul into it. Now we stand back and hope that the world will love us.'

Portia smiled at him. 'No other man could have done so much. The staff are enthusiastic from the management downwards and twenty-seven coach parties are booked so far. I wish you would take a directorship of the company. You've more than earned it.'

'Duchess darling, the poor self creates, but absolutely doesn't manage, though I shall be sad to leave you. Never again will I find a Hindlecote. It's positively my crown. I shall visit whenever chance allows.'

Grandmother, disgruntled by the chair, yet anxious to miss nothing, said to me in a penetrating whisper, 'They purr over each other like a pair of pussy-cats. I trust that man is not in love with your sister.'

'It's all right, he's fond, nothing more. He doesn't – he can't,' I stammered, hoping that Merve wouldn't hear her and give his too frank explanation. 'It's constitutional, after an illness.'

'Kindly don't maunder, Amy. I understand, though I see no necessity for the pink hair. Blue is much more suitable for an ageing man.'

Merve heard that bit. 'Do you truly think so, dear lady? You don't find it the merest touch commonplace?'

Grandmother fixed him with her basilisk stare, which he met courageously without wincing. 'No, I don't, some of my best friends favour blue. And I rather fancy that the Edwardian style is out of date.

132

The boy who delivers my groceries assures me that flares are the latest fashion, and although he looks unpromising on his bicycle I understand that he enjoys considerable success in the dance halls.'

'There,' Merve said, 'I knew the poor self had rusticated too long.'

She nodded benevolently, properly revenged for his insistence on the wheelchair. 'If I were you I should spend a little time in the capital. The name of the Castle Snackery has an American sound, but not sufficiently so for present fads, I think.'

'You don't like it? Not punchy enough? Oh dear.'

'Not punchy at all. I noticed on the way here a Hank's Place, a Drop-in Diner and a Polly's Pantry. How about something on those lines, the Smiling Sandwich for instance?' Merve twittered. Her attention began to drift. She had noticed Portia and Gerhardt standing close together and talking animatedly and she watched them with intense curiosity. From Portia one did not, after all, expect animation and laughter.

Chapter Eleven

With the renovations completed, Portia had moved back into private apartments prepared for her and Beau in the castle. Merve renamed the imposing stone chambers, complete with four-poster beds, that she and Botolph had once occupied, the Royal Suite. He wrote a piece for the brochure to the effect that Richard III of York, a couple of Henrys, and Queen Elizabeth had slept in those beds. Some of it might have been true. 'I shan't consult the castle archives, but let the imagination rove,' he said. 'One needs to believe. A good fiction, repeated often enough, becomes fact.' The Dower House was now reserved for guests. High iron railings enclosed the grounds and the pavilion, from which visitors were excluded. The garden had been most beautifully laid out with shrubs and trees and flower-beds, and the rough grass replaced by a knot-garden, edged with miniature box hedges. Beside the brick-kiln a young tree, a scented pink cherry, was in flower.

Portia's looks astonished and pleased me. Robust was never a word to associate with her, in fact for most of the time she seemed to be on the edge of some physical disaster. That had changed. She was not sun-burned, yet a pure, faint colour glowed under her fair skin and her body moved with relaxed ease. She was now a director of the company set up to exploit Hindlecote. The board retained her also as a consulta-tive expert. She smiled rather tightly when she told me this. 'As far as I know my only expertise is in the ways of adulterous husbands, though I can scarcely say so. The income is more than welcome. My life with and after Botolph was pinched and mean and small. I have to remind myself that it's unnecessary to hide my jewellery or count pound notes.'

We dined together in her private dining-room. She had placed Gerhardt Nordmann on her right and Merve on her left. I was between Gerhardt and Otto, neither of whom took much notice of me. My grandmother sat opposite, monopolized by Merve, so I was free to observe. Somebody's foot touched mine. I thought for a moment that I had made a conquest, but it was only Rudi, almost slipping under the table in an effort to get my attention. He was sitting next to a social secretary of grandly conventional manner belied by her strapless dress. It showed a restless inclination to inch its way downwards until her breasts were on the point of escaping, only to be hitched impatiently back up again. Plainly Rudi found the process bothersome and wanted reassurance. I blew him a little kiss. Grandmother saw me and raised a sardonic eyebrow. In most ways we weren't one bit alike, but she watched the company as keenly as I did and she missed nothing. My left ear tuned in to the conversation between Gerhardt and Portia. They were discussing Greek mythology and the feminine principle in creation myths and our perception of the gods. So utterly improving and harmless. A warm intentness in Portia's eyes, the inclination of Gerhardt's head towards her, his lack of interest in what he was eating, those were a different and silent conversation. They belonged more together than any couple I had ever seen. Yet a couple was precisely what they were not.

Otto, a brilliant archaeologist but a stolid man, applied himself to his food and made only an occasional remark to me. Having no education to speak of, I had nothing much to offer him. As far as I recalled, he wasn't married. Merve had told me of something perfectly scandalous that happened between Otto and the two girl students after the unveiling of the stone, so it seemed a bad idea to ask. My thoughts turned to the pavilion. I wondered whether Portia slept well in the castle or whether on restless nights she went down to lie on the day-bed in the extension behind the brick-kiln. I didn't like to think of it deserted and unloved. A strong desire to stand under the high lantern in moonlight, encircled by the dancing fauns and maenads, hit me with an anticipatory shiver of delight. I sipped cautiously at my wine and tried to hear what Portia was now saying to Gerhardt, but her voice was low and Merve was chattering vivaciously to Grandmother, inviting her to inspect his collection of old theatre bills and programmes. They seemed to have adopted each other. She had always nourished a secret liking for oddities and a passion for the stage.

At last Valentine, at the far end of the table, stood up and proposed toasts to Portia and to the success of the Hindlecote adventure. Conversation became general as we drank and then moved to the drawing-room. The entertainment was homemade and pleasing. Nobody seemed inclined to dance so Portia played the piano and Otto and Gerhardt sang traditional songs of their respective countries. Merve almost reduced us to tears with, 'All around my hat I wear the green willow', delivered in a voice of singular purity. Grandmother's chins quivered, whether with emotion or amusement was unclear. After she had gone to bed we moved to the terrace. All sound and light came from the water garden and a rising moon. The bulk of the castle, the vast acres around it and the ancient trees swallowed us in a darkness that dwarfed and reduced us. Hindlecote was not a home. There was too much of everything. Already it was fossilized, a memorial to pointless and forgotten wars, a museum. Portia and Gerhardt paced to and fro, still talking. Everything was ordinary enough. Yet I found the occasion stranger than any since a night, thirty years before, when my stepmother, Sonia, visited the Cerne Abbas Giant to ask for a child. But that was on Midsummer's Eve and in Dorset, where the old gods still make mischief. Here the legends were of men and the spirits of the dead left no trace.

Rudi and I walked back together to the Dower House. 'Is there a peculiar something in the air, Amy?' he asked. 'Or am I fanciful?'

A dim light, almost extinguished by the moon, shone up through the lantern of the brick-kiln. The door was shut and it was silent. 'May nights are always magic,' I said. 'Everything breathes and grows. It's the month of the goddess, Maia, daughter of Atlas and the mother of Hermes, the messenger. I heard Gerhardt telling Portia.'

'We were married in May, that was rather magic. It's going to be twelve years soon. How have I managed to endure so long?'

'I'm not going to divorce you, so don't ask. Didn't I promise to take care of you when you were old and wrinkled, with piles and chronic rheumatics? How *are* the piles, by the way?'

'Flourishing, thank you, Amy. Tell me, what's happened to Portia's iron-clad views on suitability? Gerhardt's emotions are plain enough, but hers? Your sister gives little away.'

'There may be nothing to give. It's a dead end. He's a dear, and if it weren't for being besotted by your wrinkles and rheumatism I could fall for him myself quite easily. But he's a man of principle too. He would

137

never desert a sick wife, and Portia would never divorce. Friendship is all they can have.'

'Let's hope that fate gives them a hand, if that's what they want,' Rudi said. He went off to bath. I heard him splashing like a whale and singing, 'Once in love with Amy', which I thought very suitable. As I was about to climb into bed, I glanced out of the window. The door of the pavilion stood ajar. Without stopping to think, I grabbed my dressing-gown, sped downstairs and crept across the grass, avoiding the thread of light cast through the doorway. Dew soaked my bare feet. The cherry tree shed petals and fragrance on the air. I began to shiver, with cold or with an emotion I couldn't have defined. Under my supporting hand I felt the curious warmth of the place. The wall breathed in and out, palpitating gently in time with the beating of my heart. I peeped through the narrow space beside the lintel.

The stillness made me believe at first that the room was empty. Then I heard a murmur and saw slight movement. Portia and Gerhardt were there, sitting as I had seen them once before, she in the blue velvet chair, he on the floor against her knees. I couldn't hear what they were saying, or see whether they were touching. Portia bent her head over something in her lap. She lifted it towards the lamp. It seemed to be transparent, an uneven lump of coloured glass through which the light shone greenish on her face. She spoke quietly. Gerhardt looked up at her and smiled. The intimacy of the scene made me catch my breath. I stifled a cough. What did I expect, a kiss, an embrace?

Suddenly the enormity of my behaviour struck me like a blow on the head. Hot shame flooded through me. Secret spying was a new low even for me, miserable snooper and busybody that I was. I couldn't defend myself on the grounds of concern for Portia, or on any grounds at all. I fled, closing the Dower House door without a sound. Hurriedly I dried my wet feet on the counterpane and was in bed when Rudi came out of the bathroom. He opened the window. For a moment or two he stood there, alert as though his attention was caught. Then he turned away and slid in beside me. He made no comment, but said only, 'How cold you are, my dear darling. Is it Portia and Gerhardt?'

'Damn! You can't possibly have heard me, you were making far too much noise.'

'Damp footprints on the path. Bare feet, about size three. Was it them or are you up to no good? Tell me all.'

'I have no statement to make at this time and I demand to see my solicitor in the morning. Good night, Sherlock.'

'Amy?'

'Oh all right then, it was them, but I'm ashamed that I looked when I oughtn't to have done. They were only sitting quietly and I'm not going to talk about it any more. OK?'

Once in the night I woke and looked out over the grounds. The pavilion was shut up again and dark.

After breakfast on the following day, Opening Day, we took up vantage points at the long narrow embrasures in the castle walls that had once been arrow-slits. The members of the staff were at their posts. Already a small, meek queue had formed outside the gates. At precisely ten o'clock they were opened and we began to count heads, until there were far too many and we had to give up. Coaches arrived, and cars, and local people on foot. Tickets were sold for the castle, for the train, for the conducted nature trails (with prizes for everyone as it was the first day). The snack-bar and souvenir shop were crowded. 'Not at all a bad beginning,' Merve said. 'Duchess darling, won't you show yourself? A glimpse, a word here

139

and there? We might all lunch in the restaurant.' I thought that Portia did wonderfully well. Of course, she knew the village people. Hadn't she ordered their lives and been a dragon to them for years? It took an effort on her part to be democratic and overcome their awe, but she decreed that every child should be given a free ice-cream, which made for much easier terms.

At tea, after the closing of the gates, I sat with Grandmother. From time to time her eyes dwelt on Portia. Then Valentine joined us. 'I thought we might leave in an hour, Grandmamma, if you're ready.'

She nodded. 'Is this or is it not a curious business?' she asked, as though she were continuing an earlier discussion. 'A late flowering? Ought I to be doing something about it?'

Val smiled slightly. He was a man too even-tempered and forward-looking for malice, yet I'm sure that the irony of the situation didn't escape him. Cristabel was a Creole from Bahama, and a Roman Catholic. Portia, firmly locked into her position as duchess, xenophobe and pillar of the Established Church as into a chastity belt, had behaved quite disagreeably when the engagement was in prospect. How greatly her attitudes had changed. He said, 'For all that's happened in her marriage, there's a tremendous, unshakable innocence in Portia. She's vulnerable of course. Any of us can fall in love, but if she does, that essential nobility – I can call it nothing else – won't, I think, be corrupted.'

Grandmother wore her sardonic face. 'Highfalutin, aren't you? I take it I'm not to interfere.' She swung round at me. 'And what's the agonized look for, miss?'

'You know I haven't been a miss for ever so long. Portia smiles now, when she used not to. She's going on for forty-seven and entitled to be friendly with anyone she chooses. Frankly, Grandmother, I don't care if she goes to bed with an entire Guards regiment, as long

140

as her heart isn't wounded and her life has interest and point.'

'That's an entirely immoral suggestion. And you think her heart won't be wounded should she fall in love with Herr Nordmann?'

'Separation would be painful, naturally: only cruelty and indifference can cause mortal damage.' Hearing the certainty in my voice, I thought, How do I know, with my small experience? I pressed on. 'Well, that's what I believe, rightly or wrongly, Grandmother.'

She and Val stared at me as though an ant had roared at them. I blushed. 'There's no need to qualify your opinion,' she said. 'It's as likely to be valid as anyone's. As you both point out, Portia's not a girl and not flighty. I'll mind my own business.'

Rudi and I drove home in the early evening. I had bought a yellow Hindlecote rose in a pot for Piers, and a china mug, showing the castle in full colour, for Roland. I searched the souvenir shop in vain for something, anything, with a picture of the brick-kiln. There were postcards showing aerial views of the castle and estate, but no Dower House, no garden and no pavilion. It was, of course, a very private place.

Mr Doolittle came to trial in the first week of July. Among others, Hattie and Mr Slade were called to give evidence. I volunteered to drive Dora and her father-in-law to London, and Hattie asked the vicar's wife to go with us as she was nervous and unsure of her ability to find the right building, let alone the right courtroom. It was a bit of a squash as Horace came along too, in case he was needed. For her father's benefit Hattie bought a defiant new cloak in Mexican stripes and another pair of wellingtons. Her curls she covered with a scarf, folded to resemble a close-fitting bonnet and tied under the chin. 'My gawd, what does she look like?'

enquired Mr Slade. We ignored him. The effect was bizarrely childlike, dowdy and, in an odd way, respectable.

Unpleasant though they had been, her experiences had firmed up her nature. She betrayed with relish. None of Mr Doolittle's schemes or words, however privately confided, went unreported. Under cross-examination by the defence counsel, Hattie freely admitted that she had once loved but now hated her father, and was of the opinion that he belonged behind bars. 'He's not just weak as I thought, but wicked,' she said, before counsel could stop her.

I had to agree with her. Doolittle's composure and self-satisfaction did not desert him. He showed his gleaming dentures to each witness, particularly Hattie, and nodded affably at us all from the dock. Hattie did not smile or return the nod until he was convicted and sentenced to another five years in prison. She nodded vigorously then, and grinned widely. I hope that Mr Doolittle saw. She took us all to El Vino's in Fleet Street for a celebratory bottle of wine and a sandwich, then, with Horace, she hurried away to another appointment. Hattie had sold her story to a Sunday newspaper. Many of the facts in the finished article were inaccurate and names were misspelt, but it was a colourful piece and widely syndicated. 'Spade,' said Mr Slade. 'Stupid buggers, nobody's called Spade. Where's the credit in that? If it weren't for me, that Doolittle would still be thieving and robbing. I ought to get a medal.' In general he was right, but that didn't stop him from being absolutely insufferable.

Dora's Olympian calm became ruffled. She had half changed her mind about marrying Reggie Bowmaker, if only in the hope of sharing out the responsibility for her father-in-law. 'It rather depends,' she said, 'on whether he thinks I'm worth the price.'

The café business Hattie disposed of at a profit to an American couple with dreams of introducing pumpkin pie and other delicacies to old England. Food was now presented with an elegance foreign to Mr Doolittle and Horace Kettle. Melon slices came transformed into boats and grapefruit halves wore cherries and little paper parasols. These embellishments were copied at The Cotte, Meadowsweet and The Paddocks. The newcomers were popular. The pies sounded rather more exciting than they tasted. With the proceeds of the sale Hattie renovated her cottage and dispensed with Horace's services by installing a new gas boiler. She never, to Dora's relief, returned to potting. Instead she took painting lessons and displayed among the rompers and nappies of Topsitogs imaginative pictures of fairies and giants. I don't know that she ever sold any. She never mentioned Atatürk again.

Gloria Hopkins was particularly bitter against the Doolittles. She had taken a fancy to Mr Doolittle, who flattered her with little attentions while consulting her on the matter of Hattie's hair-style. 'I don't care what he's done, he's a gentleman,' she told her clients. 'As for her, she's been as good as living in sin with Horace Kettle for months. Now she's left him in the lurch.' Hattie didn't hear these unkind slanders as she never again went near a permanent wave or a bubble-cut.

Unemployed, Horace wandered about for a while like a shipwrecked sailor, finding nothing to replace the Brethren of Micah, or the spaceship, or his servitude at Village Delights. He was forced to return home where he was perfectly miserable. 'It's being so cheerful as keeps him going,' said Mrs Kettle, heaving with mirth. The other Kettles obediently went into shrieks. I found him a few odd jobs on the days that his father was working on the Manor Court Estate, but he wasn't happy. 'National Service was better, Mrs Longmire,' he

said. 'I was good at that. My bed was a real picture
when I got my kit laid out, and the sergeant wasn't near
as rough on me as my father and that lot.' He gave himself an idea. Horace went off to a recruiting office and
discovered that he was just young enough to enlist for
fifteen years in the regular army. Underhallow and the
rest of the Kettles saw him no more.

Chapter Twelve

As the school summer vacation approached, we
received a note from Beau, asking if he could visit us.
He arrived, skinny and brown, carrying a rucksack and
a guitar-case. 'Mother's spending the whole of August
in Austria,' he said. 'Unless there's skiing, I find it
rather a bore. I thought I'd like to wander for a week or
two.' His manner showed signs of strain and when I
probed a little he became embarrassed. 'No, Aunt Amy,
I'm not tired, not at all. The exams weren't bad. I just
don't want to be away from England for a whole
month; it's too long.'

'And your mother doesn't mind? She's not unhappy
about anything? We haven't heard for a while, but I
imagine she's busy.'

'Unhappy, no,' he said, 'not a bit. She's fine, perfectly fine.' And he immediately changed the subject,
talking of his intentions, which were to walk through
Hampshire, Dorset and Devon, to Cornwall and Land's
End. 'I'll stick to the coast as far as possible, though the
cathedral cities interest me. And Glastonbury. One of
the chaps writes songs, modern stuff, and he's a bit
of a King Arthur freak, convinced that he did exist. I
said I'd meet him there if I can and we'd go on to
Tintagel.'

'Roland's mad on rock music and very little else. I'm
sorry he and Piers aren't here to meet you. They're in
school until Thursday, then we all go to Dorset with
Aunt Claudia's family for three weeks.' I gave the

address of the holiday house. 'If you happen to be any-where near, come and see us.'

'The twins think I'm a drip.' He smiled. 'Who can blame them? Mother was always so anxious and I had no idea of how to play. Being a cherished only son doesn't do much for the personality.'

'They changed their mind about you after the Aldermaston march, and the guitar will impress them no end. Being a twin has one disadvantage. Each of them wants to be top dog, yet each feels a need to support the other. Treat them like the puppies they still are and you'll find them friendly.'

'Didn't they think CND a bit wet? Or was that Aunt Claudia? It must be six or seven years since I last spent more than a few minutes with them. I don't recall what they did that was so wrong, but Mother made a fuss.'

'Get them to Hindlecote, they'll love it, I promise. I'm fond of the twins. They were almost born at my wedding. Claudia was the most pregnant matron of honour of the century.'

'Why am I never told things like that? My mother never does. She couldn't even manage to tell me about Father; Gerhardt Nordmann told me. He was decent about it, but it was rather like a school lecture, not comforting at all.'

'She may have thought she would be diminished in your eyes. Your father seriously damaged her pride and her ideals, and left her lonely. Of the three of us, Portia was the one to be properly brought up. You could say that she's the only true lady. When our mother died she was twelve. Portia had already absorbed her standards, which explains her reticence. It probably sounds muddling to you, but I believe that her way of managing hurts is not to talk of them, to contain them within silence.'

He leaned back in his chair and withdrew behind

146

closed eyelids, mulling things over. I noticed how like my father he was, with the same faintly humorous line to the mouth, the same air of restrained impatience. While I was shut out, I left him for the kitchen and returned with a glass of milk and a slice of Dora's homemade chocolate cake. 'Sorry, Beau, I haven't any Coca-Cola or fizzy things. I hope this will do.'

He opened his eyes. 'Milk's fine. Baby stuff but I like it.' He took a big bite of cake and, with his mouth half full, mumbled, 'I wonder sometimes about babies. Is it awful having them? I mean is it painful or dangerous? The chaps at school are clued up about all those things. They'll think me pathetic if I have to ask.'

He startled me no end. Surely I wasn't expected to give a rundown of the uses of body parts to a sixteen-year-old boy? I groped nervously for tactful words. 'You do know, er, how much do you already know? Perhaps Uncle Rudi?'

His dry, direct look again reminded me of my father. 'It's all right, Aunt Amy, we get these weird lectures about clean living and not letting ourselves be taken advantage of by older boys. One snuffy old clergyman went on, you see, about how we gave agony to our mothers when we were born, and how we ought to think before putting girls through that sort of thing. Upsetting for kids. I've wondered ever since.'

And I wondered why it had occurred to him now, and why he asked me? I said, 'Hopefully babies won't be worrying you for years yet.' He watched, expecting more. I soldiered on, thinking what a very strange conversation this was. 'Having them is painful, but worth it or it would never happen. It's a natural process. The question of risk depends on the health of the mother. If it were very dangerous there would be far fewer children around.'

'I see.' Beau had acquired the confidence conferred

by public school, yet an unease was there, just below the surface. I considered what problems there might be: unruly adolescent emotions; school pressures; jealousy of Portia's new friendship? Gerhardt had left Hindlecote. That did not necessarily mean that they never met. Having stowed away the meagre information offered to him, Beau nodded to himself. 'Wasn't I a page at your wedding? I've never seen photographs; Mother thought they didn't do us justice.'

'We were an ill-assorted group, I confess. You'd been crying. I'll show them to you if you won't be offended. You were only about four.'

Beau stared at himself, comforter in mouth, nose running, standing beside his nanny. Behind him simpered the nuptial pair with the ill-matched matrons of honour, Portia at her thinnest and saddest, Claudia beaming for once and almost bursting the seams of her dress. To my relief he laughed. 'I bet you were sorry you ever thought of having a page-boy,' he said. 'And I hated that nanny. She was forbidden to smack me, so she went in for pinching and hair-pulling when we were alone. And she stole little things. She said that God would strike me dead if I told. Mother never knew.'

'My first one said I was ugly and a throwback; the second one was all right, Gwennie, your step-grandmother. Does it satisfy you to know that you kicked your nurse in the shins that day, really hard?'

'Did I? I'm inclined to remember myself as a stupid little victim, so I'm glad I fought back.'

'You don't resent the visitors coming to Hindlecote, Beau?'

'Oh no, I shall be working hard when I get home, taking people on the nature trails, punting them around on the river, taking turns at driving the train. It's great.

148

And we're arranging a rock concert for September. I don't want to miss that.' He frowned and the embarrassment was back. 'Why don't you come down for it, Aunt Amy? I'll get Mother to ask you.' I made a noncommittal answer. When he left us the next day I felt that in some way I had overlooked a hidden question, that I had failed him. He didn't visit us at Studland.

With the memory of the previous year still overvivid, I had tried to avoid the place, hinting for a change, a safe hotel in a safe resort. In vain, since the children simply looked at me in disgust. 'Dorset,' Roland said. 'Three weeks. It's all arranged. We're buying snorkels and flippers to look for treasure and wrecks and things. Aunt Claudia says the house has been done up. There's electricity now and a proper bathroom. Lindsay's bringing her Dansette and loads of new records.'

'And Uncle Bill's going to take us night fishing, except for Alex, who cries too much if a fish gets caught.'

I had rung Claudia. 'What's going on?' I demanded. 'You've been plotting behind my back.'

'We knew you'd make a tiresome fuss. Personally I'm not at all fond of roughing it; at my time of life I need every comfort. Even less do I relish the prospect of coping with six children in an hotel. We'd have to put them in strait-jackets.'

'I'm sorry, Claudia, but I don't think I can bear to spend three weeks of terror every minute they're out of sight, even if you can. Diving, for heaven's sake, as if swimming isn't bad enough!'

She fell into a tremendous rage with me and threw something fragile across the room. I heard it shatter. 'Shut up, stupid,' she yelled. 'What kind of an idiot mother are you? Anyone would imagine that I don't care if my children kill themselves. I do. But I'll be damned if I pass my fears on to them. Turn your sons into cowards if you can. You don't deserve them. Now bugger off, Amy, just bugger off. You make me tired.'

I hung up feeling crushed and hopeless, a failure. Did I love my sons too much? Was I the kind of bad mother who tried to make them docile through fear, who ruined boys by trying to make them into the girl I longed for? Damn Claudia, I thought mutinously, why do I always have to be in the wrong, the one who worries? Her tempers passed as quickly as they sprang up, yet she usually expected me to apologize, and this time I wasn't going to, nor would I ring back. In the event, she rang me. 'I know I'm a brute,' she said unrepentantly, 'but you ask for it, so don't sulk. In this weather it's going to be heavenly.'

And it was. The summer of 1959 turned out to be perfect. The sky stretched calm and blue into infinity, the sea lay like milk, porpoises came inshore only a few yards from our little boat. At Grainger's insistence I borrowed a snorkel and swam underwater, keeping close to Piers, watching shoals of mackerel glide past and enthusing over a piece of smooth green glass that Roland assured me was a rum bottle from a pirate ship. I noticed what looked suspiciously like part of the name, R. White, makers of ginger-beer and lemonade, but I wasn't going to argue. We bathed at night, blue phosphorescence dripping from our bodies. In the evenings Bill and Rudi lit a fire on the beach and produced, with the maximum of fuss, charred sausages and bacon, and ash-covered potatoes, cooked in their skins. To me Claudia was merciless. 'Wasn't I right? Nothing bad has happened to anyone, has it? They've all enjoyed themselves, haven't they?'

'Yes, yes, yes, I'm sorry, yes,' I said. 'Please stop nagging me.'

'It would have been a bloody miserable holiday if we'd listened to you, wouldn't it?'

'Yes, Claudia, yes it certainly would. I won't do it again.'

'Just make sure you don't.' Lindsay was playing, for perhaps the fiftieth time, 'That'll Be the Day', on her record player. 'For God's sake, you poisonous little blight, play something else or I'll break that thing over your head,' Claudia yelled.

'Have a heart, Muvver dear, it's Buddy Holly. He's an immortal. He got killed in a plane crash in February. He died young, only twenty-two.'

'Not a day too soon,' Claudia said unfeelingly, her own childhood obsession with jazz conveniently forgotten.

At home several postcards were waiting for us. Portia had sent a view of a glacier and a brief message. Merve and Reggie were in Nice, wished we were there, and hoped to see us at Hindlecote in September for the rock concert. The most interesting one was from Meggie Openshaw. She had crammed it with writing. Oddly, I thought, not knowing the circumstances, she and David were touring America together, from the west coast to the east, and had visited his wartime foster parents. ('Old loves they are.') Before returning to England they intended to fly to Paris to stay with Pandel Metkin and did I think that David's mother would agree to meet her? ('The mysterious Sonia! She'll make up the set as far as parents are concerned, dear Amy. Yes, this is a good, good, good sign. Expect news when we meet.') Her question about Sonia was one that only David could answer. Although she lived not many miles away from Underhallow, she discouraged visits and had effectively cut herself off from any contact with the Savernakes. We had long since become an irrelevance. David was allowed a rare visit. Sonia never visited or wrote or telephoned. If she was unmoved now by her son, she was not likely to be much interested in a prospective daughter-in-law. Apart from that minor difficulty everyone appeared to be fine, which was satisfactory, though I felt a queer sense of hidden things, things I ought to be guessing at, though heaven only knew what.

Even Topsitogs enjoyed a boom in that long, hot summer. Hattie had been talked into buying in far more children's sun and beach suits than she could normally have hoped to sell. By mid-August they had all gone. She closed down for a fortnight and went to Clacton, where her mother was staying in a nursing home and brooding viciously on the dud Doolittles, living a few miles away in Colchester. Hattie said that the duds had tried to be friendly. She didn't think it at all a bad thing, as her mother was bound to get comfort from a mutual reviling of Mr Doolittle.

While she was away Topsitogs was broken into and some baby clothes stolen. 'It'll be the Kettles,' Gloria Hopkins said in Dora's shop. 'The youngest girl's got herself pregnant, cavorting around on Hallow Hill with any boy that gives her the time of day. Only seventeen and no morals. Serves her right.'

'That doesn't make her a thief,' I said.

'Why baby clothes, then, if they're not for a baby?' Gloria looked satisfied with this piece of logic.

Dora said, 'I'd be careful, Gloria. You can't just accuse anyone. There's some rubbishy boys round here who steal anything and sell it at Chichester market. *And* there's more than one girl about who's in the family way.'

Mr Slade, who was sitting in his favourite place by the open shop door, cackled. 'Miserable bitch, ain't she? Nobody except her's supposed to enjoy theirselves. Been nailing holes in Charlie's stocks again, I shouldn't wonder.'

'That'll do, Father,' Dora said. 'You keep out of this. It's no business of ours anyway.' He had nodded off and didn't hear. 'Or anyone else for that matter.'

'Meaning me?' Gloria asked. 'Nasty old man, talking suggestive at his age. You ought to have him put away. I was only trying to think of how I could help Hattie. She'll be fed up when she sees her shop.'

The culprit was never found, but Hattie was less upset about the trivial loss than we expected. She brought back from Clacton a thin, dreamy, unwashed girl of eighteen or so, the youngest of the dud Doolittles. When asked, Hattie was unable to explain why she had taken the trouble. 'I don't know. The girls don't get much.' Although cleanliness had small importance in her family, she made an effort. In the new bathroom at Parsley Cottage, she dunked her half-sister, scrubbed her well, washed her hair and instructed her in such basic skills of housekeeping as she could summon. The girl emerged a dark-eyed, lascivious beauty. She had no moral sense whatsoever, and thoroughly educated many of the young men of Underhallow on and around Hallow Hill, giving rise to a new verb, to doolittle. In the Castleton's Oak she was nicknamed The Fancy. Gloria Hopkins had almost more material for gossip than she could comfortably handle and passed on over a shampoo and set detailed accounts of The Fancy's depredations. Doolittling was not confined entirely to single men. Happily her Charlie's weakness was for large-breasted women so the new arrival presented no temptation to him or threat to Gloria.

'Now she's running a knocking-shop over there,' the police sergeant said of Hattie in the unsafe surroundings of the Castleton's Oak, grinding his teeth with

153

rage. 'I'll have her one day, you see if I don't.'

'Just you leave 'er be,' said the barman. 'So innocent as a babe is our Hattie. You go barging in and you'll spoil it for the rest of us.'

'Who are you to be setting yourself against the law? I know my duty and I won't be interfered with in the doing of same.'

'Balls,' said the barman, raising a quiet cheer from the patrons. 'You got a spite against 'er over half a crown for cleaning your lad's trousers. Lay a finger on 'er and that beer's the last you'll ever get on this house.'

So Hattie went unmolested. When she had drawn up a full inventory of her losses in the burglary, she found that the thief had made off with two of her paintings, showing naked wood nymphs peeping coyly out of lush undergrowth. 'Some of my very best work, Amy,' she said. It was a subtle flattery that pleased her immensely.

Chapter Thirteen

The summer weather lingered on into September.
Harvest festival took place in boiling weather and
an atmosphere of acute rivalry over the relative size
of vegetable marrows. Six of us ladies decorated
the church. We waited until the last minute to cut the
flowers and greenery and so failed to notice that Hattie
had trailed long sprays of wild hop around the plat-
form of the Sunday School room. By morning it smelt
like a brewery. The children became heavy-eyed and
sleepy and Gloria Hopkins complained to the vicar. On
the Monday morning I was helping to clear out the
mountains of produce for distribution to old people's
homes and orphanages when a new 3.4 litre Jaguar
drove around the green and stopped at my front gate. It
was driven by David. At his side sat Meggie Openshaw,
neat as a kitten, a demure and lovely smile lighting up
her face. David opened the door for her. She made a
graceful exit, showing off legs encased in sheer nylons.
'Here's Amy,' she said, and waved.

David looked at me sidelong. 'Can we stay for a day
or two?' he asked. 'The old cottage will be fine for me
if you haven't room in the house.'

I found that a mildly improper suggestion. It was in
the cottage, the oldest part of the house, that he had
first made love to a policeman's widow who was now
an extremely well-known historian. He was eighteen at
the time. That affair had lasted, intermittently and
without commitment on either side, for years, perhaps

155

until the advent of Meggie. He didn't know, of course, that I knew. To take the hopeful view, he intended a final farewell to his initiation. Men have such an extraordinary reverence for their vital parts, a dedication that women on the whole don't share, and they incline, I've noticed, to treat love as something of a defeat. I decided to be unhelpful. 'How lovely to see you, dears. The boys went back to school last week so we've rooms to spare.'

'Good,' Meggie said, 'I can bore you rigid with traveller's tales. And before I die of choked-back pride and joy, David and I are engaged. This is my ring; heavenly, don't you think?' I did, admiring it as I congratulated them. The large diamond, reset for Meggie, had belonged to a European princess. Somehow it had escaped the clutches of the late Queen Mary who, it was unkindly rumoured, helped out her impoverished relations by snapping up their jewels at bargain prices.

David, uncharacteristically hangdog and awkward, examined his feet. I lightly trod on one of them. He laughed then. 'Very well, Amy, you can crow as much as you like. This wretched girl eluded me from coast to coast, and jeered at me all the way. Never a dull moment. By the time we reached the Grand Canyon I could cheerfully have wrung her neck and thrown her in.'

'The poor old thing isn't used to respectable girls from Bolton,' Meggie said. 'He proposed instead. Isn't that nice?'

'Very nice, Meggie dear. The traffic through that London flat of his made me dizzy. I was always a couple of beauty queens behind. You'll never want to be a model or open a boutique, will you? Or travel and meet interesting people?'

'No fear, and no more Bolton or thread-winders either, so hooray! Poor old Father thinks it heaven to be connected with an earl, and Pandel threw the party of a lifetime for us in Paris.' She leaned against the wall and became dreamy-eyed. 'He's so gorgeous. I do hope David looks like that when he's old.'

Women usually lusted after Pan, which was a pity since he inclined almost exclusively towards men, or rather one man, his companion of years. It was a tribute to Sonia's allure that David ever came to be born. I said, 'I've adored him since I was eight and I still do. His nature puts princes to shame.' Davy was not pleased. I kissed him. 'And you can stop sulking and be grateful. All those women wouldn't have fallen at your feet if he hadn't made you in his own image.'

'Well of course he did,' Meggie said. 'I shall probably be fighting off competition for the rest of our lives. Fortunately I have a touch of my mother somewhere. I don't believe in fair play.'

'Is she pleased about your engagement?'

'She doesn't know yet; she can't be reached or told. Some months ago she shouldered her stock of assorted rubber goods, left Africa and passed on to countries unknown. We've heard a rumour that she woefully upset some Muslims and they've thrown her into jail.'

'Oh dear, she may be in danger. Shouldn't someone try to find her?'

Meggie shook her head. 'I expect it will do her good to be chastened. She'll make their lives such absolute hell that they're bound to let her go in time. And imagine what her wedding present would be – a book on birth control and a gross of articles out of stock.' Her look implored me. 'Amy, you are pleased, aren't you? It's for life, on my part at any rate.'

'And on mine, I'm afraid,' David said. 'I haven't the stamina to go through this again and I'm sticking with my investment. Meggie will never part with that ring.'

'I certainly won't. I wasn't brought up to be stupid.

It's my assurance of good behaviour when the aristocratic tarts from the Chelsea set start nosing around.'

I mentioned, truthfully, that I was delighted.

'Terrific,' Meggie said, 'and now comes the greatest
moment; I'm to meet the thrillingly wicked Sonia.'

David and I looked at her with pity. It was many
years since Sonia had done anything either thrilling or
wicked. In her retirement to the country and a second
marriage she had become what nature had always
intended her to be, ordinary. In the remains of her
beauty might still be read her amazing attraction. And
that was all. 'She's over sixty,' David said, 'a bailiff's
wife. She keeps hens, preserves fruit, makes jam and
sings in the church choir.'

'I don't care. She gave up everything for love, and
suffered hideously for it in the War. Those happenings
don't ever pass. On the day she dies she'll remember
the lost emotions.'

'Well, don't for heaven's sake mention them, Meggie,
or Pan Metkin, or anything at all relating to the past.
They may be romantic to you, to Mother they're
shameful.'

'My darling, you told her that we're only passing
through. I shan't utter a word except yes or no, unless
we're invited to stay to tea.'

'We won't be,' David said. 'She lost an entire life.
Robbie has made her a new one exactly as she wants
it. Old loves are an intrusion. It's her due as my
mother to be told that I'm to marry, and that's absolutely all.'

'Yes, yes, I understand perfectly how it is. But she
and Robbie are the last of the parents – at least, I hope
they are, you seem to have so many. They must all be
done as it were. Mine are dull, a trades union leader
and a doctor who's potty on birth control. The sheer
romance of Sonia is entirely for me. Private.'

'Understanding you is hopeless,' David said. 'Perhaps in twenty years.'

The visit to Sonia took place and was as brief as David expected. Meggie seemed not at all disappointed. She pored over the few snapshots I had from the days when Sonia was my stepmother, and said that the years had not so much ruined as enshrined her looks. 'You knew her then, Amy. What was she truly like?'

'Gorgeous face, luscious figure, but rather boring and proper until she discovered sex. We children didn't care for her a bit. Sorry to disappoint you.'

'Didn't that make her fall more interesting when it happened? I do wish I'd been there.'

'Meggie, it was a miserable time for all of us, including David, and I don't want to revive it. Whatever view you get of Sonia from me, the next person you ask will have a quite different one. Can we let her rest, please?'

She nodded amiably. We went on to talk about announcements. The formal engagement party, one of the chaotic family occasions we all dread and like, was to be held at Gunville Place in October, when Val proposed to close the hotel for a week and give us our heads. Before I could even begin to think of buying presents and discussing wedding dates, Beau sent an invitation for the first Hindlecote rock festival, to be followed by a firework display, the closing event of the season. The time, September, was an impossibly busy one for Rudi. As theatrical agents go, he was good, devoted to his clients and keen to nurture and place their talents. He wanted none of them to starve at Christmas. For myself, I would have refused, except for an extra message. It was brief, yet urgent. On the bottom of the printed card Beau had scrawled, 'Please come, Aunt Amy, *please.*'

159

*   *   *

My house that I so dearly love shone white and tranquil in the mellow sunlight. The garden wore its autumn splendour. The old trees on the green threw oblique blue shadows across the tired grass. I didn't want to leave all that for a single hour. Driving carefully with bad grace, I managed to arrive early. The main gate to the castle was closed and the drawbridge over the moat appeared to be raised. I passed on to a field beyond the children's playground. A stage had been set up at one end. For the rest it was a chaos of lights and cables and microphones and electricians tripping over each other and cursing. Occasionally a van arrived and disgorged strange youths and a variety of instruments. I supposed that Portia was keeping to her room. However commercial, this occasion would not appeal to her. There was nobody to ask. I couldn't see Beau about anywhere. Following the arrows, I made for the nearest possible haven, the striped and tasselled medieval refreshment tent. The bar had not yet opened. The only person present was Merve, lounging at ease, his feet planted on a table, drinking coffee and munching smoked salmon sandwiches. 'Sweetheart Amy,' he shrieked, 'join me. My last quiet moment before those adolescent zombies pierce my eardrums. The poor self is a Mozart man; I ought not to be here, my work is done.'

'I like your hair, Merve,' I said, 'it's elegant, and the flares. A tiny bit on the wide side, but you carry them off.'

'Do you truly think so, cherished girl? Was the grandmother right about blue? They call this blue heaven, a pretty name, yet I always thought pink and Edwardian was so much more the poor me.'

'That mature and dignified look makes a lovely change,' I said firmly, purloining a sandwich and

160

thinking that he now managed to resemble an emaciated dowager. 'Quiffs are out. Why are you here if the poor self hates it so much?'

'For the boy; I promised him. Had the wealth lasted, I dare say he would happily have become your everyday duke, killed things in the shires, done dukely things and been *the* perfect pain in the arse. As it is, the guitar is his salvation. I am supposed to convince the darling Duchess that a decent music school is better for him than university. But where is he? Where is she? Not in the castle, I enquired.'

This was Beau's big day. His absence from all the excitement outside mystified me. And why the urgency of his message? I felt mildly cheated, as though my habit of imagining disasters had turned on me and betrayed me into another folly. Portia couldn't need me or she wouldn't have hesitated to summon me herself. I wondered whether she was even at Hindlecote. Since her postcard from Austria there had been no word from her. Impatient at being where I had no great desire to be, I mulled over the possibility of driving home that night as soon as the concert ended. My musings were interrupted by a series of ghastly shrieks, followed by a hollow, unnatural voice mooing, 'Testing, testing, number one, testing.'

Merve covered his ears and staggered to the opening in the canvas. 'Turn it down,' he screamed, 'for Christ's sake stop that dreadful noise.'

'Hallo,' Beau said, appearing beside him and almost startling him out of his skin. 'It'll stop presently. They're only fixing the mikes.'

'Until they have done so I shall be in the dungeons,' Merve said. 'If you want the poor self to speak to the Duchess, please provide a modicum of peace and quiet.'

Beau went pale and then flushed violently. 'Will you

161

mind leaving it until the concert? She's not entirely – I mean she's all right, but she wants to talk to Aunt Amy.'

'Well, pardon me!' Merve said huffily. 'I'm sure I've nothing better to do than wait on your convenience. Just find me a bottle of gin, I shall be quite happy.' Beau opened the bar shutter and complied, adding a glass and tonic water. Merve looked penitent. 'Sorry. Sudden noises put the poor self into a tizzy of nerves. You will find me in my room.'

We watched him trip away on pointed toe, clutching the bottle like a child to his bosom. He was becoming odder, I thought. The prospect of Reggie's marriage, though distant and uncertain, worried him, and when he remembered he enquired after the health of old Mr Slade with great tenderness. Dora would never interfere in so long-standing a friendship. There was no way of telling Merve this without appearing to accuse him of selfishness or jealousy. Beau said, 'He'll come round, Aunt Amy. Will you, can you talk to Mother now? I told her you were coming. She's in the pavilion.'

My assumption that the charm of the brick-kiln had diminished was wrong then. An unreasoning elation replaced the faint depression I had caught from Merve, a sense that no harm could come to Portia there. The daylight had begun to fade. We walked in silence up from the field. The lights in the water garden came on and the castle sprang to life, golden against the evening sky. At the Dower House gate Beau left me. I moved in a dream through the almost over-scented garden, startling the moths that were feeding on the tobacco flowers. The odd sense of homecoming, of past times revived, shivered through me. The door to the pavilion stood ajar. My raised arm shook slightly as I knocked, and I waited until I heard Portia's voice inviting me in.

She held some sewing in her lap, though her hands were still. Against the velvet of her favourite chair her body melted into shadow. Her fair head inclined towards me. Beside her a dog, a Great Dane, warned softly at the back of its throat, then wagged its tail. In the mirror her reflection blurred and became distinct, haloed by the light from the single lamp. She laid aside her sewing. 'There you are, Amy,' she said in her briskest voice. 'Don't worry about the dog, he's amiable enough. I have him for company. Shut the door, please. It will keep out some of the din.'

'I'm not intruding? Beau said that you wanted to talk to me. He seems worried about you, that's why I came really. I'm not musical enough to appreciate rock or skiffle, or whatever it is at present.'

Portia smiled. 'Not precisely music, I think. A loud noise, yet thin and charmless stuff compared with the orchestras we danced to before the War, don't you agree?'

Being the youngest, my share of dancing in glamorous places had been rather small, though the War had to some extent liberated me. 'And during it too. All those romantic, nostalgic songs in little dance halls and the Blitz going on outside. How unlikely it seems now.' Portia, who had never in her life danced in a village hall, showed no inclination to pursue that line of conversation. I began to forget that Beau had summoned me for a purpose, whatever it might be. 'Thank you for your postcard,' I said. 'Did you enjoy Austria in the summer?'

She leaned back in her chair and looked past me at a beckoning nymph, then she folded long eyelashes briefly over her blue eyes. 'Yes,' she said, 'yes, I did. Those weeks were a gift out of time. I visited the clinic once. I don't expect to see Botolph again.' Beneath her calm I sensed excitement, suppressed and

163

unaccountable. Closing her work basket, she pushed it aside and stood. The dog moved with her. Resting a hand lightly on its head as though for reassurance, she gave me a funny triumphant kind of smile, glorious in a way, and happy. Deliberately she stepped forward and took the chunk of green glass from the mantel. 'Austrian mountain crystal. It's quite rare. Gerhardt found it in a rock fall when he was climbing with his nephews.'

'Yes,' I said vaguely, with a swooning sensation of being about to go off my head.

The lamplight fell strongly on Portia as she stretched out her arm, giving me by far the most stunning shock of my life. No need for me to puzzle any longer over Beau's anxiety or look for answers to his questions. She said, 'I wanted Botolph to know before he dies, to see for himself. Revenge, after all, is very sweet, you know. Now I shall forget him.' Words deserted me. Clutching the arms of my chair, I sat dumbly and stared and stared, not believing what I saw. I raised my eyes to look into Portia's face. She nodded. 'It *is* a surprise, isn't it?' That understated the situation to an unimaginable degree, but it was true as far as it went. She was forty-seven years old and she was pregnant.

Chapter Fourteen

'Six months almost,' Portia said in answer to my unspoken question. She had been, then, a little pregnant
in May, for the opening of Hindlecote to the public,
though she may not have known it. When the fog
cleared from my brain I began to wonder how long she
and Gerhardt had been lovers and how it had come
about. Perhaps they discussed it maturely first. In films
and novels bodies melt and join without volition or
forward planning, but that simply wouldn't happen in
life with the complication of clothes, and people all
over the place, and doors opening at inappropriate
moments. It was a question of striking a balance
between unromantic arrangements and acute nervous
strain. And where? Here in the pavilion, or in some
flowery Alpine meadow watched over by the eternal
snows? As though it matters, I thought, or is any business of mine.

It was peaceful in the room. The light splashed
golden on Portia's blue dress, reviving my Christmas
dream. Pregnancy added splendour to her beauty. She
stood tall and abundant as a latter-day Demeter while
the fauns and maenads pursued their eternal dance.
The round brick walls reduced the outbreak of ampli-
fied din to a far-off rumour, like a shared heartbeat.
Portia sat down and took her sewing into her lap. The
dog leaned against her knee as Gerhardt had done,
before collapsing slowly with a yawn.

Following the initial shock came a twinge of pure

envy at her daring and fear for the consequences. That singular, seductive place conveyed an assurance that all things were for good. Portia had made certain that advice and protests came too late. I put up a feeble resistance. 'You know you shouldn't, Portia; I don't have to tell you that. Surely your doctor?'

'It's going to be all right,' she said; 'I knew it could happen, I wanted it more than I can say, and in another year or two it would have been too late. I won't let it be spoilt by anyone, not even Gerhardt. He's the one who's afraid.'

'There's no possibility of marriage? That you can be together?'

'None. My views on divorce are unchanged. Gerhardt's wife has a mental disorder; he can't push her over the edge into madness, and if he did I would never see him again.'

Her tranquil acceptance almost angered me. I had to admit that she looked lovelier than I had ever seen her, alive, untroubled and young. But young was what she was not, and nor was Gerhardt. Wretchedly I recalled the lectures, arranged by Gloria Hopkins and leaning heavily towards the medical: the dissertations on internal organs and the less attractive bodily functions. Gynaecologists in particular always had statistics. Odd scraps lodged in my memory – the incidence of birth defects such as mongolism increases rapidly where the parents are over forty, risk to the mother, inflexible bones, Caesarians. How did Portia dare these dangers? Her love for Gerhardt seemed to me to be phenomenal, intense and absolute, yet selfless, demanding nothing.

I said, 'It's too little. He's not even in the same country. You'll be alone.'

She glanced up from her sewing. 'On the contrary, I shall never be alone again. I wasted so many years trying to cleanse the Augean stables.' The what? I blinked at her like an idiot. Oh yes, Hercules. 'For heaven's sake, Amy, look it up if you don't understand,' she said with slight impatience. 'Such time as remains is for me and Beau and this baby.'

'Beau, yes. He's worried, you know, and he'll suffer at school if other boys find out. They can be vulgar-minded little beasts.'

'Am I hurting him?' she said. 'I hope not; he's so dear to me. I lean on him too much, I think. But he'll leave me quite soon. In time he'll marry. Then when Botolph dies I shall be dismissed permanently to the Dower House.'

'Will you let him have the career he wants, in music?' I asked, hoping very much that she would. 'Merve's waiting to speak to you about it. I'll walk up to the castle with you now if you're ready.'

Portia shook her head slightly. 'I shall sleep here tonight, in the other room. Send him down to me. And Amy, Grandmother knows what's happening. I'll leave it to you to tell the others, but do it tactfully, please. I may be a fallen woman in need of redemption, but I don't want them panicked into a well-meaning invasion.'

Only a true and overwhelming passion could have caused the abandonment of her pinched and rigid moral standards, yet her voice and smile were as coldly distant as ever, touched with the determined arrogance that had made becoming a duchess her life's goal and, in the end, a source of misery and disgust. Claudia and some others find me sentimental and romantic, which is true only in part. I am cautious about attributing power to love. It isn't, for instance, a high road to happiness, or a therapy for damaged spirits, or a charm against evil. Wishing from Portia more sentiment and less dryness, I said, 'I don't understand you at all. You've never needed us, have you?

167

You've never needed anybody, but a time may come. Whatever you want, we'll do.'

'Is that what you think?' she asked, astonished. 'That I need no-one? People go on a great deal about their rights nowadays. Mother taught me that I am responsible for myself, able to tend my own wounds without begging for help at the first crisis. A rigid code, perhaps, but no bad one.'

'Well then, if you need us, say so.'

We must have talked together for a long time. The moment I stepped outside the brick-kiln, the craziness of Portia's attitude struck me fully. How was the child to be explained? What would people, her one-time dread, think and say? Claudia's mad involvements had caused me some dire headaches in the past, but this was madder, a bonfire of the reputation, the ultimate in scandals. Over the Dower House roof hung a quarter moon, turning the garden into a patchwork of pale light and blue shadow. With a sudden whoosh, a rocket soared and burst into flower. Others followed. The night sky coruscated with colour and the reek of smoke drifted on the breeze. A single green star hung over the roof of the pavilion. Not that, I thought, not a star, it's too much. Then it went out. Feeling chilled though the air was sultry, I hurried up to the castle to give Merve Portia's message. My lips were stiff with nervous tension. I wondered, Does he know? I let him set off for the pavilion, then followed to the Dower House. Lying alone and restless in bed, I could recall scarcely a sentence that was spoken, yet I knew everything of importance. Portia would consult no doctor. Gerhardt intended to be with her for the birth and Emmi, his sister, originally a nurse and a qualified midwife, would arrive in a day or two. 'She'll stay with me,' Portia had said. 'I shall want Gerhardt to see our child. He's given me so much.'

But what a gift, a meagre crumb or two. For Beau's birth she was surrounded by doctors, resident nurses, the ultimate in care. Portia had, I thought, always waited, hoping for kindness, some evidence of generosity and warmth. Now she faced the life of a mistress, waiting again for the letter, the phone call, the rare visit. It wasn't enough, not nearly enough. I felt rather sick. Uneasily dozing, I began to dream about the brick-kiln again, and myself in Portia's blue dress. With an effort I dragged myself back to full consciousness, only to be overtaken by all the frights and fears that save themselves up for the small hours. I hadn't brought a book with me. Roaming through the cheerless, unvisited rooms, I found an anthology of poetry lying on a chair. Between the pages was a painted bookmark, a tall angel with golden wings and halo. Poetry would have to do. I read first a verse that was marked.

> Therefore the Love which us doth bind,
> But Fate so enviously debars,
> Is the conjunction of the mind,
> And opposition of the stars.

Not much comfort there. The night seemed inordinately long. I heard the concert audience depart in a chorus of shouts and whistles and laughter, then the din as the technicians dismantled the stage and equipment and drove away. I don't know whether Portia slept at all. On my way to the castle the next morning I looked in at the door of the pavilion. She sat in the same place, but the dog was gone. 'Are you coming up for breakfast?' I asked.

'Tell them to send something down, please. Goodbye, Amy. Don't worry, and above all, don't let the others worry me.'

Why do the members of my family never expect

normal reactions to abnormal circumstances? How should I not worry? As I sat down to my scrambled eggs and bacon I managed to smile radiantly at Beau. Excitement was bubbling out of him, so I guessed that Portia had agreed to music school. Nevertheless he watched me with a doglike anxiety. 'What an exciting time this has turned out to be,' I said. 'I can't wait to tell the others about the baby. They'll be thrilled. You don't mind too much about it, do you, Beau?'

Merve, astonished at what had happened to his Duchess darling, twittered away like a cageful of budgerigars and gave him no chance to answer. 'It's just the perfect climax, perfect, with the Duke at death's door. His last gift before dying.' For a moment I thought he was making a joke in extremely poor taste, but no, he spoke in all sincerity. Beau wielded his knife and fork vigorously. I plastered my face with a mild expression of agreement, hoping that Merve would not too soon be disillusioned. 'And the unselfishness of her! Our Beau is destined for the Royal College.'

'I might not be good enough and I've one more term at school yet, time to practise, especially piano and oboe. Merve thinks I'm all right on guitar, but it isn't an orchestral instrument and not taken all that seriously. Aunt Amy, will my mother – I mean, this baby; you did say it's a natural thing and not dangerous?'

'She's in good health, Beau, and for these last months she'll have constant care. If you have the smallest anxiety, anything at all, tell me at once and I'll do what I can.'

'Thanks,' he said, 'thanks awfully. She dismisses me in a way, as if she can only concentrate on one thing at a time. It makes me feel so awkward, useless.'

Unease tied my tongue in knots. I didn't know how to give him reassurance when I badly wanted it myself. 'It's all part of the process, Beau, a kind of protection,'

I muttered, piling more marmalade on to an already laden piece of toast. Merve rescued me with a burst of joyousness about the beauty and sanctity of motherhood, and how the poor self wished that fate had not so cruelly robbed him of those organs essential to proper manhood and the creation of a dozen little ones. Beau blushed scarlet. I escaped from the castle early.

Driving homewards, I considered ways of giving the news to Valentine and Claudia, hovering in choice between the bald statement and the gradual approach. In London, I broke my journey and called to see my grandmother. 'I've just come from Hindlecote,' I said as soon as I got inside the drawing-room door.

'Do sit down, my dear. I dislike flying conversations. Did you enjoy the concert?'

'Grandmother! I didn't hear the concert and you know that's not what I want to talk about. Is there nothing I can do for Portia except fret? Do you realize that she hasn't even seen a doctor?'

'It's rather soon after luncheon,' she said, consulting a vast ormolu clock on the even vaster mantel and tugging at the bell-pull, 'however, you'd better have some tea. You appear agitated. I confess that Portia is the last woman I would have expected to become stricken with passion, but one can never tell. As for the child, she is following a traditional course. Little more than fifty years ago doctors were regarded as superfluous to the expectant mother. A competent midwife served well enough.'

'And a great many babies died, and the mothers,' I said indignantly. 'Portia's too old. It's madness.'

Grandmother compelled a change of subject while we had tea. She may have been considering deeply, but I don't think so. She talked about Grandfather and told me that Cousin Beatrice had offered to buy Ferdy a

171

villa in the south of France, though not being a French speaker he elected for a bungalow at Felixstowe instead. Mrs Smythe-Fennel was facing prosecution for false pretences. She had ordered a mass of jewels from Asprey, representing herself as the sister-in-law of a royal duchess, and forgotten to pay for them. 'Harlotry has gone to her head,' said Grandmother. When the teacups had been removed she returned to the question of Portia. 'Well, Amy, I can't pretend that there's no cause for anxiety; clearly there is. A late termination, could I have persuaded Portia to agree and a gynaecologist to oblige, is also dangerous. Let her take the risk without interference. If she succeeds it will be her triumph, a reward for the sterile, loveless years.' She eyed me sideways. '*And* one in the eye for Coritanum.'

Her forthrightness entertained me. 'Revenge without malice, I suppose. But isn't the truth bound to come out? What will people say of her?'

'The dogs bark,' said Grandmother, with a flourish that knocked a pretty enamel box filled with violet-scented cachous to the floor, 'and the caravan passes.' There was no answer to that. I crawled over the carpet, restoring the cachous to their place. She took one and sucked it noisily. Since she clearly intended that the subject shouldn't be raised, I didn't try to ask how she would feel if Portia died. She was already out of patience with death for refusing to come to her when called, and I felt that she might quite likely get indignant at the idea of her grandchildren dying before her.

The heat in London was overpowering. There had been no rain since July, though as I drove through the suburbs I noticed that a few clouds had begun to gather. My eyes wanted to droop. I sang and talked aloud to keep myself awake. Underhallow green was parched to brown and the trees drooped and were dropping their leaves early. Heavy with my tidings, I tried shock tactics on Rudi the moment I walked into the house. 'Hallo, darling. Portia's expecting a baby.' I should have waited until he had finished listening to the news on the wireless. He made noises that meant he was glad to see me and hadn't taken in my startling announcement. I let him switch off and tried again. 'I've something serious to tell you,' I said, and could have kicked myself when I saw the sudden fear on his face. 'Not me, Portia. She's expecting a baby in December.'

'Thank God,' he said. 'I thought you were ill. You mustn't give me such frights.' That settled it, the bald, unvarnished announcement it would be. 'Did you really say that the Duchess is having a baby? Are you sure? Isn't she a bit old?'

'That's the point. Honestly, Rudi, you're all going to be hopeless over this, I feel it in my bones.'

'Sorry, darling, it *is* serious of course. Hold on a moment, it can't be the blight-infested Botolph, surely.' He shook his head. 'Not in a hundred years; our singing, poetry-reading archaeologist, I'll be bound. A nice chap, but the last I should have thought to storm that citadel.'

'Kindly adjust your expression, Rudi. I see the shadow of a leer. Portia's forty-seven. She can't marry, she's six months gone, and she won't listen to reason. Also Gerhardt's the great love of her life, and I think she's bloody marvellous. I'll make coffee, I need something.' Tears had suddenly blinded me. I seldom swear, and the thought and the words took me by surprise.

'Curses upon your house!' he said. 'I do wish they'd behave and not clutter up our lives so much. We'll go to the kitchen together, hand in hand if you wish, and make something interesting. How about a white lady? Shall we venture?'

'It doesn't sound appropriate.'

'They don't do a cocktail called a scarlet woman.'

'Portia isn't scarlet, only very faintly tinged with pink. Gerhardt is the first and last passion and I'd be glad for her if she were twenty-seven, but she's not.'

Rudi messed around, separating egg whites and shaking this and that. 'Be glad anyway, Amy. Happiness won't come to her again, not in this way, to surprise and delight her. Don't you think she'll have counted the cost and found it worth while?'

Although she probably had, not being given to impulsive actions, it aggravated me that she hadn't seen fit to tell the rest of the family herself. We had several white ladies and I felt better. 'How am I to give the glad news to Val, d'you think? And Claudia? If I don't tell her first she'll be furious with me. I really hate being the messenger. She won't believe a word of it and she'll say I'm making it up. And Father and Gwennie will have to know too.'

We settled down in silence. The old house creaked a peaceable welcome. I thought of the brick-kiln pavilion, and Portia sitting there alone in apparent contentment, and how stuffy and boring she had been for most of her life. A dizzy feeling – probably a disturbed night and the white ladies were having an effect – made my head swim and drift. Perhaps I *was* making it up. Could I possibly have dreamed the whole thing? I had almost convinced myself that the next time I went to Leicestershire I should find Hindlecote Castle as it used to be, unwelcoming, unhappy, poverty-ridden, and Portia distant and cold. 'You could telephone Claudia first and ask her to tell the others,' Rudi said, returning me to the present.

'Not the telephone. The twins listen in and they'll dash off and give their version, with trimmings, before Claudia gets a chance. They're fearful liars at times.

Everyone will fall on me like a ton of bricks and think it's my doing.'

'They have an instinct for drama, certainly. If ever they need an agent, I'm their man. Don't you think it might keep for ten days or so until we go down to Dorset for the party?'

'Party? Good heavens, Rudi, I'd forgotten all about David and Meggie. I haven't even thought about their present. Oh dear.'

'It can all be arranged, and Claudia's much more receptive after a few gins.'

'Of course, that's the answer. How clever you are. I'll have to do something about the present pretty quickly. I can't think what. The usual stuff won't do. David's surrounded by rare and precious objects.'

'Perfumed silk sheets for Meggie's bottom drawer?' suggested Rudi. 'Eulalie Downcastle swears that they *made* her career. "Honestly schweetest boy, my talent would have gone utterly, utterly unnoticed!"'

'Talent for what?' I asked meanly. The fragrant Eulalie was his client and difficult to place since she was fading rather fast and declined to take character roles. I dare say the sheets saw plenty of action and wore out quite quickly. 'Does she really call you sweetest boy? She should get some spectacles, poor old thing.'

'How can she do that? She assures me that the part for her is as a Woman Who Has Lived, but she won't want to see the wrinkles that prove it. No sheets then?'

'Certainly not, it's a most suggestive suggestion.' We took our glasses out on to the terrace. The air was suffocating and black clouds piled high above the ridge of the hill. 'I shall ring Pan and ask him for the name of a modern artist worth watching. A small oil, growing in value, will be a nice insurance policy for Meggie.'

'Isn't that rather a cynical view? You trust David, surely?'

Lightning flashed. The garden leapt into view and disappeared again. 'Things happen that can't be prevented,' I said. 'Look at Portia. My family has had more than its fair share of adultery and fornication and general messiness. What do you think of a painting?'

'A good idea, Amy. Go ahead.'

'Okey-dokey, Rudi,' I said, 'I'll phone him tomorrow.' A sudden roar of thunder made me jump almost out of my skin. Rain fell in a driving sheet. 'Let's go inside. I'm glad not to be at Hindlecote in this. I'm glad to be home.'

That was the end of the perfect weather. Autumn had come, wet and cold, putting an end to doolittling on the wooded slopes of Hallow Hill. The sergeant began to keep his binoculars trained on Parsley Cottage, but Hattie had been ruminating about her sister and taking notice of her activities. She acted with unusual firmness. The delinquent was enrolled at an all-female secretarial college in Chichester. Hattie drove her there each morning and picked her up in the afternoon. It was effective as far as it went. Handcuffs, leg-irons and an armed guard would have been required to effect a complete cure. The nights were dark. However, it was cure enough to disappoint the sergeant.

Chapter Fifteen

On our way to Gunville Place for David's engagement
party, we took a detour to call on Bill and Claudia.
In her mature years Claudia found the necessity for
amiable chatter something of a nuisance and she had
implored us to be early. 'You'll give me the chance to
oil up a little without upsetting Bill,' she said.

Rudi suggested that I might find an opportunity to
tell her the news from Hindlecote in peace and quiet.
'She'll have time to get a proper grip on the facts.' I felt
that he was slighting her intelligence. Grasping facts
isn't Claudia's problem, it's persuading her to listen in
the first place. 'It comes to the same thing,' he said,
when I pointed this out. We managed to be much too
early and I was content to dawdle through the silent
autumn countryside, away from telephones and all
news, good or bad. Before reaching Blandford, Rudi
turned off the main road for the lanes through
Stourpaine towards Child Okeford. It was a cold day
with sudden spats of rain. Cloud shadows swept across
the high slopes, the valleys lay in sunlight. Under my
breath I muttered the names of the Celtic hill-forts like
a charm: Hambledon Hill, Hod Hill, Giant's Hill,
Bulbarrow.

Claudia had inherited a pleasant old manor house
near Sturminster Newton from our Great-aunt Hildegarde. The heads of the twins peered cautiously around
the door of the shed as we pulled into the drive. 'Oh
good,' they whispered, 'it's only you. Come in if you

want to, but don't let anyone see.' Vaisey squeezed past them through the gap, trotted towards us and fell into a flower-bed, where he lay, complacently patting the wet soil. I moved to pick him up. 'I wouldn't, dear Aunt Amy,' Lindsay said, 'you'll make your party clothes dirty. He can manage, he quite likes it.'

'Why the whispering, and ought you to be covered in sawdust?'

'We're making a cage for Alexander's hamsters, as a surprise. It's a lot harder than we thought. Come and see.' I went and saw, though I hesitated about going inside the shed, which held unpleasant associations for me. It had changed a great deal since Aunt Hildegarde's day. No ghosts could survive among the neat cabinets for assorted nails, and the tool-racks filled with this and that. A large, glittering saw lay on the floor underneath a saw-bench. The wobbly rhomboidal structure balanced on top was, I supposed, the embryonic hamster cage. Lindsay gazed at it thoughtfully. 'It's gone lopsided somehow, and we seem to have used a lot of wood.'

'I take it that you have permission for this enterprise?' Rudi said with mild curiosity. 'Those timbers show distinct signs of being intended for some other purpose.'

The twins exchanged identical looks of dawning unease. Grainger tried to kick a small heap of seasoned but mutilated planks into a corner. 'Wood's just wood, isn't it, for anyone to use? Father did say something about a chalet for next summer, but that was ages and ages ago.'

'Last week,' Lindsay said. 'Oh dear. Perhaps if we hide the cut-up bits he won't notice some of it's missing. We could throw them out of the car on the way to Gunville Place but they'd probably see us. Uncle Rudi, I suppose you wouldn't—'

He shook his head. 'Quite right, my dear fatheads, I wouldn't. I have more regard for your father and for my own skin. Give up handicrafts and confess at once is my best advice. You'll probably have to miss the party, but that's a small price to pay for a clear conscience.'

The winning smiles on their faces were withdrawn. 'We don't care for that suggestion at all,' Grainger said. 'In fact it stinks. We're already missing the party. I forget what we did, but it's a punishment. We're to stay in the nursery with Annie Bowells and the babies and their nanny, and only to come down to toast Meggie and Uncle David if Annie thinks we've behaved well enough to deserve our freedom.'

'I'm crazy about Uncle David, because he's so handsome,' said Lindsay. 'So's Grainger. We'd love to marry him ourselves, except that Annie says it's not the done thing to marry an uncle.'

'*And* she said that you were doomed to be an old maid because you're always tearing your knickers and looking as though you've been through a hedge backwards.'

'She did not; that was you.'

'It was not. I say, Lindsay, do you think Annie was always tearing her knickers? She's an old maid, isn't she?'

We left them vigorously squabbling. I hoped they would remember to clean the sawdust off their shoes. Vaisey, six years old and as calm as Alexander was temperamental, still sat in the dirt, apparently thinking deeply. I offered him a hand. He smiled and took it, trotting along beside me in silence. Claudia wasn't dressed. Bill greeted us warmly, looked at his youngest, swore quietly and called Annie Bowells. She sighed. 'He'll have to go in the bath again, Mr Deering. Morning, Miss Amy, Mr Rudi.'

179

'Where have we got to upstairs, Annie? Any chance of being ready to set out soon?'

'The cerise dress has come out, the one with next to no top. I told Miss Claudia it's been past its best for years and it's not right for daytime. Cerise was never her colour anyhow, but she won't have it. I'm persuading her towards that blue you like. She says can she have a drink, a sherry will do.'

Perhaps this was a good time to talk to her. 'Bill, do you mind if I take her sherry up? I want to tell her something, and I can certainly nag her out of a cerise evening dress.'

'Go with God,' he said. 'Tell her the damned thing makes her look fat; that ought to do it. She'd better make her mind up fast. By the time she's dressed and the children are clean we're going to be late.'

Meanwhile, Claudia had rigged herself out in a long black dress under an aggressively flowered, sleeveless, coatish garment. 'Heaven rest me, what on earth is that?' I asked, picking my way through the heaps of discards and taking the blue that Bill liked off its hanger.

'Oh, you're here, are you? Interesting, don't you think? When I bought it, it was the last word. That was a couple of years ago though.'

'Twenty-five I'd say, at a guess. Those patterns only appear on wallpaper nowadays. Claudia, if you can keep still just for a moment or two, I've some news about Portia.'

She scrabbled around and found a creased pink and white ankle-length Ascot dress, dense with frills and suitable for an eighteen-year-old. 'This is pretty. Does it need ironing?'

'I'll say it does, and I don't think it's a fancy dress party,' I said. 'Please listen to me.' Bill yelled up the stairs in a tone that made Claudia take notice, that if she wasn't down in five minutes he was going without her. She looked about her wildly. I abandoned hope of sensible conversation and handed her the blue dress. 'Here, put this on quickly. I'll do you up.' She dashed powder on her face, wiped it off again and walked with every evidence of calm down the stairs.

Bill dumped his sons unceremoniously in his car, not pausing to explain to Alexander why he couldn't take his guinea pigs with him. The twins prudently elected to come with Rudi and me. We walked through Val and Cristabel's private gate no more than half an hour late. The children had their own garden, with various swings and slides and a little paddling-pool. On one of the swings sat Cousin Beatrice, a regal hat with a purple cockade pushed to the back of her head, flying up and back with squeaks of pleasure while Ferdy pushed her. 'Fun,' she cried, 'such, such fun! I love a swing. It's going to be a marvellous party, dears. One more push, Ferdy, then we'll go in.'

'How I envy her,' muttered Claudia, 'primed to perfection,' and in a louder tone, 'What are you two staring at like boiled owls?'

Grainger blinked, and beseeched, 'They aren't our dread relations, are they? Just friends of someone?'

'Beatrice is your cousin three times removed,' said Claudia firmly. Grainger made a comment under her breath. 'Did I hear you say not far enough?' She received a shake of the head and a glance of injured reproach from her daughter. 'I'm glad of that as you're up for eternal punishment already. Ferdinand is Beatrice's husband.'

'Ferdinand is the teeniest bit overdressed,' Lindsay said gently, all the while moving out of reach of her mother's right hand. 'What a strange family we have to be sure.' Claudia swiped at her and missed completely. I laughed, and tried to turn it into a cough.

'I should have drowned them at birth,' Claudia said through gritted teeth, leading the way into the house. Our big family gatherings have always taken place in the ballroom at Gunville Place. Valentine and Cristabel had restored it to its Victorian elegance of velvet, chandeliers and long looking-glasses, and brought back the Chinese pots of ferns and flowers. It was a lovely room, and filling fast with guests. There were two notable absences. One, Sonia, had left Gunville Place years before, disgraced but not defeated. The hopeful Meggie had insisted that she be invited, but she had never returned to the Place and I knew that she never would. And Portia was removed from us by expectant motherhood, and by now too pregnant to make the journey.

A knot of older people had gathered around my father and Gwennie, his third wife. Uncle Henry said as I approached, 'Still here, then, Gervase? Why we hang on I can't think. I don't pretend to understand the world these days, television lounges wherever one hopes for peace and unwashed objects caterwauling like castrated polecats. They wouldn't last five min-utes on the Halls. Give me a jolly little soubrette any day.'

'Do try to keep up with the times, Henry.' Aunt Phyllida gave him a nudge. 'Gervase has never heard the voice of the polecat, gelded or whole, and neither have you.' She added an audible aside. 'I'll run him around the room a time or two and bring him back when he's mellowed.'

While we were growing, my father had been for much of the time remote, ill and disappointed with life. He viewed us, I think, with mild affection. His love was reserved for the child he hadn't fathered, David. Portia's news would not greatly disturb him. We exchanged the usual greetings and questions about our healths. 'Sit with us a while,' Gwennie said. 'It's not often we see you. Busy with the children, is it?'

'They aren't too much trouble, bless them, and they like their school. I've been to Hindlecote. Beau was anxious about his mother. After all these years she's having another baby, so she won't be here today. She seems well enough and very happy about it.'

I'm rather poor at dissembling. My father gave me a sharp look, but didn't speak. Gwennie said placidly, 'There now, and she never thought to tell us.'

'It's understandable. Society women always know an accommodating doctor and think that an abortion is just the thing. She hardly needed that, or people shaking their heads and telling her what can go wrong.'

'I should say not indeed. And I heard that the Duke was at death's door. You never know with heart trouble. He'll be better, I expect, and coming home.'

I could barely credit her reaction. Portia's reputation had become unassailable and, here at least, no doubt arose to challenge the legitimacy of her child. A life of virtue was reaping its reward. 'I don't think he'll be able to return to England. Portia visited him once or twice in Austria. She says there's no real improvement. You were a nurse, Gwennie, how dangerous is this at her age?'

She had no chance to answer me. Mr Openshaw arrived, and Grandmother with Beatrice and Ferdy. Gwennie stood up to welcome them, champagne corks began to pop and people gravitated towards the buffet. That had gone reasonably well, I thought. I heard a scuffling almost at my feet and a starched white tablecloth moved. A voice said, 'Did you hear that, Grainger?'

'Of course I heard, I'm not deaf. Aunt Portia's been doing the facts of life and she's pregnant. Little Botty is about to get a brother. Or, of course, a sister.'

'I bet it'll be another boy, or twins, two boys. Suppose Little Botty gets run over, it'll be like that film, you know the one. Douglas Fairbanks was in it. He was two brothers, fighting for a birthright. One of him got killed.'

'More like the princes in the tower, getting smothered so that there's no competition for Little Botty. Don't you think he'll smoulder with hatred?'

'Bound to. I expect he's creeping around that old castle even now, plotting. Who can we tell first?' I reached a hand under the table and hauled a twin out by the arm. It was Grainger.

'Hey, where are you going?' her sister demanded. 'Wait for me.'

'Come out of there at once, Lindsay, before you find yourself in deep, deep trouble.' A head emerged and a face wearing an expression of enquiry. 'Get up, your skirt's covered with dust.'

'Hallo, dearest Aunt, you're not shirty with us, are you? We were just keeping out of the way and talking quietly among ourselves.'

'You were nastily earwigging and making up scandalous stories about your cousin, who's called Beau, incidentally, and is a clever boy who doesn't plague us like you do.' They showed signs of sliding away. 'Don't move. You're to stand there where I can see you until I've talked to your mother. Who said you could come down anyway?'

They exchanged identical glances of disbelief and sorrow. 'Can this be our beloved Aunt Amy?' Lindsay asked. 'Who loves us to bits and never scolds?'

'We were in the lavatory and we called out that we were taking a peep. You don't truly think we'd be here if Annie told us not to, do you, dear?'

'Please don't bother with the soft soap. I'm scolding now and I suspect you're trying to deceive me. Doesn't your father think you should go to boarding school? I'm beginning to agree with him.'

They gloomed. 'You and Uncle Rudi are getting some truly odious ideas today. You won't tell on us, will you? It's not lying to use our – what's that word, Grainger? – oh yes, our sightic powers and look into the future. I don't think we ought to get spanked for that.'

'Or have Ma boxing our ears. At school we're told all the time to use our imaginations, so we do.' Some silent communication passed between them and caused Lindsay to ask meekly, 'Aunt Amy, if you're going to get us in a row, could we have some ice-cream first?'

They beseeched me with innocent blue eyes. 'You'll sit down quietly and never utter a word about Aunt Portia or Beau, on pain of my enormous displeasure? You must promise me, word of honour.'

They had been studying the Romans at school. '"We who are about to die, salute you,"' said Lindsay with tragic emphasis. 'I swear, and so does Grainger, or I'll thump her. There're four lots of ice-cream; we'd like a bit of each, please, before it's all gone.'

I spared a word of unspoken thanks that their mother, the friend and cross of my childhood and an unscrupulous arguer, had been only one and not twins. After providing them with heaped bowls of ice-cream, I sat them on an obscure love-seat behind a parlour palm and tucked napkins under their chins. They looked adorable, the wretches.

Claudia was engaged in conversation with Mr Openshaw. 'In your situation I'd go for divorce,' she was saying as I approached. 'Face it, a wife's not the slightest use swanning around Africa or Outer Mongolia, or wherever the fancy takes her. Not that I disagree with birth control. Motherhood is greatly

185

overrated. My early ambition was to live a life of unbridled sex, dancing and light wines, and now just look at this vein. A perfectly decent pair of legs ruined.' She hoisted up her skirt and showed Mr Openshaw. He gave a glance of pure terror. It seemed a propitious moment for interrupting.

'Forgive Claudia, Mr Openshaw. She's rather proud of her vein. Do you mind if I borrow her for a moment?' He backed away with a strained smile and left us, not minding in the least. The mention of unbridled sex had thoroughly unsettled him. 'You shouldn't frighten the poor man so, Claudia. Thread-workers probably don't show off their legs at parties.'

'Don't you believe it,' she said. 'I bet they have orgies among the looms. My intentions were pure. The poor man's horribly lonely and sex-starved. He needs encouragement. Did you want something or were you rescuing him from my evil clutches?'

At the vital moment I found it difficult to begin. 'Well, I've a kind of message. What I've been trying to tell you since I arrived is that Portia . . . this is just for the family, not everyone.' Claudia stared unhelpfully as I floundered. 'She should be telling you this, not me. The thing is, she's pregnant.'

'Is the point of this joke to follow?' asked Claudia.

'Oh damn, it isn't a joke. I was at Hindlecote. Portia's expecting a baby in December and she didn't tell anybody about it because she knew there'd be an uproar.' I subsided, realizing that I was almost shouting. I fancied that heads were turning and tongues wagging, though the assembled company was heartily scoffing and had no attention to spare for us. 'That's it.'

Claudia's mouth dropped unbecomingly. 'Portia's expecting a baby in December?' she repeated. 'You're raving. She's forty-seven and anti-sex. I expect she's got fibroids.'

'She hasn't got fibroids, she's pregnant, a baby, in December. How many times do I have to say it?'

Her nose sharpened in a way I knew well. 'Good God, you're serious. Not Botty, I simply won't believe she'd touch Botty with a barge-pole even as a matter of duty, so don't tell me it is. But who? Come along, my good rat, spit it out, who dunnit?'

Claudia has a keen eye for misdoings. At base she has changed little herself from the odd, uncomfortable child I grew up with. She expects no change in others. Indeed she resents it. The drab protective colouring that Portia assumed for years, her stern, conventional morality, had blinded Claudia to the possibility that the despised Duchess might have become desirable. 'Gerhardt Nordmann, of course, the nice German archaeologist. Couldn't you see? He's been madly in love with her almost since they met. How Portia got around to noticing I can't say, but she did. This baby is the result. It's the pavilion in the brick-kiln.'

'What's a bloody pavilion got to do with it?' She was in a furious rage and I knew then that she was rattled and at a loss. 'You don't get pregnant just through sitting in a pavilion. The woman's crazy, they're both crazy. Oh, I give up. And I suppose you're going to drive yourself and the rest of us crazy as well, fussing and nagging.'

'No I'm not, not at all. Portia says we're responsible only for ourselves, our own actions. No anxious phone calls, they bother her. If she wants help or company I'll give it, but that's all. And that pavilion makes things happen, it changes people's lives, I know it does. So there!'

Claudia's irritation with me died. She became thoughtful and remote and her pale blue eyes darkened in colour. 'You always were slightly cracked,' she said, 'but in a way love invents its own magic and its own disasters.' Introspection had no part in her make-up, yet there must have been times of tiredness or depression when she thought of and relived her own first and calamitous love affair. Suddenly she came to and gave my arm a nasty pinch. 'That's for not telling me what those poetry readings were all about.'

'Coming back to Gunville Place always makes you childish. If you hadn't been so jealous of Portia's looks you might have noticed for yourself.' We glared at each other and then laughed. Valentine called for silence at that point. 'Oh Lord, the speeches and the toasts. We'd better get some champagne and then circulate.'

Claudia muttered that she wanted the full story from me before I went home, and that if she felt like ringing Portia she would. Did the wretched woman imagine that she had no feelings? If so, she was entirely wrong. But Claudia did lead the way towards the buffet where I hurriedly filched and bolted a handful of canapés. Being a carrier of news had made me hungry. They were mostly posh and disgusting caviar which is like a dose of cod-liver oil on an empty stomach. I swallowed hard and thought a beautiful thought. Claudia emerged from the throng with four full glasses and passed two of them to me. 'Hurry up and get one down or you won't be able to clap when Father and Mr Openshaw do their stuff. Perhaps I ought to get the twins here from the nursery.'

I glanced around. The love-seat was empty. Two glass bowls, licked clean, reposed neatly on the floor. The significance of the look exchanged by Lindsay and Grainger became clear. They had known that they were not supposed to be with us. Getting me to bribe them with ice-cream had been one of their minor masterstrokes. 'I wouldn't worry about them,' I said. 'Let's go and stand with Pan and Jimmy.' The two, lovers of many years, had been our friends from the time that I was eight and Claudia was ten. They stood a little apart from us, contained and with a faint air of melancholy. I thought how sad it was that Pandel had never been able to acknowledge his son, and how amazingly handsome he still was. 'I'm glad you're here, both of you,' I said. 'It's an occasion not to be missed, though I wish . . .'

'What do you wish, Amy?' Pan asked. 'You're happy for David, I'm sure.'

'Of course I am. Meggie will give him what we never could, a wholehearted love. I just wish that you could speak about him openly.'

'Oh no, I might become over-Jewish and emotional and distress the imperturbable English. Also he is your father's son in all that is important. I have no right.'

Jimmy said, 'Sonia was unforgettable then. Incandescent. Every man present believed her fire was for him, every man desired her. I never saw a lovelier creature.'

'Such beauty is destructive, of course,' Pan said, 'and I helped in the destruction. It is something for which I can offer neither regret nor apology, though I have often wished to do so.'

Jimmy shook his head. 'We were spellbound. That season had a profound influence on all our lives. David's children will never understand. We're at the beginning of a new generation in a new and practical world.'

'That is either deeply philosophical or tediously sententious, my dear,' Pan said, smiling. 'Be quiet now and listen to the speeches.'

My father was brief and affectionate. Mr Openshaw explained to us that Meggie had had the best of educations and been well brought up and didn't give a fig for being a career woman. He hoped to see us all in Bolton for the wedding. 'Bolton?' Claudia said. 'I thought he intended to move to London.'

'That was before you frightened him off by showing him your leg.'

'Oh no, I remember now. He's moving *after* the wedding. I expect he wants Bolton to know that in spite of Meggie running away so much she loves her birthplace and has made a good match. Bless his heart, I wish we could find someone to get *him* off with. Listen, Amy, we have to watch over Portia whether the wretched woman likes it or not. Do you agree?'

I did, of course, though watching and waiting were about all that any of us could do. 'You could begin by not calling her a wretched woman and I don't think she would be upset by ordinary congratulations.'

The good tidings circulated through the remainder of the family at high speed. They received it with their customary lack of concern. Even Aunt Phyllida, who quite liked us all, simply gave a cheerful wave and called, 'So Portia's having a last dash at motherhood? A bit of a toss-up. Might be a genius, menopausal children sometimes are. Or, of course, decidedly not.' I found her rather less than encouraging.

Claudia gloomed at me. 'You know, Amy, I'm the smallest bit disappointed with our Duchess. Although she irritated me to bits I sort of admired her certainty. When my dubious virtue was in question I could always point to Portia as being virtuous enough for both of us, with lots to spare.'

Though I wouldn't have put it quite like that, she echoed my thoughts in part. My admiration for Portia's courage was limitless. I was overjoyed that she had rebelled against despair and loneliness and found a love that compensated for the wretched years. Yet in my heart I, too, had faint regrets that Portia had proved herself fallible and imperfect.

Chapter Sixteen

A curious enchantment enfolded Portia at this time. It was as though the gods or angels had her soul and her virtue in close keeping. She made no particular secret of her attachment to Gerhardt, yet she had no need to lie. Indeed, I'm certain that lying never entered her head. Quite simply she hid her lover unintentionally among a forest of visiting strangers, and even the villagers took the icy, impregnable quality of her nature for granted. In Sussex Reggie and Merve gave a small dinner party. They were celebrating two big new commissions that had been offered to them as a result of their work at Hindlecote. 'We're jubilant,' cried Merve, 'quite cock-a-hoop.'

Their delight that Rudi had chosen them in the first place was reinforced by the warmth of Portia's recommendation. The misery of her marriage and the nature of Botolph's illness had not, naturally enough, been mentioned to them. When Merve spoke of the beauty and tragedy of Portia's situation, and the unhappiness that the Duke might never live to see his second child, Reggie simply nodded agreement. His attention was almost entirely focused upon Dora. Her long-sleeved dinner dress was cut low, revealing the regal set of her head on smooth, rounded shoulders. Only the grey of her vigorously curling hair betrayed that she was close to sixty. Nothing in her demeanour towards Reggie indicated an overwhelming love and I thought it unlikely that after twenty years of widowhood she would ever marry him. Already he had proposed three times and three times been refused. 'He tells me that I need him to take care of me,' she said, 'but with my luck I shall simply end up looking after him. I've had enough of that.'

I waited impatiently for news from Hindlecote, but none came. At stupid times – in church, while shopping, in the middle of conversations – I experienced sudden visions of Portia in her blue dress, sitting upright and unmoving in the pavilion, looking through the door at the slowly moving constellations and simply waiting. It was in a way like a haunting. The long alienation from her had created an artificial fear of offending, of being in her bad books, that I found hard to overcome. I wrote once, an ordinary kind of letter telling her about the engagement party. I got no reply. Beau neither telephoned nor wrote. I could imagine that privacy was hard to come by at school. The sense of unreality, of cherishing a fictional memory, began to creep back.

Underhallow in winter offered few diversions. Rudi had been asked to produce the Sunday School nativity play and Dora and I helped to cut out costumes and create angels' wings from wire and sized net. Gloria Hopkins and Hattie Doolittle did the sewing. Even The Fancy proved to be useful, making creditable halos and hacking up Hattie's striped cloak to clothe the shepherds. The cloak had become redundant, along with the wellingtons. The sergeant of police still burned to lock up each and every Doolittle who crossed his path and Hattie took cover in plain hats, serviceable coats and rather nice brogues that would have been improved by polishing. Her preference for diamond-patterned golfing socks rather than stockings struck the only discordant note. The Fancy had her own lack of style. At first glance her clothes resembled multicoloured rags and she appeared to make no effort to allure, though undoubtedly she did. The Fancy exercised. Early each morning before dressing she flung open the window of her bedroom overlooking the green and breathed deeply, bent and stretched. A slow procession passed by the door of Parsley Cottage. Surprised dogs, more used to neglect, were walked back and forth until they got quite bored. Often the postman and the milkman stopped just about there to exchange opinions on the weather and were joined by those who didn't have dogs but wished they had. The constable stood casually outside the police house, gazing to all appearances at the roof-tops. He made no attempt to move anyone on. By the time that the sergeant came on duty around nine o'clock, The Fancy had reached her secretarial school in Chichester and the green was once more empty.

She and Hattie both possessed phlegmatic temperaments. They remained unmoved by bickering and the bitterness engendered by the casting of the nativity play. Personally I would ban by law any kind of entertainment involving children because of their mothers, among whom peace and goodwill were notably absent. Rudi, who had chosen a dark-haired Mary, escaped censure only because he was a man. (Women were still pretty subservient in the fifties.) There was muttering behind his back. 'Fancy him saying the Virgin Mary was Jewish. You've only got to see the statue in the Lady Chapel to know she was nothing of the sort.' Every mother of a blonde contender murmured agreement. Hattie and The Fancy went on with their sewing.

Claudia rang quite often, demanding news that I couldn't supply. By the end of the first week in December she grew impatient. 'The woman's a curse,' she said. 'If she dies in childbirth she'll be Saint Portia for ever more, and we'll be blamed for never visiting.

And everyone assumes that it's Botty's child? We'd never get away with a fraud like that.'

'She can't help other people's assumptions, you know. If we told the family she's expecting the child of Satan they'd have forgotten in five minutes. They've no grasp on detail at all.'

Rage at her own feeling of concern began to boil over. 'Why can't she be consistent and behave as she's always done? Talk about womanly weakness! Sir Lancelot turns up singing tirra lirra by the river, reads a couple of poems, gets her pregnant, and instead of chatting about it and telling all, she wuthers around like the bloody Lady of Shalott. I can't at all be doing with reticence. I want to know what's going on, so either you ring up or I do, hourly.'

There were many things that Claudia couldn't be doing with. In this instance I agreed with her. If Portia didn't need us then she ought to. 'All right, all right,' I said, 'I'll do it.'

'When? Now, today?'

'Not today. Tomorrow, I promise.' But that evening I at last heard from Beau. He was at Hindlecote and his voice shook with nerves. 'What is it?' I asked. 'Is something wrong?'

'Sorry, I don't expect so. Emmi says not – well, nothing serious anyway. It's just that I've never been close to this kind of happening before, and Mother won't stay in bed for the last weeks as Emmi wants. I can't remember her ever being ill before. It seems such an awful thing to me and I'll never understand why they're so happy about it. You did say that I could tell you if I was anxious.'

'Of course. I've been worried myself that I've heard nothing. What should I do? Do you want me to come to Hindlecote? I can manage a few days while the boys are still in school.'

'Would you, oh would you? Soon? Thank you, Aunt Amy, that's great.'

I reported back to Claudia, who was all for coming with me until she recalled that she had four children to look after. 'Damn, I can't. They're all due at the dentist next week and Lindsay and Grainger are in a play at school that I daren't miss. Their English teacher fancies that she can improve on Shakespeare and feed it to the brats in suitable doses.'

'Oh dear, I wonder whether she knows what she's doing. I'm enormously fond of your daughters, but they're even worse advantage-takers than you were at their age.'

'I can't think what you mean,' Claudia said haughtily. 'I never took advantage. This weird woman has concocted a version of *The Comedy of Errors* suitable for girls and, having two sets of twins to hand, she has cast them, surprise, surprise, as twins. My two are the Dromios. I hope she keeps in some of the ruder bits.'

'It sounds a minefield, though Shakespeare is so impenetrable they may not notice.'

'They will! I haven't looked at the play in years, but I distinctly recall wind and behinds and the kind of punning argument you hate, about the devil's dam and the burning of light wenches. Even you can understand those. Quite unfunny but the twins will think them the essence of wit.'

Company would have been pleasant, though on the whole not Claudia's. A swift pall of boredom settled on her when there was no entertainment to be had, and a castle empty of life except for the staff, a pregnant woman, a midwife and a boy, offered little. I imagined her fury if Portia declined to see us. 'I'll send bulletins,' I said, 'though I expect to be home in a couple of days, once I've managed to reassure Beau. You know how tiresome the last weeks of pregnancy are and I doubt whether Portia will want the bother of visitors.'

I wasn't home in two days, or in two weeks either. The drive was lonely and uncomfortable and becoming quite tediously familiar. Rain was falling when I left Sussex. I swooshed past the same groups of shops, the same farms, the same half-built housing estates that never seemed to get finished; even the birds and dogs and cats and people, plodding blindly in the middle of the lanes, looked as though they had been there always and would remain in perpetuity. As I went northward the weather grew colder and the car heater seemed not to be working properly. It was an act of mild insanity to persist. So much discomfort to visit a sister who showed no desire at all for my company. But there was Beau. I pitied the boy, frightened and stranded in a place and time dedicated to woman at her most critical peak of femininity. He ought not to be there. I decided to snatch him up and carry him back with me to Underhallow until the fuss was over. He met me at the gates, coatless and shivering in the bitter air. 'Hop in,' I said, opening a door, 'you look frozen. There's no crisis, is there?'

'Oh no, it's just me panicking. I don't see why I should have to; what's it to do with me after all? We were fine without my father, and now this.' He drummed irritatingly with his knuckles on the car door. I glanced sideways at him. The sullen resentful air was in evidence and he scowled, then burst out, 'Mother always spoiled me and now the closeness is sort of breaking down between us. I don't know how to talk to her any more. She doesn't tell me anything, just leaves me to guess about Herr Nordmann and Austria. I expect this sounds stupid to you, Aunt Amy, but it's as if she's gone away and left me behind. Why does she want another baby?'

The isolation of my childhood ought to have equipped me to console him instead of feeling, as I did, only a helpless fatigue. I tried my best. 'Your mother's very much aware of you, I know. If anything, she loves you too much. She had to fight hard against a selfish desire to keep you with her, knowing that some time she must let you go.' He gave a sceptical grunt. 'I'm not making this up, you know. It's what she told me. The baby isn't to replace you.'

'Yes it is, it's all she cares about. I think it's hateful and indecent and I feel an absolute fool.'

'Stop that, Beau,' I said. 'Your mother put up with all kinds of brutal behaviour for the sake of propriety. Now she's fallen under a spell, a commonplace one perhaps, and shortlived, but it's her first and last glimpse of the intangible magic of the world.'

He bent his head towards his knees and began to cry noisily. 'Sorry,' he mumbled between sobs, 'sorry to be so stupid. I'm too young for this. I'm sixteen. I don't want to have to be worried all the time.' We were almost at the castle. I stopped the car and sat unhappily brooding, thinking it no bad thing that he should get the misery out. He wiped his eyes and blew his nose violently. 'You won't want to stay, I expect. You'll want to go home when you've seen Mother. I've ordered lunch. It should be ready.'

I assumed that Portia would be in her sitting-room and prepared to follow Beau up the broad staircase, admiring the new blue carpet and a series of small bronzes, carefully placed by Merve. 'Does she manage to get downstairs at all now?'

'Oh yes. She walks to the pavilion each day and sits there. Her meals are taken to her. She's there now. Emmi called a doctor in from Leicester, hoping he'd forbid it, but Mother talked him round.' At least there was a doctor involved. I rejected Beau's offer to walk down with me and took the familiar path through the water garden. The fountains were still. Thin shards of ice lay on the pools and a cold blast blew steadily into my face. It was scarcely pavilion weather. I felt an anticipatory shiver at the thought of spending a night between the stone walls of the Dower House. Better to leave that day. Even a drive through the darkness would be less bleak. I wished I'd urged Claudia to come with me after all.

The door of the brick-kiln was closed. On the lintel the phoenix hovered above its nest of burning spices. Somewhere I had heard that the bird symbolized both alchemy and Christianity and represented the Resurrection of Christ, making the division between opposing mysteries uncomfortably narrow. I tapped and entered. A wood fire burned in the grate and the walls gave back the customary soft warmth. The dog rose growling from Portia's side. 'Down, boy,' she ordered, and a sense, half-frightening, that time had stood still assailed me. She sat where I always imagined her, in the usual chair, her head against the blue cushions, still wearing a blue dress amply flowing. A book slipped from her lap. Poetry again, I noticed, before a tall, brown-haired woman picked it up and laid it on the table. Portia said, 'Why, Amy, I didn't expect you. I wish you had let me know. Come in, since you're here. This is Gerhardt's sister, Emmi, who's looking after me.'

Sister and dog offered scant welcome. I said, 'Hallo, how are you?' to Emmi, drawing a morsel of spirit from her smile. 'We hadn't heard for ages. I was beginning to get the fidgets so I talked to Beau. He sounded anxious, forlorn too. I thought I'd drop in.' Understandably, Portia gave me a withering stare. Drop in, forsooth! Nearly six hours of driving through miserable weather. I essayed a cheery smile. 'All's well then, is it?'

Emmi answered. 'Apart from a small rise in blood pressure Portia is not too badly, though it would be better that she rest in bed now. I tell her. She defies me, yet she is tired.' Her English was even better than Gerhardt's. I told her so and she smiled. 'I had to learn quickly. I came to finish my training in London, at Thomas's, imagining I knew the language. Staff and patients, they scarcely understood me.'

Although I knew that approaching motherhood was self-absorbing, it miffed me a little that Portia showed no interest in our health and our activities. She asked after no-one. I told her just the same, struggling to find any tiny piece of news to fill the conversational hiatus. There didn't seem to be much. Were we so dull and our lives so boring? The painted face of a faun caught my attention. I hadn't noticed him before. He peered at me through the parted branches of a bush and smiled knowingly. I felt myself grinning back, dismissing a creeping fantasy that the figures changed places when I wasn't looking. 'David and Meggie were sorry that you couldn't get to their engagement party,' I said. 'They very much want you at the wedding. It's to be next Easter Saturday; that's April 16th. D'you think you'll be ready to get around by then?'

'Giving birth hardly takes that long, even at my age. Whether I shall feel like travelling to London is another matter.'

Oh hell and damnation, Portia, make an effort, I pleaded silently. Another two hours at least before I could decently leave. I tried not to look longingly at the door. 'It's to be in Bolton, Meggie's home town. I don't know whether that's easier or harder.'

'The cotton town, in Lancashire? I see.' Having dismissed Bolton, she sighed, picked up her book and began to read. She didn't suggest that I sit down. Looking at her lowered head, I felt a momentary desire to slap her, hard, and rouse her to some kind of response. I didn't. I simply stood.

We might have stayed like that until the end of time had Emmi not taken over. She invited me with a movement of her head to follow her into the back room and closed the inner door behind us. The fire was lit. A kettle steamed on a trivet. She lifted it off, replaced it with a small pan of milk and began to prepare coffee. 'It's good that you're here, Mrs Longmire.'

'Does my sister think so? I feel an intruder.'

'Be patient. It's never comfortable to be where conscience wars with love. Portia is a good woman, a Christian woman. Her priest calls often and cannot help her. She feels, I believe, separated from her God and unable to be perfect in His eyes or in her own.'

'We're not her judges. I've always wished she were less good, less rigid in her views and behaviour, so that we could be closer. And I'm frightened about what's to come. She wants this child too much.'

'So does Gerhardt, so do I,' Emmi said. 'We're very close, he and I. Our childhood was not happy. The girl he married was in Berlin when the Russians came. They used her without mercy. She can't bear a child because of it and gradually her sanity has gone. At times she is violent and must be locked up. It is terrible.' She mixed some kind of milk drink, stirring vigorously, and put it on a tray with a cup of coffee. 'Would you mind taking this to her, please. Persuade her to talk if you can.'

Emboldened, I exerted a tiny bit of authority, taking Portia's book from her hands and replacing it with the milky drink. It smelled of nurseries and children's bedtimes. She cupped both hands around it as though warming them, bending her face to the steam and sipping cautiously. 'How I long for coffee instead of this stuff,' she said, faintly smiling. 'Not long now. About two weeks. Perhaps the twenty-second or the twenty-third, a midwinter child. I love the winter.'

'Shall I read to you? I used to for Claudia when we were little.'

'If you can manage poetry I should like that.' She hesitated. 'When must you leave? Immediately?'

'Not immediately, though at this time of year I ought not to be away long.'

'Of course, Christmas. Gerhardt will be here, perhaps next week. I have no right to ask it, Amy, but I wish very much that you'll stay.'

Such an appeal from Portia couldn't be refused, though it was going to complicate our planned celebrations at Gunville Place. I thought quickly. Dora would, I knew, take care of the boys when Rudi was working, and Rudi could be trusted to pack for us and not forget the all-important presents. I had agreed to help dress the children for the nativity play. Almost certainly I would miss it but that couldn't be helped. 'Until Gerhardt comes? Yes, I can do that. I shall have to make some phone calls, if you don't mind?'

'Naturally, and borrow whatever you need. Beau will look after you.'

'Just one thing, Portia, must I sleep in the Dower House? It's not a comforting place.'

She laughed. 'Far from it. I dread the day when Beau moves me there permanently. Emmi won't let me stay here at night. You can have one of the bedrooms close to mine. Will you read me something by George Herbert now please?'

'Great-aunt Hildegarde liked his poetry a lot. Which shall I read?'

'He's a favourite of mine too. Choose what you like.' She leaned back cautiously, supporting the weight of the baby with her hands. I read three poems, ending with 'The Pulley'.

201

'Let him be rich and weary, that at least,
If goodness lead him not, yet weariness
May toss him to my breast.'

Portia's eyes had closed. She might have been asleep or praying. Shutting the book I went to make my telephone calls, feeling that half of life nowadays was spent talking into a piece of bakelite. Rudi groaned, but agreed that I couldn't desert. He promised to send a couple of changes of underwear by the next post. I then got on to Dora and reminded her of my Christmas order and The Fancy's habit of doing physical jerks in her bare skin in front of an open window. I asked her to keep Piers busy for the duration. 'He thinks he might go to hell if he sees ladies' top bits,' I said, 'though I'm sure he'll grow out of it pretty fast.'

'Most of them do,' she said, very smoothly. 'Charlie Hopkins lives for summer and sun-dresses, the lower the better. I'll make sure Piers gets no undue frights.'

Finally I rang Claudia, anticipating that she would be irritable. But in a dry, grudging kind of way she expressed concern. 'Did she actually ask you to stay on? It sounds the unlikeliest thing in the world. How does she seem?'

'Fed up with waiting, but more patient than I was. Not long now.'

'Look, Amy, if you think I ought, I'll come and join you, though to be frank it's about the worst time of year to be away, and I promised Grandmother to spend a few days in London, then drive her to Val's.'

'Better not, I think. You're rather stimulating company and Portia's been prescribed absolute peace and quiet.'

'You mean I'll be a nuisance. Well, I like that,' Claudia said. 'I'm every bit as restful as you, especially when you start panicking. She won't get much peace and quiet then. You're hopeless with blood and mess too. When the nurse tried to show you Roland's after-birth you screeched and threw up.'

'I couldn't believe I'd been carrying that around inside me. But why should I panic now? There won't be any blood. I'm only staying until Gerhardt gets here, and there's Emmi – you'll like Emmi – and a nurse. Don't be cross. I'm not enjoying this at all.'

'Who's cross? If you'd begged me to come I'd have cursed. You'll be back for Christmas, I suppose?'

'Yes. I may not have time to go home first. If not I'll drive straight down to Gunville. See you soon.'

We settled down together, Portia, Beau and I. With a little bit of extra support, Beau overcame his rather obvious reluctance to be in Portia's company and he treated her with great sweetness. I made sure that he didn't skip his music lessons and that he practised every day. On Sunday he and Portia took communion in the castle's private chapel while I sat at the back and looked at the paintings and the stained-glass windows. That was the time when I at last began to know Portia. Her need was for quietness and she would have with-drawn from me had I chattered or probed. The books she read all seemed to be concerned with religion. It still took me a while to grasp that her devotion to the Church was not, as I had assumed, a matter of conven-tion. She had an awareness of God that permeated her whole life. Spiritual argument baffles me. It took a great deal of concentrating on the few crumbs that she gave me to understand the depth of her love and guilt. 'I can't repent my adultery,' she said, 'though it's a sin, a breaking of the rules. Not for the world would I have missed loving Gerhardt. I want his child.'

'Surely not.' At this point I had to grope through a fog of ignorance, hoping no pit would open underneath me. And I was battling against a resentful feeling that

God hadn't been particularly kind to Portia. 'Isn't love and the forgiveness of sins what Christianity is all about?'

'Repentance first, then punishment, then forgiveness,' she said wistfully. 'The first is the most difficult. How can I regret the one true passion of my lifetime?' I made no attempt to answer. I couldn't for the life of me understand what she had done that had hurt anyone or deserved punishment. 'You're not liking this at all, are you, Amy?' she asked suddenly.

'It's too harsh. I don't have much religious sense and I can't possibly love a god who claims to provide all that's good but denies responsibility for the bad. It's like poisoned wine, the one who pours puts the poison in too.'

'What an odd simile.' She smiled faintly. 'Yet I'm conscious all the time of the goodness and the sorrow of God. I need that communion and I cannot find it however hard I try.' Nothing more on the subject was said, yet I became aware that she spent a great deal of time in prayer. This angered me. I hated the very idea of religion. At the same time, without realizing what was happening, I began to feel a tremendous affection for Portia.

Chapter Seventeen

Day followed slow day. Portia sewed or knitted or read devotional books; I read aloud (*Pride and Prejudice*) and to myself (*The Enchanted Castle*, a children's book that fitted my mood). In the evenings, Beau played passionately on the guitar then lazily on the piano. Except for one or two Chopin nocturnes the music was unfamiliar to me, though to hear afterwards wild, running chords and gypsyish rhythms returned me at once to that strange interlude in time and life, and the particular intensity of our waiting. Both Rudi and Claudia rang every day, Rudi to let me know that I was missed, and Claudia to ask fretful questions. Gerhardt Nordmann was due to arrive on the twentieth of December. The hours of that day passed and he didn't come. Watching Portia's tense and eager face, her patient acceptance of the discomfort of her burden, a sudden rush of tenderness washed over me. After so many years we had found an equilibrium, a way to like each other. 'Perhaps he can't get away after all,' I said.

She had been quiet, locked in with her own thoughts, as though unaware of my presence. 'He promised: he'll come,' she said, adding after a pause, 'Strange how love has so thoroughly destroyed my life and remade it. This is to be the end, but I shall have our child.'

'Why, why must it end?' I asked. 'You can still meet Gerhardt here or in Austria.'

'Amy, I haven't the temperament to be a mistress.

I've transgressed against all that I believe in, God, the Church, honour, duty, and I miss them. As the years pass and love turns into an inconvenient routine I shall miss them more. Gerhardt is my life's blood, but he isn't mine.'

I said, 'If Botolph dies, and if anything should happen to—' and stopped. Portia was regarding me as though I were a particularly nasty specimen of beetle and I realized the enormity of what I was propounding. 'Sorry,' I stammered, 'I didn't mean that the way it sounds, wishing people dead or anything like it. I was only supposing. It's the hour of night, I think.'

'Don't lay more sins on my conscience, please.' Her tone was precise, chilly and dismissive. I imagine that I had voiced a thought that she would not permit herself to think. Making excuses to someone who never excused herself was not going to save me from reproach. 'Go to bed now. Emmi will bring my supper.'

Because of her size, she found it uncomfortable to lie down. She would stay where she was all night, half-lying in an invalid-chair by the window, looking down across the water-garden to the brick-kiln pavilion. 'No. Let me sit with you. I can doze anywhere and I promise not to talk if you'd rather I didn't.' I was pleased that she nodded agreement, for a message arrived to say that Gerhardt's plane had been delayed by fog at the airport. Pregnancy had given to Portia a youthful roundness of face. Suddenly she looked old and desolate. I felt, with grim resentment, that if he let her down I might quite easily kill him. Her child was due any day and, with Christmas so close, I planned to leave the moment he arrived.

Then, after a tiny meal that she barely touched, Portia was violently sick. 'Not the baby, not yet,' Emmi said, 'something else; the pressure or perhaps only nerves. You go on home tomorrow, Mrs Longmire.

Gerhardt will come as soon as the plane can take off.'

But Portia's eyes implored me and Beau gazed at the ground with sullen, frowning anxiety. I thought, He resents the burden of worry every bit as much as Claudia does. The fear of disaster returned to me in full force. I knew that I couldn't simply walk away. 'It's all right, Portia, I'll stay another day or two.' We sat on through the night. There was a feverishness in her that kept her from sleep. She talked now and then, telling me private things in a low, unaccustomed voice. She had, she said, fallen in love with Gerhardt almost as soon as they met. For some time she failed to recognize the feeling. As for the first aches and burns of desire, they not only puzzled her dreadfully, but persuaded her that she was going down with a weird disease. Her late mother-in-law had explained to her when she was only seventeen that she should not expect to obtain pleasure from 'physical union'; it was a duty owed by a lady in return for the prestige and rank conferred on her by her husband. Consequently, Portia felt nothing but a sense of crude invasion. With a shudder-inducing creature like old Botty, one couldn't be the slightest bit surprised. One never knew, so to speak, where he'd been.

From the day of Father's wedding to Sonia we more or less lost Portia. She boarded at a prestigious girls' school and spent most of the holidays with her best friend, Hermina Swithins, Botolph's sister. I believe that from the very beginning Portia was marked down as a potential wife for Botolph, and that his character was already known in his family. Like too many Swithinses before her, the previous Duchess had married her first cousin. Throwing in a touch of seventeenth-century incest owing to isolation and chronic confusion over parentage, the ducal gore had become decidedly thin. An infusion of redder blood was needed. I recalled the old Duchess as dowdy, depressing and entirely beige, as though she could have done with a thorough dusting, but she was by no means stupid. The Savernakes were mildly scandalous, yet undeniably strong and red-blooded. Portia's youth and naïvety laid her open to influence. 'It was pathetically easy to convince me that I was in love with Botolph,' she murmured, bitterly smiling. 'It was so much what I wanted, to marry a duke, especially one with a castle. Castles are high romance, and safe. I ought to have thought more about Bluebeard.'

I raised my eyebrows, feeling that she was straying a bit far into fantasy. 'Aren't you over-dignifying a bogus little womanizer?'

'Of course I am. Doesn't one hate to be deceived? I didn't begin to know Botolph until I stopped loving him. He has a crook's sharpness, but in fact he's rather a stupid man, not worth the power of hatred. I doubt whether it occurs to him that he might be in need of forgiveness. For my own soul's sake I ought to forgive.'

I said again, 'I don't see why you should even think about it unless he asks.'

She dozed at last in her chair, a wind ripping the clouds to tatters, and the moon now and then shining in on her face. By morning I, too, had begun to long for Gerhardt's arrival. In the dead grey light of a winter's dawn Portia looked exhausted. Emmi absolutely refused to let her take her daily walk to the pavilion, and still the day ended in disappointment. Portia sipped water, but refused food and milk. When, in the evening, I left the room to wash, and change the clothes I had slept in, I found Beau huddled on a chair outside the door. His face was tear-stained. 'She's going to die, isn't she?' he said. 'That man isn't coming. He's killing her.'

'Hush, don't speak so loudly. Of course he'll come, he's been delayed, that's all.' I spoke with more confidence than I felt, but Beau wandered along with me to my room and I talked to him through the bathroom door while I changed.

'Why does she have to have this damned baby?' he asked. 'She should think about me. I don't want a brother or sister after all these years. It's stupid and wrong.'

'My dear, she's thought first of you all your life and loved you, but you'll leave her, marry one day and send her off to that Dower House. Who will she love then?' I came back into my bedroom.

'Oh, love,' he said. 'She has her dog.' I was brushing my hair and I didn't answer. He gave my reflection a faintly shamefaced look. 'I hate to be frightened.'

'You're like your Aunt Claudia in that respect. She gets into terrible rages if her rather narrow conception of normality is disarranged. I don't know whether you're allowed strong drink yet, but this is an occasion that calls for one. I'll join you.'

'I can mix a Harvey wall-banger,' he said.

'I don't know what that is, Beau, but lead me to it.' It turned out to be something rather strong with vodka. I gulped a couple down quickly. They didn't make me feel better, but removed me by a hair's breadth from worldly anxiety. Down below, at the front of the castle, voices sang to a flute accompaniment. 'It's the carol-singers,' Beau said, uncheered by the wall-bangers. 'This is a rotten awful Christmas. Let's go down.' The strangeness of our situation (or perhaps it was the vodka) gave the scene a faintly nightmarish quality as though the comfortably smiling faces might change and become monstrous. For all the sweetness of the singing I could not feel festive. The unobtrusive staff, who wandered daily like ants around the empty rooms, cleaning and mending, totting up sums in ledgers, writing letters, making bookings for the new year, now emerged in force, bearing mince pies and hot cocoa. The waits sang on in the great hall among the pagan marbles. The vicar was with them. Beau mixed a fresh batch of cocktails for him. 'Wall-banger, Vicar?'

'Later, please. Her Grace wants to take communion,' he said. 'I'll go to her now.' He took off his overcoat and draped a stole across his shoulders, fished out chalice, consecrated wine and wafer and, to my blurry eyes, floated up the staircase like some great black, sanctified bird. I sneaked another drink. Perhaps with sleep oblivion would come and when I woke the world would have gone back to being normal.

It hadn't of course. Emmi and a couple of secretaries were on ladders, decorating a Christmas tree. Beau watched morosely. But as if to reward Portia's faith, Gerhardt arrived that afternoon with the fading of the light, two and a half days late, haggard and bone-weary. He fell on his knees beside Portia's invalid-chair and laid his head against her as though he were listening to the baby. 'Heart's dearest,' he murmured, 'oh my dear love.' It was tremendously mystical and European, and embarrassing to the onlooker. I retreated. Tomorrow was Christmas Eve. Rudi and my sons would already be gathered with the rest of the family at Gunville Place. I faced an early start and a long, cold drive in the morning.

Sleep poleaxed me. I dreamed that Claudia was dressed as a Christmas angel and reading the burial service. 'I'm an expert on Shakespeare's jokes,' she said. 'You won't understand,' and advanced on me with long fingers ready to pinch. I tried to shout at her, but nothing happened. Waking with an awful start, I looked at the clock and saw that it was almost eleven. A tray with tea and bread-and-butter stood beside me.

The tea was stone cold. As I hurled myself out of bed, Emmi put her head round the door. 'Chef says will you have breakfast here or in the dining-room?'

'I'd rather not bother, thanks. I ought to set out right away. I can stop somewhere on the road.' I ran into the bathroom, dashed a wet flannel at my face and began to throw on clothes at lightning speed. Fortunately I had brought so little with me that I managed to cram everything I wasn't wearing into my small bag. I was ready to go.

Emmi said, 'Have you looked out of the window? I think you'd better.' She drew back the curtains. The world outside had vanished. The fog that had delayed Gerhardt had followed him, shrouding the landscape, locking me in. On unfamiliar roads did I dare to take a chance on running into clearer weather? I needed petrol; how would I manage to find a garage? And even if I set out at once, I couldn't hope in this murk to reach Dorset before midnight. I was trapped. Since we were married I had never been separated from Rudi at Christmas. I wanted to weep very loudly.

'I'm not hungry, Emmi. Can I just have some coffee, then I'll go in and see Portia.'

She drew down her mouth. 'Gerhardt has taken her to that brick house. What is it that attracts her to it? She begged to go.'

'Stupid as it sounds, I believe there's a kind of spell in the pavilion,' I said, feeling a quivering sense of alarm at putting the thought into words, in case the spell should turn out to be an evil one, 'an atmosphere of comfort. And I rather fancy that they fell in love there.'

'*Bezaubert?* They say such places exist, that the dead walk and witches fly. I don't believe it. A pretty play-house for the rich, no? Beau cares little for it, so tonight we celebrate the feast properly, here in the castle. I've told Gerhardt. He must bring her back.'

Shunning the pavilion, I walked to the Wodsbridge field with the dog racing ahead of me, and leaned over the parapet of the medieval bridge. I could hear the flow of the river, invisible in the fog. A bitter cold and damp pierced through my clothes to the skin. Hoar frost outlined a nettle growing from a crevice in the wall beside my hand. The reeds rattled idly, the water made tuneless sucking noises, the bare tree-branches creaked. An eerie menace lurked in the stillness. My shallow, nervous breaths puffed out extra spurts of mist. Resentment against Portia and Gerhardt made my heart jump and hammer and I gritted my teeth with frustration. Christ was not going to visit this miserable old place. Why would He? I didn't even want now to go to Gunville Place. I wanted my sons and my husband; I wanted to go home. Padding silently, the dog nuzzled my hand and made me jump. I went back to the castle and began making yet more phone calls. Rudi volunteered to drive with the boys to join me. 'It's too dull for them,' I said. 'They'll hate it and you might not make it. There's no sign of the fog lifting.' He could hear the misery in my voice as clearly as I could and I felt ashamed.

Piers asked if he could talk to me. 'Aren't you coming for Christmas, Mum? Does that mean we can't have our stockings?' For a second I forgot whether he still believed in Santa Claus or not. Then I recalled Roland in a scornful, dismissive mood telling him that parents made it all up, and Piers saying with relief, 'Good. I don't want a fat old man coming down my chimney at night. It's stupid.' I assured him, wistfully since he seemed otherwise unmoved by my absence, that Rudi would manage everything. 'I got you a thing,' he said, 'and I want to give it to you.'

'We'll have a little Christmas of our own and you can

212

give it to me then. Shall I try to guess what it is?'

'No. Aunt Claudia's cross. She says it's just like bloody Porsheler to put a blight on things. If you don't come home soon she's goin' to drag you. And she says love.' There was a long, effortful pause, then, 'Me too.' He hung up before I could get sentimental or ask him to put Rudi back on the line.

We did our best with Christmas Eve, giving small presents and drinking wine. All the staff joined us. The lights were lit on the tree, and we linked hands and wished each other a happy Christmas. Gerhardt, looking like a monk on the point of martyrdom, sang, '*O Tannenbaum*', and a song about the Christchild. I hoped we wouldn't get 'Silent Night', which is too sentimental when the family is together and happy, and sheer bloody murder to the emotions when in exile from home. There was no escape. The secretaries and estate guides favoured us with 'Silent Night'. I stared glumly at the star on top of the tree, ignoring the noise and laughter, deciding that I wouldn't try to be jolly and wishing they would all go to bed. The next day we had to endure the whole thing again, but with turkey and pudding and a Yule log that managed to singe the dog and set the rug on fire. The dog rolled over and put itself out. Beau threw the rug out of the window onto the terrace with considerable force. I think the gesture made him feel better.

On Christmas Day Portia stayed away from the pavilion. Her child was already, according to the doctor's calculation, a few days overdue. In the afternoon he visited. I don't know what he said, except that he mentioned that the fog didn't seem to be clearing. Emmi looked cheerful enough. I went to bed as soon as I could. In spite of tactfully placed radiators and huge fires in every room, the temperature in the castle was dropping and the cold made my clothes feel as though

213

they were made of paper. Huddled under the covers, I wept a few tears of frustration and then slept.

I woke early and wandered downstairs in my dressing-gown. Living was definitely gracious in the renovated castle. Coffee kept warm over a spirit lamp. Under a single cover sat a boiled egg in a silver cup, wrapped in a napkin. The door of Portia's room opened. Supported on Gerhardt's arm and wrapped in an enormous sable coat that had belonged to the Duchess before last, she rolled to the door and out of the house. I knew where they were going; to the brick-kiln pavilion. They were mad, both of them. When you came to think of it, I mused, admiring the neatness of the egg, mammals have a raw deal when it comes to reproduction. On the wall opposite to me hung a painting by Alma-Tadema, of laughing maidens sporting around in their bare skins. 'Put some clothes on or you'll be laughing on the other side of your faces,' I informed them darkly, crunching toast, and deciding that it would make this lost Christmas no worse were I to make a run for Sussex and home.

When I descended for the second time, Emmi and the nurse appeared and made for Portia's room. Emmi saw the open door and said something fluent that sounded rude, in German. 'You'd better fetch them quickly,' she said to the nurse. I walked down with her to say goodbye.

The light over the fields was a dirty yellow colour that I didn't much care for. Portia's dog followed us. The nurse shooed it and when it didn't move aimed a kick at it. Happily she missed. I was quite ready to kick her too. She stumped into the pavilion ahead of me. 'I'm to bring you back,' she said, flat-faced and flat-voiced. From the way Portia stared at her, I decided that she had little future at Hindlecote once the crisis was past. Gerhardt helped Portia rise to her feet. She gasped, gave a startled, 'Oh,' and sat down again, grasping her bulge. The nurse raised bored eyebrows. 'There, you're starting. Hurry up, you can't have it here.'

'I don't pay you to give me orders,' Portia said, 'and I don't care for your face. It resembles a dead flounder. Go away.' A direct and startling insult, worthy of Claudia: I cheered silently.

'Compliments fly when quality meet,' said the nurse with a toss of her head. 'Suit yourself. You're late anyway. I shouldn't still be here, not over Christmas. I'll see what Mrs Emmi's got to say about you.'

A certain liveliness entered the proceedings. Emmi came running, followed by a secretary and a grounds-man pushing a tea-trolley bearing an electric urn from the café, a heap of towels and a couple of large metal bowls. Hot water, the great necessity, was not provided in the pavilion. Gerhardt bumped the trolley through into the back room. 'Plug that thing in, please, and hold these towels for me. I'm to call the doctor again when the contractions are closer together,' Emmi said, throwing a mackintosh sheet onto the day-bed. 'The dear God knows what he'll think of a place like this. Is there a telephone?'

'In the Dower House,' I said, 'and there's an Ascot over the kitchen sink if you need more hot water.' Beau trailed along in the wake of the procession, kicking viciously at stones on the path. I sent him back to the castle. 'It's a slow process. Will you make sure a good fire is kept up in your mother's room? We'll call you when there's news.'

The nurse, blood-sister to Mrs Gamp, leaned against the mantelpiece and watched the struggle without much interest. She picked up the piece of green crystal. 'Tell her to put that down and leave things alone,' Portia said and bent over with pain. Gerhardt spoke sharply, took the crystal and returned it to its place. The next time I looked for the nurse she was dozing.

Portia's labour began around eleven in the morning and lasted for twenty hours. It was terrible. I'm not as stupid about blood as Claudia makes out. What destroyed my self-command was impotence in the face of my sister's pain. I could have borne my own better. Portia made scarcely a sound, moaning slightly as the contractions became more insistent. Gerhardt sat at her head, not daring to touch her and growing greyer in the face with every spasm that racked her body. There was nothing for her to pull on. I gave her my hands, grateful to feel the bruising strength of her thin fingers. We had no gas and air to help her. As the hours passed, I thought that no woman at Portia's age could go through this for so long and survive. Gerhardt seemed on the point of collapse. Sweat and tears were rolling down my face as Emmi stood, timing contractions, sponging Portia's face, sterilizing thread and scissors in a small pan balanced on the trivet. At four in the morning she sent the nurse to ring for the doctor. An hour later we heard him arrive, stamping his feet and saying something facetious about the roads and the weather. 'Go out now, Gerhardt,' Emmi ordered. 'We shan't need you on our hands.' I moved to the outer room, feeling warmth and reassurance flood through me, listening to the doctor making sounds of approval. Then I went into the garden to report to Gerhardt.

He stood by the door of the pavilion, his shoulders bowed. A thin snow was falling, whitening the garden and dusting his hair, and I thought he was crying. I touched his arm. 'It's all right,' I said, 'going well. It oughtn't to be long now.'

'As God judges me,' he said, 'I didn't intend this. She let me believe it wasn't possible. How can a man worship a woman and cause her so much suffering?'

216

'Portia wanted it. It's her own private miracle considering her age, and it means a great deal to her.'

'I want only her. And I shall never see her again, unless by chance.' The snow fell faster. The air was filled with wildly dancing flakes that drove into our faces and transformed the ugly Dower House into a pure white palace. 'Our child is arriving in snowy weather,' Gerhardt said. 'I'm glad. We both love the snow.'

The end came suddenly and my intimations of disaster proved utterly false. I stood by with a towel. Portia's daughter, Rose, shot into the world a few minutes before seven o'clock on the morning of December 27th, with an apologetic little cry. 'Healthy as they come,' the doctor said.

Emmi put her into my arms the moment the cord was severed. 'Wash her – gently, if you please.' I sponged away the stains, marvelling. She was so fair, so perfect; I never saw a lovelier baby or one who more aptly suited her name. I gave her back to Emmi with a small pang of regret. The doctor left, saying cheerfully, 'You won't need me again, but I'll call anyway.' I heard him talking to Gerhardt. 'Odd thing, you know, it wasn't snowing in Leicester or on the road. You must be low-lying here. Good morning to you.'

Portia lay back in a clean white nightgown, looking down the bed to her liberated stomach, and smiling. Emmi put the baby into her arms, fished a bottle of schnapps from her professional midwife's reticule, and poured some into a glass. 'Come in, little brother,' she called, 'and take a drink. Not too long. Portia must sleep and so must I. Can you and Mrs Longmire watch for just another hour?' The nurse was sitting in Portia's chair with her feet on a stool, picking at her fingernails. Emmi surveyed her with disgust. 'What have you stayed for? Out!'

I borrowed the Duchess-before-last's sable and went into the still whiteness of the garden. The fur was heavy but not very warm. Portia's dog lay on the freezing path, its head resting on its forepaws. I covered it with the coat. Short of giving it back to the animals it had come from, that seemed the best thing to do with it. The dog whined softly. At the far end of the path I turned. Through the open door I could see straight into the back room where a single lamp burned. Gerhardt was on his knees holding one of Rose's tiny hands and murmuring to Portia. A golden light surrounded them. Good heavens, I thought, the Holy Family; all we need is an ox, an ass and a shepherd or two to have the first Christmas all over again.

I walked up to the castle with Emmi to tell Beau that he had a sister. When I returned the sable lay on the path and the dog had gone. Rose was bundled up in her crib, Portia slept, and Gerhardt sat motionless, watching them as though he wanted to learn them by heart. Gratefully, I sank down in Portia's chair. After a while Emmi relieved me, gave me some arnica for my bruised arms, and told me to go to bed. I dozed for an hour or two. Beau wakened me with a woeful expression and a tray. Settling apologetically on the end of the bed, he said, 'It's ages since you had any food, Aunt Amy. I thought you might be hungry so I've brought us some turkey sandwiches.' We munched away in companionable silence, then he sighed heavily. 'You're quite sure that Mother's going to be all right, aren't you? You wouldn't pretend?'

'No, I wouldn't, but surely you've seen her? The doctor thinks she's done wonderfully well.'

'I saw her for a moment when she was brought back to the castle. She was tired and the baby was asleep so I didn't stay long. Shall I take the tray away now so that you can dress? It's much milder outside and the snow's gone.' He seemed patient and older than his years and his departing back looked lonely.

Portia's secretary told me an odd thing, that it had not snowed anywhere else in the country. Considering the remarkable advent and birth of Rose, and the changes in my sister and her castle, I wasn't a bit surprised.

Chapter Eighteen

That afternoon, the pantomime version of the three wise men appeared: Claudia, Merve and Rudi, bearing gifts. Merve, who had not previously experienced Claudia's driving, tottered whey-faced from the car. 'Madwoman, my intestines are all of a hurly-burly and my pancreas fit to burst. Of my poor heart I cannot even speak!'

'That's good,' Claudia said amiably, as Rudi and I kissed and hugged and generally behaved like frustrated lovers. 'Dear me. Hero and Leander Meet: Hellespont Boils Over!'

Rudi smiled. 'She also sings, you know. If a partridge in a pear tree is mentioned in my hearing again I shall throttle both partridge and singer. Is all well, my darling? Baby here yet?'

'Yes, this morning, and they're both fine. Where are the boys?'

'I sold them to a baby-farm. I hope you'd finished with them. They didn't fetch much of a price. Roly sends love, and instructions to stay bright. Piers painfully searched his soul and came up with the message, "Say hallo to Mum." A brilliant child; we don't deserve him.' I gathered from this nonsense that he was pleased to see me.

'Hallo, Amy,' Merve said in a die-away voice. He was wearing a furry, yellowish garment of a type I hadn't seen for thirty years, known as a teddy-bear coat. It reached his ankles. 'Your hair's a mess, dear.'

'I expect I forgot to comb it. It was a busy night. Where on earth did you get the coat? Don't tell me they're in again.'

'In? Not at all. I picked it up at Fulham Market for two pounds seven and six. Isn't it something? Hardly worn.'

'One can see at a glance why,' Claudia said. 'In my youth it would have been accompanied by a pork-pie hat, Oxford bags and a sports car, and thought rather caddish. American college boys were fond of them for seducing girls under. Never mind. It matches your present complexion.' Normality had arrived. The night in the brick-kiln pavilion might never have been, except that my eyes felt ready to drop out with tiredness. Soon I could rest as much as I liked. Meanwhile, I expanded with cheerfulness, beaming on them and disconcerting Claudia. 'Amy, could you stop grinning, please, you're blinding me. And you didn't say what kind it is.'

'What kind's what? Oh, you mean the baby? A girl, quite tiny considering how huge Portia was, and absolutely enchanting. Come and meet her.'

Upon our arrival Gerhardt tactfully disappeared. Merve's illusions about Botolph, firmly entrenched by now, remained unshattered. 'Such a heroine, Duchess darling, but such a prize! Shall you take her to Austria? Of course, of course, you will want to show her to her father.' Claudia showed signs of an impatient desire to tell him the truth until I nudged her. Merve was in a wallow of emotion. I thought, If he gets unbearably sentimental I shall howl myself into hysterics. We escaped quite lightly. 'Rose, a sweet Christmas rose. I envy you so much. My homage to you, and now I must fly. It's the milky scent, you know. I'm allergic.' He bowed himself out, leaving behind a rich assortment of antique rattles and ivory teething rings.

We didn't stay long. I yearned to crawl into my own bed and sleep. Also I knew that Gerhardt had only another night to be with Portia before they parted for ever. They ought not to miss a single second of it. Merve absolutely refused to be driven back by Claudia and climbed into our car beside Rudi, who wasn't entirely pleased. Claudia's driving was fast but safe. I was prepared to dare anything for the sake of peace. 'Merve's bound to twitter, and screech every time he sees another car. I'll come with you. Avoid the pot-holes and don't sing. I intend to doze all the way to London.' To tell the absolute and shabby truth about myself, I needed to get my demons under control. Portia had emerged victorious from her battle against disapproval, pain and the possibility of loss, and yet I coveted Rose.

We had our late Christmas in Underhallow, with extra presents. The butcher parted joyfully at next to nothing with an emaciated turkey that he had never expected to sell. 'It seems a cruelty to cook it,' Rudi said. 'We could give it a decent burial and open a tin of corned beef.'

'I've no idea of how to stuff corned beef, and Roly's the only one who'll eat it.' Before I could sink into despair, Dora contributed a sumptuous ham and the gossip. In missing the nativity play, I had also missed the police sergeant's dilemma, though as soon as I ventured out of the house I was told about it. Many times and in many versions. I discounted most of what Gloria Hopkins told me as being low on facts and high in moral reproof. Rudi's account and Dora's were, I'm sure, more accurate. The children's play passed off reasonably well. The sergeant, not a notable lover of the young, most of whom he regarded as criminals in embryo, softened his stony heart at Christmas. He and his constable attended, sitting foursquare in the front row. Well content, he nodded and smiled. His dossier on the Doolittles was coming along promisingly. They provided him with a nice little hobby. The only evidence he lacked was that of money changing hands for favours received and, he boasted in the Castleton's Oak, that was simply a matter of time. In the church hall he relaxed. Hattie and The Fancy dodged about behind the scenes, helping to dress the children, pushing them on stage for their entrances and pulling them off if they inclined to hog the limelight. The play drew towards its end.

After an interval for light refreshments, carol-singing was to follow. 'I like a good rousing hymn around Christmas time,' the sergeant announced. 'My constable's going to miss his mince pie if he don't get a move on. I hope he hasn't got the runs again. He's a bit prone.' Having obtained a cup of tea and his own mince pie from Hattie, he looked around in the lavatory. Drawing a blank there, he wandered behind the stage. In the now deserted changing-room he came upon his stray lamb lost in the busy embraces of The Fancy and not worrying about his mince pie one bit. The sergeant's temper proved unequal to the situation.

'Most of us heard the rumpus and went to see,' Rudi said. 'We thought the hall had caught fire. I must say that the sergeant is a virtuoso with the truncheon. He bruised the constable's rear quite severely, and crushed his mince pie to fragments in the process. It rather served him right, I felt.'

'It's put him in a quandary over The Fancy,' said Dora.

'Doesn't that strengthen his case?' I asked. 'Direct evidence.'

'My word, the constable was mad. He asked since when had fornication been a criminal offence or even a breach of discipline off duty? Being a single man who's suffered an unwarranted assault, he reckons he could sue.'

The sergeant had often boasted in the Castleton's Oak that his subordinate was a good, clean-living lad and an example to the riffraff propping up the bar. He was disappointed. But he didn't care at all to be sued. His attitude became placating, and the constable enjoyed a new power. After the spellbinding unreality of Hindlecote Castle, I found the rough and tumble of Underhallow infinitely soothing.

Dora and Reggie joined our late celebrations. A price was exacted for their company in the form of Mr Slade who, to Reggie's fury, refused to be left behind at the shop. 'I'm not having him in the dining-room while we eat,' Dora said, 'and that's flat. He's been an old horror all over the holiday. He can stay in the kitchen.' She cleared a space of useful furniture and took away his walking-stick so that he couldn't wander. Throughout the proceedings his moaning could be heard like the chatty ghosts that haunted Scrooge, and when Dora went to pull a cracker with him, he threw a bowl of Christmas pudding and custard. It missed her, but smashed on the floor.

'We had this last week,' he said, 'I'm sick of it.'

She cleaned up, sticking a green paper crown on his head. 'There's a coincidence,' she said, smoothly, 'I'm sick of you too.'

'Ho yes? Well, you're not getting rid of me. You can tell that fancy man of yours I'm good for another twenty years yet, unless you poison me first.'

'Don't tempt me,' said Dora. 'Have a chocolate and try not to dribble.'

'That was my Peter Rabbit dish,' Roland said. 'I wanted it. What's a fancy man?'

'You haven't used it for ages, Roly,' I pointed out,

'and I think Mr Slade's just being rude about Uncle Reggie.'

'Just the same I wanted it. Why do we have to have him when you wouldn't let me invite Miss Doolittle? He's *awful*. I don't think Uncle Reggie's very fancy, that's Uncle Merve.'

We let the rudeness pass; there was no gainsaying that Mr Slade was awful. I had drawn the line at Hattie, not so much for her own sake as for The Fancy's. I very much preferred that Roland and Piers should not be too well-informed about her spare-time activities.

Rose was christened early in February in the private chapel with none of the pomp that had attended the christening of Beau. This time there were no strange dukes or baronesses. Claudia and I were godmothers, Valentine and, to my intense surprise, Merve, were asked to stand as godfathers. Portia did stipulate that Merve should wear an appropriate dark suit. He appeared dressed in a black frock-coat and trousers, looking uncommonly like an extremely camp under-taker. He was thrilled to bits.

Now that Rose had become a reality and no longer a threat to Portia's life, Beau had decided to love his half-sister. He had never disliked Gerhardt, but he was glad to have seen the last of him. 'Mothers shouldn't have lovers,' he said. 'I share a flat now with three other chaps and their mothers are ordinary, like you. They make cakes and stuff, and darn our socks.' I'm sure he meant it nicely, which didn't stop me from feeling a complete drudge.

'I'm not much use at cake-making and I hate darn-ing,' I said, feeling a lot of prosing arguments coming on. 'Falling in love is mostly an accident anyway, and I'm glad it didn't miss your mother altogether. She has the rest of her life to be ordinary if she feels like it.'

Before we left I wandered down to the Dower House.

The brick-kiln pavilion was deserted, the door pad-locked, the garden not yet emerged from its winter sleep. I climbed over the wired-up gate. The beginning and ending of Portia's love affair with Gerhardt lay here, yet the charm for her seemed to have faded. She was again the Duchess in her castle. I circled the building, reaching up to touch the strange incised decorations, staring at the constantly burning, constantly reborn phoenix on the lintel. For a brief spell I listened, hoping for what, laughter, a voice, a sigh? Nothing spoke to me, no spells were there. The enchantment had been, I decided, a thing of my imagination.

'After David's wedding, I'm taking Rose to stay with Emmi,' Portia told me. 'The meadows begin to flower at Easter and I want her to love the mountains as much as I do.' She winced then, as though she had stabbed a needle into her finger. 'Gerhardt is in Egypt and likely to stay there. I'm not breaking my vow.'

'My dear, I never for a moment imagined you would.' Far worse to me would be her absolute retreat into the isolation of the past. I had become deeply fond of the Portia who confided in me on wakeful nights and I didn't want to lose her entirely.

'Amy,' she said in a low voice, 'I'll never manage to be light-hearted as Claudia is, or to make jokes, or to be other than I've always been, but believe me I'm grateful and touched that you stayed with me.'

I smiled and said it was an unforgettable experience, feeling a bit choked. Had I stood by cheerfully and in a spirit of ungrudging self-sacrifice, I might then have felt good about myself. But I hadn't, so I couldn't. The entries in my journal for those days are brief and peevish. I was a fraud. Conversation became general, flowing around us and separating us. I couldn't speak to Claudia about the pavilion; she would think I'd gone entirely off my head. I wrote down a description and an account of the emotions and sensations I had experienced, or thought I had experienced, there. Even to my own eyes it seemed crazy.

I didn't manage to speak to Portia again until the day of David's wedding. Lancashire mystified her. She struggled valiantly with the accents and, as far as was in her, behaved like a democrat. 'Why do they call me Doochess?' she asked in a whisper. 'It's quite incorrect.'

David overheard. 'Sorry, Portia, they seem to think it's your Christian name, like Duke and Earl in America. I hope it doesn't offend you too much.'

'Not at all,' she said graciously, 'I simply wondered.' But she still looked puzzled. Mr Openshaw took her under his wing and discoursed (he could not be accused of mere speaking) about the poverty of the area and the solid worth of the workers. He was so effective that Portia ended up as a patroness of the local girls' club. Not that she ever went to Bolton again; she simply gave money. 'Is your wife here today, or is she still abroad?' she asked.

'I did my best,' he said. 'Messages to every capital city I could think of. There's that many countries now in Africa alone, and I barely managed to touch the Far East.'

'Isn't that rather worrying?'

He shook his head. 'Not if you know her it isn't. She feels she's got a mission. If our Meggie was an African or Indian, she'd be back here like a shot, interfering. I'm not sure I'd know her if she walked through that door, it's been so long.'

The wedding seemed to embrace much of the town population. I was thoroughly enjoying the abundance when I saw a face that I recognized, Josie Knapp, who had once lived in Underhallow. It shook my confidence in David. His affair with Josie had been a scandal in its day and had thoroughly upset Gloria Hopkins. My impression was that it had continued in an uncommitted fashion more or less until the present. Her eyes lighted on me and she made her way to my side, wreathing like a cat, her hips inviting and receiving notice. In more than ten years she had scarcely aged. Still lovely, still voluptuous, and now both notable and rich, a formidable combination. 'Quite an occasion, Amy! I glimpsed Rudi just now, then I lost him in the crush. Clever of David's Meggie to invite me, don't you think? I would have done the same.' She smiled, pushing her hands through her dark hair in a familiar gesture, showing off her breasts to advantage. And it occurred to me that Meggie knew when to gamble and how to win. This was Josie's final dismissal.

'Gorgeous, isn't she,' Meggie said when I had a chance to speak to her. 'Quite old though. Too bad she has to go. I frightened David out of his wits when I put her on my guest list.' She studied her glass of champagne thoughtfully. 'Perhaps the poor innocent believed she was a secret. Unless we leap at them accusingly, men do think we women are awfully dense and unobservant. You know, Amy, one can have too much of this wine stuff. Sometimes I pine for a glass of bitter and a cheese and onion sandwich with the girls from the mill. It's my secret vice.'

'We'll try it together some time at the Castleton's Oak. The beer's well spoken of. You seriously misled me about the thread-workers. They're full of fun and positively delightful.'

'Ah yes,' she sighed, 'but you've never been expected to marry one when you were pining for freedom.'

'Are you happy now, Meggie? No more running away?'

'Never, as long as David behaves nicely. I'm Lancashire through and through and I'm a sticker. Heaven help him though if he gets ideas about Josie Knapp. I can be quite rough in a dire emergency.' So that seemed to be all right, and Davy, though still wearing his faintly bewildered air, told us all how blessed he felt in snaring Meggie. During this speech she grinned at me and gently shook her head.

Botolph, having survived long enough to give credence to the view that he had fathered Rose, died three days after Easter on the day that Portia arrived in Austria. Beau, singularly indifferent, became Duke of Coritanum. The body was flown to England for interment in the ornate family vault. We all dutifully trooped off to Leicestershire again to attend the funeral. Portia felt only mild relief. 'He died to me as a husband and a man ten years ago,' she said when the pomp was over. 'I grieved then. It wasn't pleasant knowing that he was alive and hating me.' Nothing was said about her moving to the Dower House.

In May, before the year could settle into anticlimax, Claudia and the twins came to stay for a night or two. 'The unnatural little beasts want to see Princess Margaret getting married, and wave to the Queen. Sickening!'

'We're about the only girls anywhere in the world who haven't seen *someone* royal, let alone the Queen,' they explained together, 'and we don't even have television. I suppose you haven't thought of buying one, have you, Aunt Amy?'

Rudi had one in his office, but I shook my head, not wishing to draw attention to our London retreat. 'I expect Mrs Slade would let you watch hers if you can put up with her father-in-law.'

'The horrible old man who swears and spills his

food?' asked Lindsay. 'We like him, don't we, Grainger?'

'Are you two quite right in the head? You've seen a woman before,' Claudia said, 'and that's what the Queen is, minus her trappings. This jaunt's costing a mint. A television set would have been cheaper, and if you'd thought about it earlier I expect your grandfather could have arranged something. He used to know all those creaking antiques at Court.'

'We don't want to dress up and be stuck with a lot of old frumps. If we could just have a television. They're educational.'

'Well you can't. Listen to the wireless or go to the pictures the way we did, and watch the news there.'

'In the year of the flood? I tell you what, Aunt Amy, you can look at Mrs Slade's set. We'll wave our Union Jacks at the camera and you see if you can spot us. Ma might as well stay with you. She's only going to grouse all the time and we're groovy chicks, quite capable of looking after ourselves.'

Claudia ground her teeth and told them that chicks, groovy or otherwise, were liable to have their necks wrung. She then showed them what to do if they were molested by strange men. This involved a variety of painful moves taught to me years ago by Great-aunt Hildegarde and later passed on by me to Claudia. For once the twins seemed impressed. Dutifully we went to view the affair at Dora's. Mr Slade fell asleep with a mouth full of rice pudding that slipped gradually onto the front of his shirt. Dora wheeled him away. 'Now,' Claudia said, 'we can pull everyone to pieces. I can't be doing with unlimited rejoicing.'

At one point, very close to the Abbey, a twin's face, huge and grimacing, appeared on the screen. (Claudia said it was Lindsay; I can only tell them apart in the flesh.) Behind them I glimpsed Beau. 'Did you see me?'

Lindsay asked when they at last got back. 'I got right up close to the camera and then the cameraman told me to bugger off or get a clip round the ear. I bet I looked lovely.'

'You looked mad and hideous,' her mother said unfeelingly. 'Was that Little Botty with you?' ('Beau,' I muttered.)

'We ran into the old thing with some of his friends. They got us a place. It was fun. We didn't have to torture any of their squashy bits.'

Claudia took us to dine that evening at Village Delights. The twins liked Princess Margaret's tiara, but found the Queen something of a disappointment. 'She certainly looked glum,' Claudia commented. 'Not a groovy chick, we gather. One never exactly associates them with whole-hearted jollity at the best of times, though they could, of course, be holding themselves in to set a good example to us vulgar plebs. She may absolutely long to have a good cry at weddings.'

'Dismal,' said Lindsay through a mouthful of devil's food cake. 'One would have liked a radiant smile and a couple of handfuls of confetti. But an experience to be treasured. Could we try some waffles with maple syrup and a sliver of toffee pecan pie with ice-cream, please? We only had a bag of peanuts for lunch and that cake wasn't very filling.'

'It wasn't devilish either,' said Grainger. 'I don't quite know what I expected, but not just an old chocolate sponge. Imagine Beau turning out to be a swinger, Aunt Amy. Not a dukely bore. The boys are all coming down with some of the parents to stay at Gunville Place in the vacation, and we're having a day out.' I missed them immensely when they went home.

Chapter Nineteen

My contact with Portia steadily dwindled. She mentioned that she had given up her presidency of village guilds and organizations and taken on an active involvement with the promotion of Hindlecote. She guided parties round the castle, took tickets, even sold ice-cream. I suspected that she felt a need for self-punishment. Without a doubt she loved her daughter deeply, yet old customs are a long time in dying. Because her days were work-filled she had small time to spend with Rose, who lived in the nurseries with a nanny. I should have liked to discover how close Portia had come to making her peace with God. She found my views on religion simplistic. They were, I knew, and I felt unable to put the question. At Christmas she sent us a card and photographs of Rose, mentioning that she proposed to spend a week alone in France. She gave no address. I should have been thrilled to look after the baby while she was away, but to suggest it seemed like an accusation of neglect.

The persecution of Hattie by the sergeant had been brought to an end in the autumn of 1960 when the constable announced that he intended to marry The Fancy. The two men had an acrimonious argument in the Castleton's Oak. 'She'll make your life a bleeding mockery,' said the sergeant. 'Off with any man when you're on nights. You want your brains testing.'

'Just leave us be,' retorted the constable. 'My mum's taken her on and they get along famously. She's a different girl now she's got someone to keep a proper eye on her, *and* she's loving.'

'I'll say she is! Too blasted loving, as half the men in this pub'll tell you. I've been like a father to you. Don't do it, lad, don't do it.'

'Some father. You're over-handy with a truncheon, you are. Get yourself a woman and leave me to run my own life.' Most people took the sergeant's view, but the marriage went ahead in record time. 'Look at it like this,' said the happy bridegroom to his superior, 'Mr Doolittle won't be bothering you none when he gets out, not with his girl married to a copper.' The Fancy quickly became pregnant and, to the relief of the rehabilitated Hattie, retired from the sport of open-air doolittling.

I telephoned Portia on New Year's Day of 1961. Her visit to France wasn't mentioned. She chatted happily of Rose's first birthday and Beau's musical progresss. Before she hung up she told me that she thought of buying a small house of her own nearer to London. When, at the beginning of February, I received a note from her asking whether she could come to stay for a few days, I assumed that the visit was in some way connected with properties. She arrived in Underhallow on a cold, wet afternoon. I had expected her to bring Rose with her, but she was alone. As she climbed out of the taxi and straightened, I noticed anew her extreme thinness. An air of absolute weariness about her touched me with deep unease. I asked no questions, settling her in the drawing-room with tea and some of Dora's homemade scones. She ate nothing. A long silence passed that was not unfriendly, but difficult to break. At length she leaned forward, clasping her knees and said, 'I don't suppose you ever knew how Mother died, Amy. You were very young.'

At once the sense of foreboding, of impending

disaster, returned, focused now. Portia could not know, since I had told no-one, either at the time or afterwards, but I knew precisely how our mother had died. She had told me herself, had even shown me the ravages of disease on her own body. One of the causes given on the death certificate was pneumonia, the other, primary carcinoma of the breast, and only her doctor and I had known for certain that she had courted the pneumonia, rather than wait to die of cancer. In those days there was virtually no hope and small help for pain. I said, 'I was five. I saw her, spoke to her, ten days before she died. At the time I didn't fully understand, but I knew what was wrong, and I've always remembered.'

'Well then, I needn't explain. The doctors say it can pass through the generations. I imagine that's what the specialist will find.' She leaned back in the chair with a faint smile. 'I'd forgotten how you watched us all and listened.'

I thought, Does she, can she know what she's saying, and if so, how can she smile? A kind of paralysis struck me. I tried to speak and was dumb, the breath filtered out of my lungs and I gasped for air. Eventually I stammered out, 'Couldn't it be something else, something to do with having the baby?'

'It isn't confirmed, I had the X-rays only this morning, but I perfectly understood the cautious manner. Ought I to be very frightened? I can't seem to be.'

My fear was enough for both of us. It settled over me in a grey, persistent cloud. 'When will you know?'

'In two or three days. If I may stay? I've given them this number.'

I'll never know how she got through the waiting in absolute calm, compelling me to remain calm with her. Alone, I wrestled with panic and tears. Seeing my helplessness, Rudi took charge of us both with perfect tact, seeking Portia's company, though like most men he was not at ease with illness. A superstitious dread settled on me. I looked for signs: if it doesn't rain today before ten, Portia will be all right; when the phone rings I'll let it ring five times, then it will be good news. The call came. The news wasn't good. I drove her to London and saw her directly into a hospital bed. 'Beau will have to know,' she said. 'I can rely on you not to alarm him unduly.'

That same night one of her slight breasts was removed. 'They were never much to look at,' she said, and I went back to the waiting-room and at last cried my eyes out. The task of telling everyone again fell to me and it was the worst thing that I ever had to do. Beau came to the hospital, sullen and aloof. I had no consolation to offer. I didn't even venture to touch him, knowing it wouldn't be well received. When he left I watched him go, clattering down the stairs at breakneck speed, and running anywhere or nowhere. Grandmother came to my aid. Drawing on heaven knows what reserves of strength and purpose, she took him over, securing him under her capacious and unsentimental wing. She was a magnificent woman.

A series of radium treatments followed Portia's convalescence, bringing alternate wild hopes and despairs. They made her dreadfully sick. I wanted her to send a message to Gerhardt, but she wouldn't. 'He's had his fill of illness. When I'm well again Emmi can tell him, not before.'

Claudia drove down to Underhallow. White-faced and subdued, she sat with Portia and scarcely talked to me. I knew that she was finding it unbearable. When she left she was crying secret tears and her car veered all over the road before she got it under control. In April the weather was mild and Portia expressed a desire to go back to Hindlecote. Rudi and I took her and, with his blessing, I stayed. She seemed stronger and the doctors forecasted a slow recovery. Once again I was ashamed of my fears, but Portia certainly never believed for a moment in their optimism. One morning, quite soon after her return home, she said that she wouldn't get up. She lay in bed and dozed while I read to her. The nurse brought Rose in to see her for a few minutes, then took her back to the nursery. It was the beginning of a terrifying decline. The doctor from Leicester chose and hired nurses to provide by day and night those cares that a sick woman needs. At night I went exhausted to sleep. I awoke free for a split second of forgetfulness before knowledge flooded back.

To my anxious observation Portia put up no fight at all. She seemed composed. Even when the doctor's morphia failed entirely to control the pain she neither wept nor complained. Her mouth curved perpetually in a faint untroubled smile. The habit of acceptance was strong in her and perhaps, too, with her abandonment of love she felt that life offered less than enough to make it worth while. As for me, I loved her fiercely now that it was too late.

She remained sensible and controlled. One afternoon she said, 'Amy, you will take care of Beau and Rose until they're of age, won't you? If I don't recover. There are trust funds and I've written a guardianship clause into my will. I want Rose to be brought up wholly as an English girl and I hope you'll feel able to love her. She's too young to miss me. But poor Beau, I do worry for him.'

I said yes, and croaked out that I already loved Rose and that Beau had a strength of character that would bring him through in time. What has it all been for? I wondered bitterly: a travesty of a marriage, a brief love affair and the effortful childbirth. Unconsciously Portia answered me. 'Rose was made and born in absolute love. It couldn't have been sustained, not at that pitch. It was perfect. God knows when to call a halt.' Then, when she slept, I climbed in my misery and impotence to the top of the castle tower and wailed until I could trust myself to be calm. With the advance of summer, I suggested out of desperation that we might take her down to the pavilion during the day-time. She refused. Could I truly have been so stupid as to believe that an enchantment lay there, that an arrangement of bricks and stucco could change events, that it could heal? I know that I accepted at last what I couldn't change.

Beau came home. Portia's beauty had already become that of the dead. She was almost unrecogniz-able. Only her huge eyes remained wholly alive, vivid and blue. He said nothing to me. We had no way of helping Portia or each other. 'Let me send for Gerhardt,' I begged her again. She raised an arm and examined it. It was fleshless, the fine skin wrinkling over bone. She shook her head. Then in spite of her veto I made a decision and telephoned to Emmi in Austria, leaving her to tell Gerhardt or not, as she thought best.

She set out with him for Hindlecote at once. That evening the vicar made his daily visit and Portia received communion. While he was sitting with her she passed into a coma and never recovered con-sciousness. So quietly did she leave us that it was difficult to know the precise minute of her death, though it must have been less than an hour before Gerhardt's arrival. In two weeks she would have reached her forty-ninth birthday. I think that Portia had a more vivid awareness of God than most people ever experience, and I'll swear that she was content. The nurses took over. I stood with Gerhardt and Emmi by the open window, hating the buzz and laughter of the visitors, hating Gerhardt's difficult and uncontrolled weeping.

Portia was not buried among the Coritanums. 'I don't want to lie beside Botolph in that gloomy place for all eternity.' So we laid her to rest in a plot that she had purchased herself, in the parish churchyard under a golden yew. It had taken me too long a time to understand her goodness and courage, and even longer to love her. Portia left in my life an area of desolation and fruitless regrets. I grieved for her bitterly. Some times and some events are too painful simply to be written down, put away and forgotten, and at this point in my life I stopped keeping a journal altogether.

Rose came home to Underhallow, unaware of her loss. Beau declined to leave Hindlecote. When he did, he went straight back to London. He would never, I knew, regard me as a substitute mother, though we learned to rub along together, avoiding painful places.

Claudia, angry with grief and more subdued than I had ever known her, said, 'To the very end I never managed to understand what Portia was about. Now I never will. Why, when I rarely saw her, does the world seem so appallingly empty?' Rose was staggering around the room from knee to knee on some mysterious mission of her own. 'That poor child, it's a mercy she has you. You've always longed for a daughter.'

'But not at this price, not for Portia's life. What have I done to deserve such a gift? Nothing. It was her risk, her pain, not mine.'

'The two things are separate, loss and gain. They have to be. If you think of death every time you look at the baby, it won't exactly make for happiness. As I see it, that's what you have to do, give Rose a happy life.'

Cold comfort, I thought, but perhaps that's what we ought to expect, for every gain a loss, sadness for every moment of joy. 'We mean to give her everything we can,' I said. Rudi poured Claudia a drink. Rose gurgled at us and said, 'Um mum mum mum mum.' I tucked her under my arm and took her upstairs to the boys' old nursery. It would need decorating for a little girl, a daughter. She went graciously into the cot. I sat with her until she fell asleep, then I pulled up the covers and kissed her good night.

THE END

A SELECTED LIST OF FINE WRITING
AVAILABLE FROM BLACK SWAN

99313 1	OF LOVE AND SHADOWS	Isabel Allende	£6.99
99630 0	MUDDY WATERS	Judy Astley	£6.99
99619 X	HUMAN CROQUET	Kate Atkinson	£6.99
99687 4	THE PURVEYOR OF ENCHANTMENT	Marika Cobbold	£6.99
99624 6	THE COUNTER-TENOR'S DAUGHTER	Elizabeth Falconer	£ 6.99
99721 8	BEFORE WOMEN HAD WINGS	Connie May Fowler	£6.99
99657 2	PERFECT MERINGUES	Laurie Graham	£5.99
99611 4	THE COURTYARD IN AUGUST	Janette Griffiths	£6.99
99774 9	THE CUCKOO'S PARTING CRY	Anthea Halliwell	£5.99
99754 4	CLOUD MUSIC	Karen Hayes	£6.99
99742 0	THE CONSTANT MISTRESS	Angela Lambert	£6.99
99771 4	MALLINGFORD	Alison Love	£6.99
99696 2	HOLY ASPIC	Joan Marysmith	£6.99
99696 3	THE VISITATION	Sue Reidy	£5.99
99747 1	M FOR MOTHER	Marjorie Riddell	£6.99
99732 3	A PRIZE FOR SISTER CATHERINE	Kathleen Rowntree	£6.99
99777 3	THE SPARROW	Mary Doria Russell	£6.99
99763 3	GARGOYLES AND PORT	Mary Selby	£6.99
99753 6	AN ACCIDENTAL LIFE	Titia Sutherland	£6.99
99700 5	NEXT OF KIN	Joanna Trollope	£6.99
99780 3	KNOWLEDGE OF ANGELS	Jill Paton Walsh	£6.99
99673 4	DINA'S BOOK	Herbjørg Wassmo	£6.99
99723 4	PART OF THE FURNITURE	Mary Wesley	£6.99
99642 4	SWIMMING POOL SUNDAY	Madeleine Wickham	£6.99
99591 6	A MISLAID MAGIC	Joyce Windsor	£6.99
99651 3	AFTER THE UNICORN	Joyce Windsor	£6.99